THE MOST Wonderful CRIME OF THE Year

ALSO BY ALLY CARTER

The Blonde Identity

THE MOST Wonderful CRIME OF THE Year

a novel

ALLY CARTER

AVON

An Imprint of HarperCollinsPublishers

This is a work of fiction. Names, characters, places, and incidents are products of the author's imagination or are used fictitiously and are not to be construed as real. Any resemblance to actual events, locales, organizations, or persons, living or dead, is entirely coincidental.

Interior text design by Diahann Sturge-Campbell

ISBN 978-0-06-327668-0

If anyone has ever tried to gaslight you into thinking you're the problem, congratulations! This book is for you.

PROLOGUE

Excerpt from the Official Police Interrogation
of Margaret Chase and Ethan Wyatt

December 25

Ms. Chase: Well, of course I have his blood on my hands.

Mr. Wyatt: It was just a scratch.

Ms. Chase: I obviously didn't try to kill him.

Mr. Wyatt: Maggie's more of a lover than a—

Ms. Chase: If I'd tried to kill him, he'd be dead.

Mr. Wyatt: She's such a good person. [*Mr. Wyatt pats his heart.*] Right here.

Ms. Chase: Of course, I'm not offended that you'd accuse me of murder. I'm offended you'd think I'd be bad at it.

Mr. Wyatt: It's a point of professional pride. Ha! Wait. That was a joke. Can you please write down that I was—

Ms. Chase: You should have separated us, you know? We shouldn't be together for this. Not that we're together! Oh no! We are not a *we*. He is *he* and I am *me* and we are not . . .

Mr. Wyatt: We're colleagues.

Ms. Chase: I prefer nemesis. Nemesis is a far better word.

Mr. Wyatt: It's a big market, and we appeal to different— Have I mentioned they're making one of my books into a movie?

Ms. Chase: I'm sorry, but are we seriously still sitting here, doing nothing? Am I really wearing this ridiculous sweater, answering these ridiculous questions when she's . . .

Inspector Patel: Why don't you start at the beginning?

Mr. Wyatt: I . . . uh . . . I don't understand the question.

Inspector Patel: When did it start?

Mr. Wyatt: Oh. It started—

Ms. Chase: In the elevator.

CHAPTER *One*

One Week Earlier

It wasn't until the elevator doors were sliding open that Maggie realized she was about to come face-to-face with her three least favorite things in the world:

Christmas. A party. And Ethan Freaking Wyatt.

For a moment, she just stood there, the cacophony of carols and chatter fading to a low hum as she stared through the open doors at the smug look on his smug face—at his trademark leather jacket and the strand of twinkle lights wrapped around his neck like a scarf. There was a Santa hat on his head and, of course, a copy of *Silent Knight* ("Now a #1 *New York Times* Bestseller!") in his hands. The fact that it was just a cardboard cutout and not the man himself should have softened the blow for Maggie, but it was all she could do not to punch him in his cardboard teeth.

At the very least she should have reached for the button and made the elevator doors close faster—and maybe she would have if a voice hadn't cried out, "Oh my gosh. You're here!" Which was when Maggie knew she'd made a terrible mistake.

She should have slipped away when she'd had the chance, down in the elevator. Through the lobby. Then out onto the cold and crowded streets of Midtown Manhattan seven days before Christmas. She should have gotten out of there—and she would have—if Cardboard Ethan hadn't distracted her. But now it was too late and two tiny but deceptively viselike hands were dragging her off the elevator and into the big open lobby of Killhaven Books.

"Shellie bet me five dollars that you'd show, and here you are!" Deborah had to raise her voice to be heard over all the small talk and laughter because, oh yeah. There was a party going on. *A Christmas party*. And Maggie had waltzed right into the middle of it. A tree was blinking and music was playing and the room was swirling. Just a little.

"Maggie?" Deborah's voice was closer. Softer.

"You know, it's a miracle there aren't more murders at Christmas."

"Oh, here we go," Deborah mumbled, but Maggie never took her eyes off Cardboard Ethan.

"Think about it. People who hate each other crammed together in hot rooms with too much alcohol. Scissors and strangulation devices lying around."

"Strangulation devices?"

"You know . . . Lights. Tinsel. I bet you could do some real damage with garland." In spite of everything, Maggie felt herself perk up at the possibilities. "Even mistletoe is poisonous."

"To dogs," Deborah said.

"In large enough quantities, *everyone's* a dog," Maggie pointed out as she slowly turned to face the woman beside her.

Deborah Klein was five-foot-one inches of power. Gray hair. Chanel suit. And eyes that had seen it all during her forty-nine-year rise from the mail room to the most feared woman in publishing.

"I say all this because *I* am going to murder *you*."

"Who? Me?" Deborah brought one tiny hand to her chest.

"Yes, you! *It's just lunch, Maggie. You need to get out of the house, Maggie. We need to talk marketing, Maggie.*"

"One, I don't sound like that."

"You sound exactly like that."

"And two—"

"This is a party, Deborah. There is a tree made out of paperbacks right over there. Half the marketing department is singing karaoke. And . . ." Maggie trailed off as she realized—"Lance VanZant is literally wearing a T-shirt that looks like a tuxedo."

Deborah waved the words away. "Lance VanZant wrote one half-decent book nine years ago. No one cares about Lance VanZant."

"What about him?" Maggie pointed to Cardboard Ethan and Deborah had the good taste to look guilty.

"I'm told it's not exactly to scale."

But then a thought occurred to Maggie. "Ooh. Can I have it when this is over? I've been wanting to learn how to throw knives."

Deborah's mouth was opening, slowly, like she couldn't figure out what to say when a woman walked past, chiming, "Merry Christmas, Maggie!"

She was new and Maggie thought her name was Jen. It was probably Jen. Statistically speaking, one-third of the women who worked in publishing were named Jen, but Maggie wasn't thinking very clearly because the room was too loud after a year of constant silence. It was too crowded. And Maggie, who had never loved crowds or parties to begin with, felt her hands start shaking.

"Let's get you something to eat." Deborah had a hand on Maggie's elbow. She could feel it through her Joan Wilder coat, puffy and too hot in the crowded room. She'd always thought it was an excellent coat to disappear inside, but Deborah was still there, whispering near her ear. "I'm sorry. It's been a year and I thought . . . Stay five minutes. For me. I'm sorry I tricked you into coming, but there really is something we need to talk about."

Maggie was starting to waver. She'd already spent fifty bucks on train fare and taxis and lost a whole day of work, so it might not be that bad. After all, she didn't have to go *to* the party. She just had to walk *through* the party, and she could do that. She'd been walking every day for a year—for almost thirty years. She could make it to Deborah's corner office.

But then the elevator dinged. The doors slid open and a deep voice boomed, "Ho! Ho! Ho!" First, he spotted the cutout. "Well, who's this handsome fella?" Then he spotted her. "Hey! It's good to see you, Marcie!"

And Maggie started looking for some tinsel.

CHAPTER *Two*

Maggie hadn't always hated Christmas. There had been a time when she'd loved the lights and the presents and the trees. She knew all the words to at least thirty different Christmas carols and used to sing them in July. She had a sweatshirt with a reindeer on it that she always wore to school on the Monday after Thanksgiving. (Did the nose light up? Yes, yes it did. Did she wear it that way? Absolutely.)

Twelve-year-old Maggie had baked sugar cookies and organized Secret Santas and terrorized her mother with multipart questions like (1) *Why don't we have a big family?* and (2) *Why don't we spend Christmas with our big (fictional) family?* and (3) *Can this fictional gathering of this fictional family take place in a location that always has snow?*

But Maggie was an only child born late in life to only children. Maggie didn't even have grandparents, and it was almost always too warm for snow in Texas.

So the problem wasn't that Maggie hated Christmas; the problem was that Christmas hated Maggie. Every terrible thing that had ever happened to her had occurred with a backdrop of carols and lights, and, eventually, Maggie had no choice but to start taking it personally.

Her dog ran away when she was thirteen. When she was sixteen, their car caught fire and the next day all the presents disappeared out from under the tree. A week later, the car was running again and Maggie never asked a single question.

Her senior year of high school, they *did* have snow, but it knocked out power to half the state and Maggie spent the holiday huddled around the fireplace with her parents, hoping the water didn't freeze.

Of course, at the time, she didn't know that was the last Christmas they'd have together. She'd joked about how next year would be better—telling her parents they had to wait until she was home from college to put up the tree and wrap the presents.

But twelve months later, her parents were gone and Maggie was alone and . . .

"I need to go."

Deborah pushed her into a chair then moved to the other side of the desk. "You need to sit."

"Look"—Maggie started to stand—"I appreciate what you're trying to do, but I'm really not good at parties, so let's catch up after the new year, okay? Let's—"

"Sit. Down." Deborah didn't raise her voice. Deborah didn't have to. When she was nothing but a nineteen-year-old intern, Deborah had pulled the greatest crime writer to ever live out of the slush pile, so when Deborah whispered, people listened. Even people who hated the smell of peppermint and eggnog and pine.

"I have a surprise for you." Deborah eased into her leather chair then tossed something onto the stack of manuscripts that rimmed her massive desk. It was just an envelope, square and the color of eggshells, but for some reason Maggie was almost afraid to touch it.

"Oh. I'm afraid I . . . uh . . . didn't do cards this year."

"You never do cards and neither do I. That's not from me."

The card was heavy in Maggie's hand when she reached for it. The paper was smooth and soft and— Money. The envelope felt like money in every sense of the word. Her name was scrawled across the front in the most pristine handwriting she'd ever seen. *Ms. Margaret Chase.*

"Well. Open it," Deborah dared, and Maggie turned the envelope over to break the wax seal on the back. The card inside was even softer.

You are cordially invited to—

"No."

"You haven't even read it!"

Maggie couldn't help but whine, "You tricked me into coming to one party just so you could invite me to another one?"

Deborah's laugh was almost maniacal. "Oh, that's no invitation, sweet Charlie. That is your ticket to the chocolate factory."

Maggie had known Deborah for almost nine years, but she'd never seen her look like she looked then: giddy and sly and almost ravenous. She imagined that's how nineteen-year-old Deborah must have looked when she'd pulled Eleanor Ashley's first manuscript from the pile on the mail room floor. Like a woman whose evil plan was just getting started.

"You've been invited to the home of your biggest fan for Christmas."

"Deborah—"

"In England!" Deborah said with a flourish, as if that made everything better and not infinitely worse. "All expenses paid. Now before you tell me I'm crazy—"

"You're crazy! Do I need to remind you that I write mysteries?"

"So?"

"So my fans like murder! And murderers! And—"

"Your last book was about a woman whose cat could smell poison."

"Hey! *The Purrrrfect Crime* sold very well in Brazil," Maggie said, but Deborah was determined. There was no teasing glint in her eye, no mischievous twinkle.

"I can personally vouch for this particular fan. And I'm telling you"—she lowered her voice—"you *want* to get on that plane. You are positively *dying* to get on that plane."

Maggie ran a finger over the heavy paper. It really was a lovely card. "I don't want to spend Christmas with strangers," she admitted and Deborah's eyes went soft.

"Then who are you spending Christmas with? Because you know I'm a heartless old crone but when I think of you rattling around that tiny apartment all by yourself . . ."

"I'm on deadline." Maggie held the words like a shield.

"I'm your editor, and I just decided to move your deadline."

"But I . . ."

"Have nothing planned for Christmas, do you?" Deborah glanced toward her open door. The sounds of the party were a low din in the distance, but she inched forward, arms on the desk. It was a posture that screamed *you didn't hear this from me.* "Look, I don't want to get your hopes up, but something is coming next year. Very big. Very hush-hush. And I think you're the person for the job. But I need you to *get on that plane.*"

Maggie fingered the wax seal on the back of the envelope. "What kind of fan flies their favorite author to another country for the holidays?"

"The kind with money and good taste in books."

"This can't be safe."

"It is."

"This can't be smart."

"Oh." Deborah laughed. "It is."

"This can't be—"

"Maggie. Dearest. Most prolific and professional writer I know, I say this with love. I say this with kindness. I say this in the truest spirit of holiday cheer: you need to get a life."

Deborah had never steered her wrong—not once in nine years and dozens of books. Deborah believed in her. Deborah wanted the best for her. Deborah was the closest thing Maggie had to family, which was perhaps the only thing sadder than having no family at all. And all Maggie could do was look at her mentor who would never be her mother and draw a tired breath.

"Maybe. But that doesn't mean I have to get a Christmas."

"Okay." Deborah sat back. "Then what does the next week and a half look like for you? Sitting around, thinking about your former husband and your former best friend unwrapping presents in your former house?"

Some might have thought the words were cruel, but Maggie recognized them for what they were: a challenge and a dare. That was her cue to start fighting, but all she could do was eke out a half smile and the words, "Presents they bought with my former money. Don't forget that part."

She eyed the envelope again, imagining snowy fields and

garland-laden banisters, carol singers and horse-drawn sleighs be-cause, evidently, to Maggie, English Christmases take place entirely in BBC adaptations. "No. I . . . I shouldn't."

"What you should do, Margaret, is trust me."

What Maggie didn't say was that she had no intention of trusting anyone ever again. Especially herself.

CHAPTER *Three*

Twelve Years Ago

It wasn't that Maggie's parents hadn't wanted a big family. It was more like they'd never really learned how to have one. They'd been older when Maggie was born, and sometimes she got the feeling they were like the staff of a restaurant, ready to close up and go home when she'd stumbled in five minutes before closing.

So it shouldn't have come as a surprise when, two weeks after moving into a dorm in upstate New York, Maggie's parents put their little Texas house on the market. They bought a condo in Florida and two matching golf carts that neither one of them knew how to drive, and that year, Maggie spent Thanksgiving eating dry turkey sandwiches and sleeping on an air mattress surrounded by unpacked boxes.

She was already back on campus when she got the call, alone in her dorm room when a stranger told her about the accident.

She was alone when she went back to Florida to pack up the condo and sell the golf carts and ship a half-dozen boxes to a storage unit not far from campus.

She was alone when the boy from the Office of Residential Life explained, "I'm sorry, but students aren't allowed to stay in the dorms over winter break."

Because Christmas was coming. Of course it was. Christmas was *always* coming, but Maggie couldn't go back to Florida; and she couldn't go back to Texas. And she probably couldn't stay in the storage unit where she'd placed her family photos, the good dishes, and seventy-seven novels by Eleanor Ashley.

"But I have to stay here," she'd pleaded with the RA who was looking at her over the top of a giant box labeled *Garland and Shit*.

"You can't," the boy said, like maybe the university had admitted her by mistake. Like no one could be that stupid.

"No. They can't kick me out just because it's Christmas. I live here. This is where I live."

"Look, I know it sucks and parents are the worst, but most people just go home." He looked at her like the solution was both obvious and inevitable. "You should just go home."

Then he turned, shifting the box like it held the weight of the world—like no college student had ever had to bear a greater burden—and Maggie felt her throat start to burn.

"But what if . . ." She'd never had to say the words out loud before. "What if you don't have one?" Her voice cracked, and her eyes watered and maybe that's why he didn't quite get it as he glanced back over his shoulder.

"What?"

"My parents died and the golf carts were nonrefundable and I need the condo money for tuition."

She'd said it all too quickly—like those were excuses that he had to hear all the time—and, suddenly, Ryan from Residential Life stopped looking at her like she was stupid and started looking at her like she was crazy. And also pitiful. Which was okay. At that moment, pity was almost all she had going for her.

"I can't go home." She ran a hand over her eyes like she could push the tears back in. When that didn't work, she looked away. "I don't have one."

"Look, I'm really sorry. But . . ." His voice was lower, softer. Closer. "They turn down the heat and cut the lights. There's no food. There's *no heat*. It's three weeks. You literally cannot stay here."

He was right, of course. The heat was the deal-breaker, which meant she was going to have to dip into her meager savings and get a motel. Maybe an Airbnb. She could get a part-time job. Maybe go to the nearest airport and start impersonating long-lost relatives in the hope that someone might take pity on her and take her home. It was either that or—

"You could come home with me," a voice said from behind her.

And that's how she met Emily.

And that was the beginning of everything.

Even the end.

CHAPTER *Four*

Seven Days Before Christmas

Maggie was fine. Really. She was totally and completely—

Resigned. Yeah. That was more like it. She'd learned long ago that the firsts are always the hardest. The first birthday. The first round of holidays, cycling throughout the year. But the year was almost over, and her first Christmas was coming, so she might as well experience her first party, soldier through and get it out of the way.

Because Maggie wasn't fine—but she would be. As soon as her stomach stopped growling and her head stopped hurting and this last first was finally over.

So she piled a bunch of cheese cubes on a napkin and grabbed a sparkling water that was probably going to make her burp. She managed three whole minutes of small talk with two different Jens before Ethan Wyatt started a conga line.

"How's it going, Marcie?" he shouted as he congaed by, and Maggie started doing Party Math in her head.

If she hid for thirty minutes, then waved at three more people on her way to the elevator, maybe no one would notice if she spent the rest of the party hiding in an empty room, reading her Purse Book and eating her Napkin Cheese. It was a genius plan, really. She should have thought of it from the start.

But as she darted down a darkened hall, looking for an open door, Maggie felt her footsteps falter. She had to stop. And stare. Because, officially, the display might have been called the Wall of Fame, but according to Deborah, everyone at Killhaven just called it The Eleanors.

Tucked away behind polished wood and (supposedly) fireproof glass stood ninety-nine novels by Eleanor Ashley. First editions, unlike the used and frayed and dog-eared copies Maggie's father had once called her only friends—a joke that would have been funny if it hadn't also been true. And for a moment, all Maggie could feel was wonder, followed quickly by shame because Eleanor Ashley wouldn't hide at parties. Eleanor wouldn't have been tricked into coming to begin with. Eleanor would have—

"Yo! Ethan!"

Only a man who wears T-shirts that look like tuxedos could ever shout "Yo!" in a professional setting. Maggie barely had time to dart into an office and hide behind a half-closed door before she heard two sets of footsteps come around the bend in the hall.

"Lance. Hey. How's it going?"

"Oh. You know." Lance gave a coarse laugh. "I dressed up for the occasion."

"I see that. Nice."

If Killhaven were a high school, then Ethan was the golden boy, player of sports and breaker of hearts. The kind of guy who could get voted prom king at a school he didn't even go to. Meanwhile, Lance and the other Leather Jacket Guys were nothing more than Ethan's asshole acolytes. Or Assolytes, as Maggie liked to call them. She half expected Lance to offer to polish Ethan's leather jacket or do his homework. Maybe dispose of a body.

"Yo. Man. Did you see the ice queen?"

"Who?" Ethan sounded like he was only half listening—like maybe even the Assolytes were beneath him.

"That Maggie chick. You know. That one who thinks she's the queen of the cozies." Lance laughed and Maggie bristled. "I can't believe she came!"

"Why?" Was Ethan's voice sharper than usual? She couldn't tell. "Is she sick or something?"

"No, man. She got divorced. And her husband took *everything*. It was a whole thing. Messed her up. She went full arachnophobic and hasn't left her house—"

"That's agoraphobic—"

"—in like forever." The hallway was a little too quiet for a little too long and Maggie started to worry they were going to hear her heart trying to pound its way out of her chest.

"You know"—Lance's voice took on a lascivious tone; he sounded like the reason they invented penicillin—"she's probably starting to get real lonely. Maybe I'll go see if I can't get her to stuff my stocking, if you know what I mean."

"No, Lance. What *do* you mean?" Something about the sound of Ethan's voice made it feel like the temperature was dropping fast. Like she was going to see her breath.

"Come down her chimney? Mistle her toe."

"Mistletoe's poisonous." Now Ethan sounded annoyed.

"She might need someone to frosty her snowman—"

"Leave her alone, Lance."

"I'm just saying, it's getting cold. She might want to share body heat."

"She just left her husband, and she doesn't need you—"

Lance gave a quick, sharp laugh that cut him off. "But that's the best part. *He* left *her*. Wait. You look surprised, man."

"No—"

"Lance!" someone called. There were voices at the end of the hall, followed by the sound of fading footsteps, and for a long time, all Maggie could do was stand there, telling herself it was over. They were leaving. They were gone.

But then she heard a low, dark laugh. A subtle huff. And Ethan Freaking Wyatt saying, "No, I'm not surprised he left her."

There was a roar in Maggie's ears then. A rush of blood and gravity and rage. It felt like she was flying—faster and faster, hurtling out into a vast and endless void. A black hole was swallowing her whole as the footsteps and the party faded away and only the words remained.

I'm not surprised he left her.

There wasn't enough tinsel in the world. No scissors sharp enough. No garland strong enough. She was going to kill him with her bare hands. With her teeth. With her . . .

When Maggie stepped into the empty hall, she froze. Because what she saw in the glass surprised her.

The Eleanors were gone, replaced by a woman with Maggie's hair and Maggie's face, but she was little more than a shell, pale and fragile. It was like looking at the ghost of a girl who had frozen to death twelve Christmases ago. Someone who was *afraid*.

Maggie didn't want to be that girl—she'd shoved her down and hidden her away. She'd spent years clawing up from nothing to that New York skyrise. She'd written and she'd bled, and she'd done it all on her own, no matter what Colin told his lawyers.

I'm not surprised he left her.

No. Even the great Ethan Wyatt had the story wrong, and Maggie wanted to shout it from the rooftops and shove it in his face. She wanted to be stronger and tougher and . . . Eleanor. Maggie wanted to be Eleanor, but she'd settle for being the girl in the reindeer sweatshirt.

And that was the thought that made her storm down the hall and back through the crowd and walk up right to Deborah.

And say, "So when do I leave?"

Three days later, Maggie was in the back seat of a town car, watching the skyline of Manhattan pass by the tinted windows. They were almost to the airport when she felt the car slow and turn too soon.

"Oh, no." She leaned up to talk to the driver. "I'll need the main entrance. I'm on . . ." She twisted in her seat, looking for her itinerary, but what she saw out the window made her stop. And stare. Because there was a private jet idling on the tarmac.

She heard the driver say, "This is it, ma'am. You've arrived."

And she thought, *Maybe I have*, as she crawled from the car.

And again as she climbed the stairs.

And once more as she stood in the cabin, surrounded by glossy wood and rich, soft leather, wondering if New Jet Smell was a thing because, if so, this jet definitely had it.

It felt like more than just the start of a trip. It was the start of a new chapter. And for the first time in almost a year, Maggie felt herself begin to smile. And hope. And wonder—

A toilet flushed. The lavatory door opened. And a deep voice exclaimed, "Marcie!"

Maggie spun around, but the jet door was already rising—already closing. It was too late to turn back now.

CHAPTER *Five*

Maggie was having a nightmare. Yes. That had to be it. Her teeth were falling out and she'd just remembered a class she hadn't been to all semester and, oh yeah, she was locked inside a metal tube that would soon be hurtling over open water . . .

With Ethan. Freaking. Wyatt.

She was going to wake up, though. It was going to be okay. This wasn't actually—

"Hi there."

At first glance, Maggie had thought the jet seemed huge, but it suddenly felt small. Very small. Entirely too small! Because Ethan Freaking Wyatt was stepping out of the (presumably even smaller!) lavatory and . . . Had his shoulders always been that wide? And had he always been that tall? He started forward, squeezing down the *entirely too small* aisle of that *entirely too small* airplane, and, really, did no one care about carbon emissions? Aeronautic safety? Maggie's sanity? There was simply no way this teeny tiny plane was large enough for Maggie. And her luggage. And Ethan Wyatt's shoulders. And arms. And ego.

"Crime-fighting cat got your tongue?" Ethan flashed a mischievous grin that he'd probably been giving his whole hot guy life. It was no doubt heavily insured. He could probably use it as collateral for a loan.

It was almost worth being stuck in this terrible dream to watch the smirk slide slowly off his chiseled face. He was looking at her curiously, like maybe he'd never met anyone who was immune to his particular brand of charisma. Like he didn't know whether that should make him respect her more or resent her less. But more than anything, he seemed confused.

"Well, Marcie, my dear, we seem to be going on this little adventure together." When he reached for the safety rail that ran along the ceiling of the jet his shirt rode up and— Was *that an ab*? Yes, there were definitely abs under there—the kind that you can *see*. And presumably *touch*. But Maggie wasn't thinking about touching. Nope. Not even a little bit.

"Why are you here?" Was she shouting? It was hard to tell over the pounding of her blood and that persistent ringing in her ears.

But Ethan merely raised an eyebrow like *isn't it obvious?* "Mysterious invitation from a mysterious benefactor to . . . well . . . mystery writers?"

And then Maggie didn't speak: she laughed. The quick kind. The loud kind. The *guffaw* kind. "I write mysteries. You write . . ." She stopped herself, but Ethan simply raised an eyebrow in a way that looked like a question but felt like a dare. "You know what you write."

"Oh, no. I think I want you to tell me." There was a smile in his voice, like this was fun and not a nightmare come to life. "What kind of books do I write?"

"You're a leather jacket guy." He was currently *the* Leather Jacket Guy, but Maggie didn't say so. "You write leather jacket books."

He gave her a look like *I know I'm going to regret asking this but* . . . "What, exactly, is a leather jacket book?"

As if he didn't know. "They are books with car chases and gunfights and back covers that are nothing but giant author photos of dudes who are always—*always*—wearing a leather jacket."

"I see. So you know everything there is to know about me, then." His tone was a mixture of wry amusement and intimidating calm. "So what about you?"

"What about me?" Maggie's voice was suddenly a half octave higher than it should be.

"What do I need to know about you?" He adjusted his grip on the railing, shirt riding up and abs peeking out again, and Maggie totally forgot the question. "You know . . . Hi, Ethan." His voice went slightly higher too. "I'm Mar—"

"Maggie," she cut in before he could get it wrong.

"—ga-ret," he changed on the fly. "I'm a Sagittarius—"

"Capricorn."

"Virgo rising."

"I have no idea what that means." Maggie looked around the cabin. She really needed to pick a seat. Put her things away. Die.

"I like long walks on the beach, warm chocolate chip cookies, and finding fun ways to kill a man with a knitting needle."

Oh. That was too much and, suddenly, Maggie couldn't stop herself. She whirled on him. "Really? A knitting needle?"

"Yeah." He actually looked surprised. "What's wrong with—"

"If you can't figure out how to kill a man with a knitting needle, you're in the wrong business."

"But I—"

"There are actual weapons that are less inherently dangerous than knitting needles."

"What I meant was—"

"Nobody ever died because they tripped and fell on a nunchaku."

Had he moved closer to her or had she moved closer to him? Maggie wasn't sure. She just knew that his smirk was slightly crooked and a strand of light brown hair that had probably been blond when he was a baby had curled over his forehead as he stood there, looming over her, and for a moment Maggie wondered if the jet was already moving. She felt a little unsteady on her feet.

I'm not surprised he left her.

It was like they were already in the air, like the cabin had lost pressure. It was getting hard to breathe when a young man in a smart navy suit appeared at her elbow saying, "Ms. Chase? Mr. Wyatt? My name is Peter and I'll be taking care of you. If you'd like to take your seats, we'll be taking off soon. There's a storm in the forecast, and we'd like to land before it hits."

Oh. Right. Because they were on an airplane. Together. And they were going on this bizarre trip. Together.

"This yours?" Ethan reached for the tote at her feet. Her laptop was in there. And her favorite notebook. And her backup notebook. And her *other* backup notebook. But he lifted the heavy bag with one finger, sliding it into a tall cabinet as his shirt rode up.

Again. This time she saw two abs because he couldn't keep from showing off.

But she didn't say a word as she settled into a plush leather chair and fastened her seat belt. It was okay. He'd probably go to the back of the plane and they wouldn't even have to talk until—

Zzzzzzzzp.

She turned to see him in the chair across the aisle, pressing a button and adjusting the seat. The slide of leather on leather made a humming sound that filled the cabin as he went lower.

Zzzzzzzzzzzzzzzzzp. And lower.

"Look, I think we need to get something"—*zzzzzzzzzzp*; his seat started back up again—"straight. You and I have, for whatever reason, been chosen for this . . . this . . ."

"Mission?" he offered up.

"No."

"Endeavor?" *Zzzzzzp.* He was heading back down.

"No."

"Quest? Ooh! Can we call it a quest?" *Zzzzzzzzzp.*

"No!" *Zzzzzzzzp.* "We have been invited on this trip, and I think we need to—" *Zzzzzzzzzzzzzzzzzzzzzzzzzzzzzzzzp.* He was fully horizontal and the plane was starting to move. "Will you stop that?" The *zzzzz*ping stopped, then started again as the seat reversed, rising slowly to the upright position as the plane began to pick up speed. "As I was saying, we have both been invited on this—"

"I still think we should go with *quest*." He nodded decisively.

"And I think we should—if possible—put aside our issues with each other—"

"What issues?" His voice sounded different this time.

"—and try to just . . . get along." Maggie ground out the words as the plane roared down the runway. For a split second, she felt almost weightless as they started to rise.

"What issues—"

"Call a truce," she went on. "A détente."

"A what?" Now he sounded upset.

"It means a cease-fire—"

"I know what détente means. What I don't know is why you and I need one."

He couldn't be serious? Of course not. Ethan was never serious.

Deborah had asked her once why she hated him so much, and the answer had been easy: Ethan Wyatt wasn't a person—he was *a persona*. A social media feed brought to life. A human sound bite comprised of charming quips and clever banter, carefully constructed to make people fall in love before they got bored enough to swipe.

He was pretend. An illusion. A lie. Maggie had known him for five years, and they'd never had a single conversation. Not one. Not until . . .

A memory landed, unbidden, in Maggie's mind and she rushed to shake it off, while, across the aisle, Ethan blinked.

"I'm a little confused, Marcie, my dear—"

"Maggie," she forced out.

"Why are you acting like we're enemies?"

"Why are you acting like we're friends?"

"What . . ."

"Either we're"—Maggie made a gesture—"finger-gun buddies—"

"I don't think that's a real thing."

"—or we're not. But please don't try to gaslight me into thinking we're friends when you don't even know my name."

"Marcie . . ."

"*My name is Maggie.*" She died a little when her voice cracked. "It has always been Maggie, and if you can't remember that, just don't call me anything at all. Please."

For a moment, all he did was stare. And blink. When he finally spoke, his voice was softer. "Are you serious?"

"Of course, I'm serious! Just like I was serious at the American Library Association when I told you I didn't want your sticker."

"How was I supposed to know that adhesive allergies are a real thing?"

"And I was serious at the Edgars when I told you—"

"Hey! The fire marshal said that could have happened to anyone."

"And at ThrillerCon? What about what happened at Thriller-Con?"

"One: I think shorter hair looks great on you. And two—"

"I can never go back to Houston!"

He had the nerve to roll his eyes. "Of course you can go to Houston. Murder by the Book would have you. Do you want me to call Johnnie? I can call Johnnie."

She couldn't even look at him. "And Tucson . . ."

The plane leveled off and the cabin lights went dim and Maggie wished she could pull the words back.

"I thought we weren't supposed to talk about Tucson." His voice was soft and low, and the bad part was that he wasn't lying, wasn't teasing. The worst part was that it was true.

"Just . . . please. I'm asking for a few days of peace, and then you can go back to mocking me and I can keep on avoiding you and we can both live the rest of our lives, blissfully having no respect for each other. Do you think you can do that?"

The cabin that had seemed so lush a few minutes before was suddenly like a spaceship—foreign and cold. Lights the color of amber were shining through the darkness, directing them to the emergency exits, but Maggie knew better. There was no way out but through.

"Can we do that? Please?" Maggie thought she might break under the weight of all that silence, but Ethan wasn't speechless. If anything, he looked like a man who had so many things to say he couldn't possibly pick just one.

Then he shook his head and settled on "Yeah. Truce. Whatever you want."

Maggie turned and watched the lights of the city fading behind them, the dark waves of the Atlantic stretching out ahead. She couldn't shake the feeling that the man beside her was like that water, sweeping and powerful and beloved. But Maggie had spent the last year feeling like an open wound. She was an open wound and he was full of salt.

"I really do like your hair."

Colin hadn't. *I didn't marry some short-haired girl*, he had muttered when he saw it, not quite loud enough to prove she'd actually heard what Maggie knew she'd heard. It was one of his greatest skills, like poking a stick through the bars of a tiger's cage—irritating, taunting—and always protected from the consequences of his own actions.

But Maggie had kept it shorter anyway. A few inches above her shoulders but long enough to pull back because, the truth was, she liked it too.

Ethan went back to poking at buttons and opening compartments while the lights of the city were swallowed by the sea.

"Do you know where we're going?" she had to ask.

"Nope."

"Are you . . ." Maggie looked down at her hands. They were chapped and raw but not quite bleeding. They looked like how the rest of her felt. But for the first time in a long time, there was another heartbeat in the darkness. She was scared but not alone. "Aren't you at least a little bit curious?"

She could barely make out his face in the shadows. He should have been less powerful with his million-dollar looks off the table, but it wasn't Ethan's face that made him. It was his presence. And, if anything, it was heightened in the dark. She could hear him breathe. She could see him shift. She could feel him—thirty inches and a million miles away.

"Whatever happens, I'm with you. Whatever comes, I'm in."

Zzzzzzzzzzzzzzzp. The chair slowly descended until it lay fully flat and he turned on his side.

"Hey, wanna make out?" he asked. She glared. And then Ethan chuckled and closed his eyes. And slept.

CHAPTER *Six*

"Maggie." The voice was low and close and almost familiar. Like a dream she couldn't quite remember but wanted to have again. "Maggie . . . Margaret Catherine Chase, you're going to be late!"

Maggie bolted upright and remembered: She was on an airplane. She was with Ethan Wyatt. But she was also possibly (probably) covered in drool, and he was trying very, very hard not to laugh, so Maggie gave him a drooly scowl and told him, "That's not my name."

"And a good morning to you too!" His hair was mussed and his grin was crooked as he stood above her, haloed by a bright, clear light. The plane smelled like coffee and bacon, and out the window . . . "Welcome to England."

She'd never been because there had never been money, and once there was money there wasn't time. It was the catch-22 of her life, and she felt a little naive as she looked down at the frosty hillsides.

"We'll be landing soon." Peter slid an omelet and a cup of coffee in front of her.

"Thank you," she said. "Could I have—"

"Cream, two sugars?" he guessed, then gave her a wink. "Already in there."

Wow. Whoever their mystery benefactor was, he'd done his homework.

"So on a scale of one to ten, how freaked out should I be that these people know how I take my . . ." Maggie trailed off when she realized Ethan wasn't beside her.

She turned to see him near the back of the plane, digging in a suitcase and pulling out a fresh shirt. When he grabbed his old one by the collar and slid it over his head in one smooth motion, he looked like an ad for bodywash or body spray or just bodies in general because the move revealed muscles she'd thought only existed on book covers. Killhaven was making a mistake, Maggie realized, because it turned out Ethan Wyatt looked far better *without* his leather jacket.

Which he knew. Of course he knew. So she was going to turn around and stop staring. She had to. Any second now. The last thing Ethan needed was another woman fawning over him, so she was going to turn around and eat her omelet. Yup. She was going to get right on that. But then he bent to dig in the bag again, pivoting slightly.

And that was when she saw the scar—long and jagged, starting at his shoulder and then running down the right side of his back. The wound was old and healed but still angry—as if something dangerous lived inside of Ethan and was still trying to claw its way out. And none of it made any sense.

Ethan Wyatt was smooth perfection and effortless charm. Easy smiles and clever quips. The product of focus groups and Photoshop and at least ten thousand dollars' worth of high-end orthodontia.

Ethan Wyatt wasn't *real*, but that scar was. Two minutes ago, she would have sworn he was the kind of guy who would tell everyone his war stories, play them up for the ladies and the press, but Maggie had never heard a word about an injury. She'd only ever heard . . .

Come to think of it, Maggie had never heard anything about his past at all. And for the first time she had to wonder what was the bigger mystery: this trip or the man who was taking it with her?

When he turned, Maggie whirled in her seat and went back to her omelet. She didn't ask a single question. She didn't say a thing.

A Rolls-Royce was waiting on the tarmac and a hard wind was blowing off the sea as Maggie climbed down the jet stairs thirty minutes later. They were somewhere in the country, surrounded by miles of rugged coastline and frothy water and Maggie couldn't help but shiver as she watched an older man climb out of the long black car and head toward them with a wave.

"Welcome!" He wore a tweed coat and a little tweed hat and looked like someone who would know what a marchioness was even if he'd never read a romance novel in his life. "Glad you made it. Good thing too. Before it gets a wee bit chilly."

"This is *not* chilly?" Maggie's hair whipped wildly around her head and blew in her mouth. Even Ethan seemed disheveled, but with his collar turned up and his hair mussed, he just looked a little extra roguish—like he'd had a rough night, but the *good* kind—while Maggie stood there, trying to peel her hair off her tongue.

She was still spitting and flailing when she heard a chuckle and felt a hand on the small of her back. "Come on, Margaret Louise."

The driver had gone for their luggage and Ethan was leaning around her, reaching for the door and pressing close enough to block the wind. He hadn't shaved and dark stubble covered his jaw. He smelled like peppermint and smooth, soft leather, and even after she heard the *click* and felt a rush of warm air at her back, Maggie just stood there, frozen.

"What?" Ethan looked like he didn't know if he should be amused or afraid.

"That's not my name," she said, because it was safer than admitting that she wanted to feel his stubble to see if it was as soft as it looked. She wanted to ask about his scar and his past and his secrets. She wanted to know how someone like Ethan was spending Christmas with someone like her, but the words froze on the wind, and all she could do was shake her head and crawl inside, then watch in confusion as he bent down to carefully tuck the hem of her coat where it wouldn't slam in the door.

He started to rise, but stopped midway when he realized Maggie was staring. "You know, some women think I'm chivalrous."

"Some women think the earth is flat."

"Oh." He bit back that million-dollar grin. "You wound me."

Maggie smirked. "Is that an offer?"

A thousand scenarios flashed across his face when he said, "Maybe later." And then he winked and slammed the door and Maggie tried to stop herself from smiling.

CHAPTER *Seven*

Twelve Years Ago

The first time Maggie met Colin Livingston he insisted on riding in the back seat. That was what she noticed first and remembered the longest. Not the frayed and beer-stained fraternity sweatshirt. Not the red-rimmed eyes and beleaguered grin of a guy who never rolled out of bed before ten.

But as she stood on the dormitory steps waiting for Emily, her smallest suitcase at her feet even though she'd had absolutely no idea what to pack for three weeks with a stranger's family, her only goal was to take up as little space as possible, make as little noise as possible—to not eat too much or take showers that were too long or do any of a hundred things that might get her sent out into the cold by herself. Again.

So Maggie wasn't sure what to think when a little red BMW came flying through the parking lot, then slammed on the brakes in front of her.

"I'm gonna change my name to Rudolph," Emily chimed from behind the wheel. "Get in!"

Maggie wasn't expecting a boy to climb out of the BMW's passenger side. When he flipped the seat up, allowing entrance to the back, Maggie started to climb in, but he cut her off. "I'll ride back there." Then he practically folded himself in half to fit.

Some pop star's version of a Christmas carol was coming out of the speakers and Emily turned down the volume. "New Friend Maggie meet Old Friend Colin." She was wearing earrings that were tiny bells with sprigs of fresh mistletoe in them, and when she smiled and popped a bubble it didn't even mess up her lip gloss. Maggie had never been so envious of anyone in her life.

Not because Emily had a BMW or pretty things or even some-one she could introduce as "old friend." It was more because Emily belonged. In that car. On that campus. In this world. In a way that Maggie never would.

Emily had spent the last week assuring Maggie that no one would mind one extra guest. She wasn't an imposition. And she absolutely didn't need to chip in for gas or food because Emily's father managed a hedge fund and Emily's mother managed Emily's father, and be-tween all their society friends and business acquaintances, chances were halfway decent they wouldn't even notice Maggie was there. They certainly wouldn't care.

"Colin's family always spends Christmas with mine," Emily ex-plained.

"We have a house next door," Colin chimed in from behind them.

"The three of us will be the only people under forty, and we'll be glorious," Emily said, then popped another bubble.

"Hey, Em—" Colin started, but Emily was already turning down the heat because she knew what he was going to say. She knew *him*. And something about it made Maggie feel even lonelier.

"Are you . . ." Maggie looked back at the boy whose head brushed the ceiling. "Sure? That you want to ride back there? I don't mind."

"Oh, this isn't for you," he said. "It's for me. The back seat is way safer than the front."

He caught Emily's gaze in the rearview mirror and she stuck her tongue out at him. "Colin is still mad that I beat him at go-carts when we were seven. He doesn't appreciate my driving."

"So I should put my seat belt on?" Maggie asked and Colin laughed. Then Emily slammed on the gas and peeled out of the park-ing lot, running over the curb on the way.

By the time they reached the eleven-bedroom mansion on a rocky beach in Rhode Island, Maggie knew three things: Emily was a fashion major and a terrible driver and Maggie's new best friend.

By the time New Year's Eve rolled around she knew one more: she was in love with Colin Livingston.

CHAPTER *Eight*

Three Days Before Christmas

The car wasn't a cherry red BMW. There were no Christmas songs on the radio. And absolutely no one was going to teach her a made-up version of "The Twelve Days of Christmas" or give her five golden Chandler Bings for a silly present.

This was a whole new Christmas adventure, so Maggie tried to focus on all the ways that it was different. Like the chauffeur's little tweed hat or the surreal sensation of riding on the wrong side of the road as they drove across the frosty hills.

Or, Maggie reluctantly admitted, the man on the other side of the car.

A *ding* pierced the silence.

Ethan hadn't spoken since the airport. He hadn't looked at her since the wink.

Ding.

She watched him tap his phone to check a text from Amber. Where are you, Mr. Hotstuff?

Oh please . . .

Ding.

This one was from Maya: WE MISS YOU.

Ding.

Brooklyn: You seriously aren't coming?

Ding.

Kimmy: I refuse to have Christmas without you.

Ding.

Rachel: I can beg, you know? Do you want me to beg?

"Say whatever it is you're thinking over there before your head explodes."

Ding.

Maggie could have denied that she was snooping, but she was far too tired and too jet-lagged to try. "You're . . . popular."

"These are from the last eight hours. We must have just gotten service."

"Oh." She looked at her own phone. Twenty percent battery. Two bars. And not a single sound.

Ding. Ding. Ding. Ding. Ethan barely glanced at a string of texts from "Do Not Resuscitate," then sighed and powered off the phone. "Please tell me they don't have cell service wherever we're going," he called up to the driver.

"It comes and goes," the older man said simply, and Ethan leaned back against the headrest and closed his eyes.

"Won't your girlfriends worry if they don't hear from you?" she couldn't resist saying.

"Oh, they're trained better than that." He flashed a mischievous grin, practically daring her to start a fight, so Maggie turned back to the window and the winding road.

They'd passed through a quaint little village as they left the airfield, but they hadn't seen another town for almost an hour. They were surrounded by rolling hills and sweeping vistas, grazing sheep and long stone walls that seemed to stretch forever, but an odd sense of foreboding was starting to grow inside of Maggie.

"Excuse me, uh . . ." She leaned closer to the driver.

"James, ma'am."

"James. Hello. Um . . . where are we? Is that a silly question?" It was probably a silly question.

But James merely laughed. "Not silly at all, ma'am. Let's just say we're closer to Scotland than London and if the wind at the airport felt straight off the North Sea that's because it was."

"I see." She didn't really see, though, and the countryside was growing rougher.

When they reached a rushing river and a deep ravine, the only way to cross was an arching stone bridge that looked like something straight out of a fairy tale—the kind that was incredibly dark before Walt Disney got ahold of it. And Maggie wanted to ask a thousand questions. Like *Did his employers have guests often?* and *Did those guests ever disappear without a trace?*

"Uh . . . James? How far is it?"

"Oh, we're here, ma'am." *Here? Where?* Maggie saw a lake shimmering in the distance, but there wasn't a town or a house in sight. "The estate is over twenty thousand acres. And it abuts a national park."

"Oh. That's"—*convenient if you need to dispose of a body*— "lovely."

"It certainly is," James said as the car crested a hill and, suddenly, Maggie wasn't in a Rolls beside her nemesis. She was in a movie. Or a time machine. Or someone else's life. Because there, in the valley below, stood the grandest home that Maggie had ever seen.

It must have been some kind of castle. Or manor house. Or abbey? Maggie didn't have a clue. She just knew that it was three stories tall with probably hundreds of rooms and belonged in the kind of movie where hot guys with accents wear cravats.

It was a palace from another era—made of stone and glass and centuries. Kings and queens had probably slept there. Wars had no doubt been fought there. Emily's parents' seaside estate would have looked like a McMansion in comparison and for one brief moment, Maggie forgot to be afraid.

"Welcome to Mistletoe Manor," James said when the car slowed and stopped in the driveway.

"Ten bucks says there's an old guy here who wants to hunt us for sport," Ethan whispered once James was out of the car.

"I hope not." She looked across the back seat at Ethan. It was the first time they'd felt together in something—like they were in on a secret. "I'm pretty sure there's an Eleanor Ashley novel that starts that way."

They both climbed out and Maggie braced against the cold.

"Oh yeah," Ethan said over the top of the car. "I've heard of her."

Surely it was the wind? Sleep deprivation? The world's worst case of jet lag? Because there was no way that he meant . . .

"You've *heard* . . ." Maggie tried to keep her voice down. "You've . . . *Have you never read Eleanor Ashley?*"

He shrugged—an actual shrug! "Is she any good?"

"*Is she any good?* Is she . . ." Maggie wanted to crawl over the car and strangle him. "Eleanor Ashley has written ninety-nine novels of perfection. She's the world's greatest living author and the greatest crime writer of all time, and so help me if you mention Sir Arthur Conan Whatshisface I'm going to disembowel you with an emery board. Eleanor Ashley came from nothing. She was born in a house with no plumbing and only went to school through the sixth grade because her family needed her to work. She wrote her first novel on scraps of paper she pulled out of the trash at the office building where she was a cleaning lady.

"Eleanor Ashley *invented* the modern crime novel. She revolutionized the genre and . . . Killhaven—you know the publisher that just paid you seven figures for your next book? It wouldn't *exist* without Eleanor Ashley. So yeah. She's good. She's amazing. She's . . ." Maggie trailed off, confused and annoyed, as Ethan's gaze drifted over her shoulder. His lips quirked. His eyes twinkled. "She's . . ."

And then there was a new voice flying on the wind. "She's standing right behind you."

CHAPTER *Nine*

At first, Maggie thought she was dreaming—or possibly dead—because she couldn't believe she was in England. With Ethan Wyatt. Standing in front of a mansion. That belonged to—

There was a gentle push at her back and suddenly Maggie was stumbling away from the car and closer to the woman with white hair and sharp blue eyes. Eleanor's left hand rested on her hip and her right sat atop the silver handle of a cane. She looked like a painting come to life, the story of an avenging angel who fell to Earth a thousand years ago, then decided to stick around.

Maggie had read every book—every article—every word ever written by (or about) Eleanor Ashley, but all she could think as she stood there was *No wonder they call her the Duchess of Death.*

"So happy you could make it. I would have given you more notice, but, well . . . I like a twist." Eleanor's smile was quick and sharp and teasing. A little self-deprecating, too, because when you've sold more books than the Bible you can afford to be the butt of your own jokes.

Maggie knew Eleanor was in her early eighties, but the woman before them seemed timeless in a black sweaterdress that was probably decades old but had never gone out of style, kind of like the woman who wore it. Her only item of jewelry was a pearl and silver brooch in the shape of a magnifying glass. It felt whimsical and out of place but also extremely, exactly perfect.

"You're . . ." Maggie barely recognized her own voice. She thought she might pass out. And maybe she would have if she hadn't felt a pressure around her waist—a strong arm pulling her tight against far too many muscles.

"How was your flight?" Eleanor asked.

The pressure on Maggie's waist tightened, like Ethan was trying to squeeze a reply out of her. "Uh . . ."

"It was great!" Ethan beamed. "Thank you so much for having us. We're honored to be here."

He squeezed again. *Ouch.* "Hi. Hello. Hi."

"We're big fans." It was a lie, of course, but Maggie was probably fan enough for both of them and Ethan *was* practically carrying her toward the door—like they were contestants in a three-legged race but only two of their legs were working properly and they both belonged to him.

"You're . . ." *Eleanor Ashley. My favorite author. The reason I do what I do. My idol. My favorite. My oldest friend even though we've never met.* "You're . . . You're . . ."

"—home is lovely," Ethan filled in, giving Maggie a look that said *get it together*, so she did the only thing she could think to do in front of the Duchess of Death: she dipped slowly and—

"Did you just curtsy?" Ethan whispered.

"I . . ."

"We're both just thrilled to be here. Right, Maggie?" He glanced down at her. "Maybe a little tired, though? Didn't you say you were tired?" he prompted, then gave a low, soft laugh. "It was a long flight."

Maggie felt the weight of Eleanor's gaze then. Appraising. Calculating. Like at any moment she was going to order Maggie back into the Rolls, the airplane. The sea. Like Maggie was going to get sent away before she'd even stepped inside. But that would have been okay, Maggie told herself. The last two minutes were already the best Christmas of her life.

But Eleanor simply turned to lead them inside, and Maggie couldn't keep from staring at the way she leaned heavily on the cane, not quite limping, but moving slowly. Carefully. For the first time, she seemed frail. And she must have read Maggie's mind because she gestured to the cane with her free hand.

"Don't mind this. I just carry it to keep the boys away." Eleanor gave a weak chuckle, then admitted, "And I slipped on the stairs a few weeks ago. Thought I might as well use the damn thing. I've had it forever. There's a dagger inside. See?"

She picked up the cane and twisted and then, *click*, out popped a dagger. Even on the overcast day it glistened in the sun. "I have another one that will shoot a tranquilizer dart twenty feet if you press the rose on the handle."

There was pure mischief in the older woman's eyes. And sheer adoration in Ethan's.

"I love you," he said. "Will you marry me? Or adopt me? I'm happy either way. Totally your call."

"I like you." Eleanor smiled like a woman who had heard far worse offers, and then she cocked her head and said, "We'll see."

CHAPTER Ten

Maggie had no idea what to expect from an English mansion that was probably hundreds of years old. Suits of armor? Small, interior moats? Maybe a jester in residence? But what she found on the other side of the door was a wide, open space that stretched to the back of the house. Giant columns rose into a high, arching ceiling and the floors were polished wood. It felt more like a cathedral than a home, and there wasn't a doubt in Maggie's mind that, if she'd yelled, she would have heard an echo.

The only thing out of place was the staircase, which was two different colors—like patchwork. *Eleanor fell on the stairs*, Maggie's tired mind remembered. Someone had started a repair job that they hadn't quite had time to finish, but aside from that, the whole house seemed to be brand-new and incredibly old at the same time. She was just starting to wonder how that was possible when she heard footsteps and a high voice crying out, "Well, there you are!"

The girl couldn't have been much over twenty, with long blond hair pulled back in a headband that matched her pale pink sweater. There were pearls at her neck and French tips on her nails, and when she stopped beside a pair of antique dueling pistols, she looked like she was getting ready to pledge Kappa Kappa Murder.

"You went outside!" the girl exclaimed in an accent that sounded more like Alabama than Great Britain. "In the cold! Without a coat!"

"And lived to tell the tale," Eleanor replied in a singsong tune.

"Now, Aunt E, you know what the doctor said—"

"Cecilia." Eleanor cut off what was sure to be a lecture she'd heard before. "Come meet our guests. Ethan. Maggie. May I introduce Cecilia Honeychurch?"

That was when the girl seemed to notice the guests. Or, well, *guest*. Because her eyes went to Ethan and never left. His hair was wavier than usual and his eyes a little sleepy but, wouldn't you know it, Ethan Wyatt made jet lag look good.

Meanwhile, Maggie's hair was tangled and her skin was dry, and when she looked down, she saw a blotch of omelet on her sweater. Not that anyone was looking at her.

"Well, hello there." The girl held out her hand to Ethan. "I'm Cece."

"Eleanor?" Ethan's voice held a teasing lilt. "Why didn't you tell us we'd be meeting your slightly younger sister . . ." He trailed off, realizing . . . "Too much? I think that was too much?"

But even *that* sounded charming and Eleanor smiled. "I appreciate the effort."

Cece batted her eyes and slapped him playfully on the arm, lingering on those frankly ridiculous biceps. "Oh, you're a big flirt."

He lowered his voice. "Among other things." He dropped his hold on Maggie and she stumbled away. "And who might you be, Cece?"

Cece tucked a piece of hair behind her ear as if she wasn't already wearing a perfectly adequate headband. Then she exclaimed, "I'm Aunt Eleanor's niece!" as if aunts and nieces weren't typically related. "When she heard I needed a job, she said I could move to England and be her companion and secretary and . . . well . . . just sort of all-around aide." She turned to Eleanor and raised her voice. "We have a lot of fun together. Don't we, Aunt E?"

If the look on Eleanor's face was any indication, she and Cece had very different definitions of the word *fun*, but there was something else in her eyes, too: patience and curiosity—like someone who was working on a plot and pulling at strings, not sure which ones would make a knot and which would make them all unravel.

But then something over Maggie's shoulder caught Eleanor's attention. "How is it out there, James?"

Maggie turned to see the driver walking down the hall. He must have come in through a servants' entrance because he'd traded his coat for an apron and carried a stack of mail on a silver tray.

"Gonna be a bad one, ma'am. Glad you folks landed when you did. Now, I'll take your bags to your rooms. If you need anything, just let me or Miss Cecilia know."

Cece reached for the tray. "I'll take that, James."

"I've got it." Eleanor started flipping through the letters and Maggie couldn't keep from staring because even Eleanor Ashley's mail was fascinating. Red envelope (*probably a Christmas card*). Green envelope (*Christmas card*). White envelope with a picture of a light bulb (*utility bill?*). Blue envelope with a staff and snake (*medical bill?*). White envelope (*personal letter?*).

Maggie was just standing there, thinking she would happily read Eleanor Ashley's utility bill cover to cover when Eleanor shoved the mail under one arm and leaned a little heavier on her cane. "Cecilia, would you mind showing our guests to their rooms? I'd prefer to stay off the stairs as much as I can."

"Oh, of course! You poor thing." Maggie might have been stunned and exhausted but she knew one thing: there was nothing poor about Eleanor Ashley. Still, that didn't stop Cece from shouting, "Why don't you go lie down?"

"I'll do that." Eleanor pasted on a smile but whispered, "Perhaps you can tell her there's nothing wrong with my hearing?" And then she walked away.

As Maggie watched her go, it felt like coming awake after a long nap—the kind where you're not sure if it's day or night, summer or winter. Like you don't know if you've been sleeping for an hour or a year. The one thing she knew was that Ethan's arm was heavy and warm as it fell around her shoulders, guiding her toward the stairs.

"That's Eleanor Ashley," she mumbled numbly. "We're . . . we're spending Christmas with Eleanor Ashley."

She kept waiting for Ethan to tell her she was crazy, that she was wrong. But he just kept looking down at her with something like fondness in his eyes. And when he said, "Let's get you to your room, Maggie," her name sounded just right on his lips.

CHAPTER Eleven

"We are *so* happy y'all could join us," Cece said when they reached the top of the stairs and started down a drafty hall. "She's been a little mopey. *Since she fell*," she added in a whisper. Like it was a crime to admit that Eleanor was human. And frail. And, in fact, an eighty-one-year-old woman and not just the icon who lived in Maggie's mind.

"How bad was it?" Ethan asked.

"Oh, it was more scary than bad." Cece waved the worry away. "The runner was loose and the railing was old and, well, she's just not a young woman anymore. It could have been a lot worse."

Maggie had lost her mom and dad at eighteen. She'd never even known her grandparents. Maggie didn't have family memories or family heirlooms or family in any way at all. Maggie had no one. Maggie had nothing. But Maggie had always had Eleanor, and the thought of what might have happened . . .

"This is her office." Cece paused for a moment in front of a large door and Maggie stumbled to a stop. "But I wouldn't go in there if I were you," Cece warned. "She doesn't like people touching her new book. Even if they were just dusting and didn't mean to mess up chapter twenty—"

"New book?" Maggie didn't even try to keep her voice down. "She's writing number one hundred?"

"Oops." Cece's cheeks turned pink. "I wasn't supposed to mention that."

Maggie was aware, faintly, of footsteps walking away, of the air growing colder and stiller around her. But, mostly, she could feel herself leaning, teetering, starting—

A warm hand slipped into her cold one. "Come along, Margaret Grace." She forgot to put up a fight as Ethan dragged her away.

Five minutes later, Maggie was starting to wish she'd run a string, left a bread trail, maybe invested in some high-end walkie-talkies because she was pretty sure the only way she was going to find the first floor again would be to go to a window and jump. The halls were long and twisty and the whole house felt like a maze as they followed Cece up staircases and down corridors, past bookcases and alcoves and windows that overlooked twenty thousand acres of very empty England.

"Your rooms are just up . . ." Cece trailed off as a sharp scream pierced the air outside.

"Is this place haunted?" Ethan whispered to Maggie. "Five bucks says it's haunted."

And maybe he was on to something because all the color drained from Cece's face as she went to the window and started wiping condensation off the glass.

"They're early." Cece groaned as the sound of slamming car doors echoed up from the drive below. "They must have tried to beat the storm . . ." She was already walking away when she stopped and pointed to a pair of open doors. "Those are your rooms. We have cocktails in the library at six. Don't be late for cocktails. Aunt Eleanor hates it when people are—" More shouts sounded from outside. "If you need anything, there are bell pulls and—" A baby's cries echoed through the glass. "Library. Six o'clock." Then Cece turned and dashed away.

"My money's still on ghost." Ethan sounded smug.

"That was a baby."

"Name me one thing that's creepier than a baby ghost." It was the most serious she'd ever seen him and Maggie bit back a smile because she didn't dare agree.

Instead, she chose a room at random, but before she could step inside, Ethan eased in front of her and rested a forearm on the doorframe and just kind of . . . leaned. He looked big and strong and confident while Maggie stood there, grateful she hadn't fallen on her face in Eleanor Ashley's driveway. Worse: she knew her ability to stay upright had been largely because of him, and Maggie knew she should say thank you. Or something. She should definitely say—

"So how will we pass the time? Wanna make out?" He flashed a grin and Maggie darted under his arm.

She could still hear the deep timbre of his laughter long after she'd closed the door and thrown herself onto the four-poster bed and screamed into the pillow.

You've been invited to spend Christmas with your biggest fan, Deborah had said. It was probably an exaggeration. Maggie didn't actually believe that Eleanor Ashley had read her books. But Eleanor knew Maggie's name. She'd invited Maggie into her home.

The mattress bounced. The bed-curtains jiggled. And Maggie let herself think that maybe—just maybe—Christmas might not be so awful after all.

CHAPTER Twelve

"You know, you really shouldn't sleep after a red-eye."

The voice was too deep to be Colin's. Too warm and too close and too . . .

"Ethan!"

He was lying on the bed beside her, rugged jaw propped on his upturned hand. "There's a reason they call jet lag the silent killer."

"No one calls it that."

She tried to push her hair out of her face. Then she gave up and tried pushing him off her bed, but he was like a Greek statue, fully clothed but just as heavy as if he'd been carved out of stone.

"Why are you in my room?" Her mouth was too dry and her eyelids were too heavy and there was nothing but darkness outside the window. She had no idea what time it was. She just knew that Ethan Wyatt was on her bed and that wasn't even the weirdest part of her very weird day.

"I knocked," he told her simply.

"You should have—"

"I knocked *loudly*," he cut her off. "And repeatedly. You didn't answer."

Had she swallowed wool? Is that something that happens in England?

"Why—"

"It's almost six," he told her. "And Eleanor doesn't like—"

Shoot. Maggie looked at the darkened window again as if it were a clock, but she knew he was right. It felt like she'd been out of it for hours, and now Maggie had sleep in her eyes and wool in her throat and she was still wearing her omelet sweater and she didn't have any idea what one wears to cocktails in Eleanor Ashley's library!

She flew from the bed and toward the pair of giant suitcases that sat inside the door.

"I brought those in for you." Ethan sounded smug. "You're welcome."

Luckily, Maggie had packed options. So many options. Every possible, conceivable option, but as she unzipped the biggest bag she realized she was frozen. Precious seconds were ticking by and Ethan was still there. She saw his confused face reflected in the mirror.

"What?" Maggie snapped, waiting for a joke but he just shook his head.

"Nothing. I just thought you'd be a little roll-y suitcase kind of person, not . . ." He gestured to the giant bags.

"I used to be," she said, but she still couldn't move.

"You don't know what to wear, do you?" He gave her the kind of grin that said he'd figured her out, cracked her like a safe. She couldn't possibly have any more secrets.

So she whirled on him. "No. I don't know what to wear for Christmas cocktails with Eleanor Ashley!" She threw her hands out wide, then grabbed her toiletry bag and most basic little black dress and ran into the bathroom to change because that was no doubt faster than trying to push Ethan out.

"Technically, it's Christmas Eve Eve Eve," he called from the other side of the door.

"Get out!" she called back.

"You're gonna need help zipping that," he said as she threw water on her face and some dried-out mascara on her lashes. It flaked and got in her eyes and she only had twenty seconds to brush her teeth.

But the worst part was when she pulled the dress over her head and remembered why she hadn't worn it in a year. First, because she'd barely left her apartment, but also . . .

She remembered standing in a dressing room and watching Emily roll her eyes. *"Come here. You never were good at zipping."* *Maggie turned but Emily caught her eye in the mirror. "Just make sure you wear it when Colin is home. And make sure he doesn't just unzip it,"* Emily had said with an exaggerated *wink wink.*

Maggie couldn't wear that dress. She couldn't even *zip* that dress. But there was a voice on the other side of the door, calling, "Oh, Margaret Lavinia, we're going to be late."

So Maggie twisted and turned and—"Ow!"—banged her elbow on the doorframe, trying to ignore the little voice that was telling her she really only had one option.

"Come on, Margaret Eugenia."

Reluctantly, Maggie opened the door and Ethan went silent at the sight of her.

She'd barely had time to twist her hair on top of her head and slap on the only lipstick she owned—something called *Heathen* that Emily had gotten in a goodie bag at Milan Fashion Week. Maggie had always liked the color but from the look on Ethan's face she probably had it all over her teeth or something. And she didn't dare say he was right about the zipper. She'd rather die first. But she somehow managed to step into the room and turn around.

She waited for a joke about the fact that she was wearing the world's most utilitarian bra or how she had two freckles on her back that were positioned like teeny tiny nipples. Colin used to tease her about them. Or *mock* her? Maggie was no longer sure of the difference, but Ethan didn't say a thing.

He just studied her face in the mirror, and when she met his gaze, she didn't recognize the Ethan who stared back. There was no teasing, no taunting, no too-cool, too-clever, too-charming grin. It was as if a mask had slipped and for one split second, she saw *Ethan, the man* and not *Ethan, the Guy in the Leather Jacket*. And for that split second Maggie forgot how to breathe.

"Hey. She's gonna love you." A warm finger brushed down the line of her spine. He was looking at her like he knew her—like he'd *always* known her. Better than Colin. Better than Emily. Better even than she knew herself. And all Maggie could do was stand there as one heartbeat turned into two. Then three. And then her heart stopped beating altogether and Maggie felt herself sway. The touch broke and the moment ended and Maggie watched his mask go on.

The persona flickered to life as he said, "Besides, your boobs look amazing in—"

"Zip it," she ordered and the zipper slid into place and he didn't say another word as she stormed back into the bathroom and slammed the door.

"Do you want me to wait?" he called. Wordlessly, she opened the door and pointed. "Downstairs. I'll wait for you downstairs."

CHAPTER *Thirteen*

"You're two minutes late to my party."

Maggie skidded to a stop on the stairs, breathing hard and still trying to put in her earrings. For a split second, she wondered if she was hearing things, but then she saw Eleanor in the foyer below, standing at a window and looking out over the drive.

"I'm so sorry. I only meant to lay down for just a minute, but . . ."

Wait. Was it supposed to be *lay* down or *lie* down? Maggie didn't know. Maggie never knew! But if she was wrong, Eleanor hadn't noticed or cared. In fact, she hadn't even turned. She just kept staring out the window and Maggie tried to keep her footsteps soft—like Eleanor was sleepwalking and she didn't want to wake her.

"Thank you for having me. Your home is"—*Massive? Just as intimidating as you are?*—"lovely. It's—"

"Too old and too big for its own good and worth far more money than it should be. Just like me." Eleanor didn't laugh and didn't smile and Maggie didn't know what to say as her idol's breath fogged against the cold, dark glass. "It's quiet, though. I like the quiet."

Maggie remembered the long drive and empty landscape—twenty thousand acres of no neighbors and no streetlights. On a clear night, they could probably see a million stars.

"I was born in a house with a dirt floor, did you know that, Maggie? The biographies like to talk about how poor we were, but they always miss that detail. Which is a pity. It's a good one. My mother was sixteen and her parents had kicked her out. She was basically squatting in what was basically a shack and . . . The only thing she knew how to write was her name."

"She must have been so proud of you."

Outside, snowflakes streaked through the porchlights, making little white dashes in the sky. The wind howled and the house moaned, but Eleanor Ashley seemed stronger than it all. A force of nature.

"I'm glad you made it before the weather turned. It's going to be quite a storm." She sounded a million miles away, like she was talking to herself when she added, "I didn't plan on the storm . . ."

"Excuse me, ma'am." Maggie turned to see James standing in an arching doorway. "Inspector Dobson is on the phone. There's a possibility he will not make it until morning."

"I'll talk to him." Eleanor turned and, for the first time, looked at Maggie. "You go on to the library, dear. I'll be right there." Eleanor drew a ragged breath, bracing, like someone about to dive into an ice-cold lake. "We might as well get started."

And Maggie couldn't help but wonder: *Started with what?*

Excerpt from the Official Police Interrogation
of Margaret Chase and Ethan Wyatt

December 25

Inspector Patel: Who else was there that first night?

Mr. Wyatt: Ooh! Is this the part where we lay out the suspects? Finally. Let's lay out some suspects.

Ms. Chase: Well . . . there was Eleanor's nephew, Rupert.

Mr. Wyatt: Yeah. There was that guy. And that guy's wife.

Ms. Chase: Kitty's sweet. A little—

Mr. Wyatt: Fertile. Very, very—

Ms. Chase: Tired. She'd have to be. The children are a handful. Let me see. There was Dr. Charles.

Mr. Wyatt: Yeah. I can't tell you much about him. I think Charles was his first name. No. His last name. You know, I have no idea.

Ms. Chase: And, obviously, Their Graces.

Mr. Wyatt: Wait. I thought her name was Grace?

Ms. Chase: I'd never met a duke or duchess before.

Mr. Wyatt: Don't forget the lawyer.

Ms. Chase: Right. And I guess that leaves Sir Jasper.

CHAPTER *Fourteen*

The good news was that Maggie had no trouble locating the library. The bad news was that she found it mainly by following the voices. *Plural.* Because, evidently, she and Ethan weren't Eleanor's only guests. And that was how she found herself inching toward her second party of the week, holding her breath as she peeked through a pair of wide double doors into . . .

Heaven. Or what Maggie had always imagined Heaven would look like.

The room was two stories tall and the walls were rimmed with shelves, but Eleanor didn't have a cool, rolling library ladder. No. Eleanor had *two.* One for each long side. It was all Maggie could do not to push them to the back of the room and challenge Ethan to a race.

She imagined soaring past a thousand books and photos and pieces of Eleanor's life—like the oil painting that had been the cover of her tenth book. A Venetian half mask that had been in the movie they made of her third. Black-and-white photos hung over a fireplace that was surrounded by overstuffed couches and comfortable chairs. Dotted throughout the room were daggers and clubs, sickles and shields. It was like Murders-R-Us had had a sale and Eleanor had bought one of everything.

And yet the most unexpected thing was the Christmas tree, twinkling and glowing by the wall of windows that overlooked the grounds at the back of the house. It was tall and perfect, and suddenly Maggie was eight years old again, wishing Santa would bring her cousins for Christmas.

"You found us!" Ethan was standing by the fireplace, flames leaping and crackling as he stood close to Cece. They'd been talking, bonding. Probably on the verge of getting engaged as far as Maggie knew—not that she cared.

"Maggie?" Ethan sounded worried as he walked toward her.

"Yes. I found you."

He looked from Maggie to Cece then lowered his voice. "Why, Margaret Olivia—"

"That's not my name."

"—are you *jealous*?"

"Don't be ridiculous."

Maggie tried to laugh but the only sound she heard was a cane pounding against the library floor and Eleanor commanding, "Come on." She was heading their direction—shoulders thrown back. Eyes sharp. She was the Eleanor they'd first met and not the sad, tired woman by the windows when she said, "You've got people to meet."

The first stop was Eleanor's nephew.

"Rupert Price. Lovely to meet you."

Rupert Price did not, in fact, think it was lovely to meet them. Maggie saw it in the way he wouldn't meet their gazes or shake their hands and didn't even bother to hide his contempt at sharing his family holiday with riffraff—which was a bold stance for a man wearing a sweater with Santa Claus on it.

"Why are you here?" he asked pointedly the moment Eleanor turned away.

"Excuse me?" Maggie asked.

"How do you know my aunt?" There was an edge to his voice, like at any moment he was going to shout "Intruder!" and call for the guards.

"Oh, we . . ." Maggie started but an arm fell, heavy and warm, around her shoulders.

"We're writers." Ethan took a slow sip of his drink and Rupert tensed in the way slightly insecure men always tense when faced with that much Ethan. "Eleanor invited us."

"So she's inviting strangers to Christmas now?" Rupert said, almost to himself. Like he couldn't decide if that was very good or very bad, but one thing was certain: he hadn't been expecting it.

"Oh, you must be our Americans!" A woman wearing a sweater that featured Mrs. Claus appeared at Rupert's side. She had a baby on her hip and a wide smile on her face. "I'm Kitty. Rupert's wife." She bounced the baby and pointed to the two little boys and one girl playing (and screaming) twenty feet away, all of them in sweaters with tiny elves. "And these are ours."

"I can tell!" Maggie was honestly delighted.

"Oh, and this is Nanny Davis. Can you believe she was Rupert's nanny when he was a boy?"

Ethan looked at the woman who was approximately five hundred years old and sleeping peacefully by the fire. "You don't say . . ."

"Oh yes. I couldn't do it without her. These kids run me . . ." Kitty's gaze drifted over Ethan's shoulder. "RJ! Eli! Eloise!" Kitty called to the children playing at the other end of the room. "Rupert, will you go check on them, please?" she asked her husband, who didn't go check on anyone. He just took a long swig of his drink and tried not to stand next to Ethan, who was taller. And broader. And who was smiling at Kitty in a way her husband probably never had and for a moment Kitty just stood there, blinking until—

"Mine!" a little boy shouted and took off running through the crowded room with—

"That's not a real sword, is it? Rupert? Rupert!" Kitty asked and Rupert drained his cocktail just as Ethan spun to pull the very real, very sharp sword from the hands of the very small child who was running past, screaming at the top of his lungs.

Next up was—

"Dr. Charles," the man said, gripping Maggie's hand. He was the kind of man caught perpetually in between. Neither old nor young, handsome nor ugly. Probably nice but perfectly nondescript. He seemed as confused about why he was there as Maggie felt, but he also seemed to have made his peace with it, judging by the way he reached for a tray of shrimp puffs.

"Friend of the family, eh? I used to work with Kitty. Best nurse I ever saw, but then she left to be a mum. Rupert invited me. Say," he called to a passing Cece, "got any more of these?" He pointed to the empty tray and Cece gave a tired nod but kept walking.

David and Victoria Claymore, the Duke and Duchess of Stratford, were unamused. Perpetually. They looked like *Horse and Hound* magazine had become sentient and started to speak. Maggie waited for the inevitable discussion of horses. And also hounds. But they just stood silently, drinks gripped tightly in their pale hands. The duke had a vacant smile on his face, but the duchess was looking at Maggie like she might be something a dermatologist was going to have to burn off.

"So you're Rupert's sister?" Maggie tried. She even pointed to Rupert in his Santa sweater as if his sister might need a reminder.

"Yes?" The duchess made it sound like she wasn't so sure. But just then, one of the kids pulled a ceremonial dagger off the shelves and Kitty yelled, "Eloise! No! Eloise, come back here and give Auntie Eleanor a kiss. Eloise!" and the duchess looked like she might be considering changing her answer.

But something had just occurred to Maggie. "Oh my gosh! You're the Duchess of Stratford, and your aunt is the Duchess of Death!" Maggie thought that was an extremely fun and excellent point, but the duke simply looked at her, confused and a little dim.

"Death is not an actual title in the peerage," he said. Then he and his wife turned and walked away like they would rather be literally anywhere but there.

The lawyer was a young man named—

"Fredrick Banes III, nice to meet you. But I'm Freddy to my friends." He was in his late twenties and had a crisp, British accent that called to mind boarding schools and polo matches and names that were spelled Chumbledown but were pronounced *Randolph*.

"I'm with Proctor, Banes & Jones." Out came a pair of business cards. "I'm not the one on the masthead, though. Ha. No. Baby Banes, right here." He forced a laugh. "My father and grandfather are the real Baneses of the operation. We're Ms. Ashley's solicitors. So glad you made it in before the storm. I was worried when we booked the jet."

"Lawyers do that?" Maggie asked.

He blushed. "At PB&J we do whatever Ms. Ashley asks us to do. Or so they tell me."

"I see."

"Have you been with the firm long?" Ethan asked.

"Almost a year. Not really sure why the old man walked into my office this morning and told me it was my turn to do Eleanor Duty, but . . ." He seemed to hear what he was saying. "Not that I'm not honored! She's a legend, you know. And, well, we all have to take our turn, make the pilgrimage, so to speak. Kiss the ring."

He was reaching for a shrimp puff—his hand was just an inch away—when Cece jerked the tray back and left Freddy "Baby Banes" standing there, looking like a little boy who might be sent to bed without supper.

Eleanor's final guest was someone Maggie actually knew, at least by reputation.

"Sir Jasper Rhodes, at your service."

He was twenty-five years younger than Eleanor and far less prolific, but no mystery collection would be complete without at least one book by Sir Jasper.

Maggie had always assumed that the stories were exaggerated, but no. At nearly six foot five, Sir Jasper was even taller than Ethan and somewhat thick around the middle, but, amazingly, that's not what a person noticed first—not when he was standing there in a long black cape and deer hunter cap.

Maggie didn't know whether he was going for "recently retired superhero" or "*Hound of the Baskervilles* cosplayer." She'd always assumed Sir Jasper's persona was a gimmick—an act—but the man couldn't have been more sincere as he gave a gallant bow and placed a faint kiss on the top of Maggie's knuckles.

"I have long dreamed of the day when I might kiss the hand of the great Margaret Chase. I am honored. I am enchanted. I am—"

"Laying it on a bit thick," Ethan mumbled.

"Excuse me?" Sir Jasper asked.

"I said you don't want to get sick." Ethan pried Maggie's hand out of Sir Jasper's. "Airplanes, you know. Germs."

"I washed my hands," Maggie mumbled.

"You can never be too careful," Ethan growled back then dragged her to the other side of the room.

CHAPTER *Fifteen*

There had been a time when Maggie might have paid what was left of her life savings for two hours alone in Eleanor Ashley's library, but as she inched toward the shelves, the party seemed to fade in the background, and for the first time, it didn't feel like some grand adventure. It felt like coming—*RJ! Bring Mummy the hand grenade, darling!*—home.

Her fingers ran down spines like the keys of a piano, playing a tune that only she could hear until, suddenly, she stopped. And gasped.

"See anything you like?" A soft voice came from behind her, and Maggie spun to see blue eyes twinkling back.

"I . . ." Maggie must have forgotten how to speak, so she just pointed to the books on the shelf. At least a dozen of them. All by Margaret Chase. "I wrote . . . You have my books."

Eleanor laughed in surprise. "Of course I do. I make Deborah send them to me. Didn't she tell you?"

You've been invited to the home of your biggest fan for Christmas.

"Well, yes. I mean no. I mean . . . You're Eleanor Ashley, and I'm . . . no one."

"Are you? *No one?*"

It felt like a trick question.

"I'm . . ." She was twelve years older, but Maggie would always be the girl who had woken up one Christmas morning in a mansion where there wasn't a single present for her under the tree. "I'm just honored to be here." It seemed like the safest answer.

"I'm glad. Because you're one of *my* favorite authors."

And then Maggie died.

The End.

Well, not exactly. But it felt like it. And she might truly have expired on the spot if Eleanor hadn't gestured to the next section of shelves and asked, "What about those? Do you have a favorite?"

"Oh, I couldn't possibly—" Eleanor gave her a look. "This one." Maggie pointed to the copy of *Roses Are Dead, Violets Are Blue*. It wasn't Eleanor's best-known title, but— "It was my first. When I was thirteen, my mom decided to go back to college, which was great, but my dad had to work double shifts and I spent most of my time at the library so we didn't have to run the air-conditioning during the day."

For a moment, Maggie froze, sure she'd said too much. But Eleanor wasn't going to use that fact as a weapon, and Maggie didn't want to think about how she'd spent so much of her life around people who would.

"And . . ." Eleanor prompted.

"I read it so many times the librarian told me not to bring it back. She said they needed a new copy. It took me years to realize it was still in good condition and she was just being nice. It was the first book I ever owned." Maggie was babbling and rambling. It left her feeling guilty for reasons that didn't make sense and embarrassed for reasons that did. But, most of all, she felt . . . strange. Like there was something hot on the back of her neck, a tingling and a prickling and—

She turned to see Ethan staring at her from the other side of the room.

"And him?" Eleanor's voice pulled her back.

"Excuse me?"

"What do you think of him?"

"He's very popular." It wasn't opinion; it was fact. Millions of copies sold. Signings that lasted well into the night. Fan groups and podcasts and (allegedly) a need to check into hotels under fake names to keep groupies from tracking him down. Maggie had it on good authority that there was a store on the internet that specialized in T-shirts with his face on them. (Not that she'd looked. Much.) "With . . . everyone."

"But not with you?" Eleanor asked.

"I don't really know him," Maggie said quickly—not just because it was the safest answer but also because it was true. She *didn't* know him. Not where he was from or where he lived or . . . anything. Because Ethan was an enigma. The mystery was part of the brand and the brand was *everything*.

"Well, somehow I doubt he would say the same about you." Eleanor's voice was low and her eyes were mischievous and Maggie was just starting to wonder what it all meant when James cleared his throat and announced—

"Dinner is served."

CHAPTER Sixteen

"So how do you know my aunt?" Victoria, the Duchess of Stratford, held a gin and tonic in one hand and a healthy dose of skepticism in the other as they settled around the dining room table. The words were innocent enough, but the tone made it sound like no one would voluntarily spend Christmas with Eleanor Ashley unless there were something in it for them.

"Oh . . . I . . ." No one should have been looking at Maggie, not when Ethan was three feet away, but the duchess had already sized up the outsiders and determined that Maggie was the weak antelope. This was how she got weeded from the herd.

"As I told you, Victoria, Maggie, Ethan, and Sir Jasper are my guests," Eleanor said from her place at the head of the table. Her gaze was sharp, but her tone was overly indulgent. "I'm a great admirer of their work. Besides, it seemed we were going to have more than enough room this year." She shook out her napkin. "Tell me again why your boys couldn't make it?"

The question was just innocent enough to disguise that it had teeth. Victoria smiled but took a sip of her drink, leaving the duke to explain. "Switzerland. Skiing. Couldn't miss it." He gave a nervous chuckle. "Simon's new girlfriend is thirty-seventh in line for the throne, you know," he added, like he didn't want to brag, but, really, how could Eleanor compete with that?

"Well, I hope you don't want me to plan thirty-six murders. I could make ten look like accidents. Twelve at the most," Eleanor said, and Maggie could have sworn the duke looked disappointed. "And . . . oh hello." Eleanor turned to Dr. Charles like she'd just laid eyes on him for the very first time. "And who are you?"

"This is *Dr. Charles*, Aunt Eleanor." Rupert's voice was a touch louder than it needed to be, emphasizing every few words as if she might not know which ones were important. "Kitty's *friend* from her days at the *hospital*. He didn't have anywhere to go for the holiday so *you* suggested he *join* us. Remember?"

"No, I don't remember." For a moment, Eleanor looked like the woman by the windows, distant and melancholy and . . . homesick. She looked homesick in her own house. But then her gaze turned sharp again. "Probably because it didn't happen." Rupert cut his eyes at the doctor. "But any friend of Kitty's is welcome, Doctor. Lord knows we have the room. I'm glad to have you."

Dr. Charles gave a warm smile. "Thank you, ma'am. It's an honor."

"Aunt E . . ."

"That's not her name," Victoria muttered, but Cece went on as if she hadn't heard a word.

"Are you cold? Should I get you a shawl?"

"I own a shawl?" Eleanor sounded surprised. "I must be older than I thought. Mr. Wyatt?"

"I left my shawl upstairs," Ethan deadpanned and Eleanor's lip ticked up, fighting a grin.

"You know, I like to do my research, but I'm afraid I could find very little about you."

Honestly, Maggie was impressed that Eleanor had found anything at all. As far as Maggie could tell, Ethan Wyatt had been born five years ago, a six-foot-two-inch baby in a leather jacket. No résumé. No bio. Just a runaway bestseller and a jaw that could cut glass.

"You were born in Germany, I believe?" Eleanor asked.

Most people would have missed it, the split-second gap in Ethan's facade—two film reels that didn't quite line up and if you replayed the moment in slow motion, you could see the place where he was spliced together.

"I am a citizen of the world, ma'am." His voice was low and rich, but for one brief moment, Maggie could have sworn she saw his hand shake.

"But you're American?"

"I am."

"And your background? Your training?"

"Oh . . ." He chuckled. He smiled. He did everything but wink and ask Eleanor if she came here often. "A bit of this and that."

And so it went. No matter where the conversation meandered, it always came back to a game that Maggie liked to call *What's Not to Love About Ethan?*

After two hours, they'd been through a soup course, salad course, main course, and cheese course and were waiting on dessert while the Duke of Stratford snapped his fingers and tried to find the words—

"What are those chaps called"—*snap, snap, snap*—"the dolphins?"

Ethan bit back a grin. Probably because no one could take the full force of his smile without protective equipment. It was like looking at the sun. Or handling nuclear waste. "They're called Navy SEALs. And no comment."

"Marine sniper!" Cece guessed.

"No comment." Ethan gave her a wink.

"Army Ranger?" Cece guessed again.

"No comment."

"International assassin!" Dr. Charles tried, but Ethan simply shook his head, slow enough to be a bit dramatic.

"No comment."

"CIA?"

"I could tell you, Duchess, but I don't think you'd like what I'd have to do next."

And then everyone laughed and laughed and Maggie wondered how hard it would be to kill a man with a dessert fork.

Eleanor would know. Maggie should ask. But their hostess was quiet, watching, lips turned up in something that wasn't quite a smile while her blue eyes twinkled in the candlelight. She looked . . . amused. Not with Ethan, but with the night. Like they were at the start of one of her favorite scenes and she was trying not to shout spoilers.

"The truth is . . ." Ethan rested a forearm on the table and angled closer, like they were all friends now. He might as well let them in on a secret. "I'm not vague about my background because of some marketing ploy. I don't keep people guessing because it sells books . . . though it does." He flashed a self-deprecating grin he probably practiced in a mirror every night before bed. "I don't talk about my past because *I'm* not the star of my books. Ultimately"— dramatic pause—"*my characters have to speak for themselves.*"

Maggie had heard him use that line a thousand times. It was his bread and butter, tried and true. She watched the people at the table absorb those words like the first drops of water on parched earth. They were all getting sucked into the Vortex of Ethan—swirling, drowning—but then Maggie shifted and her chair squeaked and Sir Jasper seemed to remember she was there.

"What say you, Ms. Chase? What brought you to our humble profession?"

Maggie suddenly wanted to go back to five seconds ago when everyone had forgotten she existed. That was vastly superior to the feeling of ten sets of eyes turning and settling on her.

"I . . . Well . . . uh . . ." Her foot banged beneath the table and her chair squeaked again and she started wondering if it would be possible to just walk back to New York. The Atlantic had to be iced over by that point.

"I liked to read." Maggie's cheeks flushed. "Her." She pointed at Eleanor and, instantly, Maggie wanted to pull the words back. It was like she'd said way too much and also too little and the awkwardness descended like a fog.

It reminded Maggie of her engagement party and the three— count them, *three*—different society matrons who had kissed Emily on the cheek and asked to see the ring only to be told that, no, Colin was marrying the other one.

Maggie was the least famous, least successful, least charismatic author at the table, so she looked at Ethan, willing him to tell another story or show off his abs, but he stayed silent for the first time in his hot guy life and Maggie felt personally betrayed.

"Lovely," the duchess said dryly, then drained her glass of wine.

"Speaking of which"—Eleanor pushed back from the table and reached for her cane—"you must excuse me. I've written five hundred words before bed every day for fifty years. I'm afraid to-night cannot be an exception. If you need anything, James or Cecilia will see to you."

She was almost to the door when she stopped and lingered for a moment, looking over the assembled group. There were people who were related to her and people who worked for her and people who wanted to be her (*Maggie. Maggie wanted to be her.*) But as Eleanor took in the people at the table, Maggie realized that not a single one of them had introduced themselves as Eleanor Ashley's friend.

She'd written nearly a hundred books. She was wealthy and fa-mous and powerful. But she was also an old woman with a bum leg and a drafty mansion.

And she was alone.

So perhaps she was a little bit like Maggie after all.

CHAPTER *Seventeen*

Jet lag might not have been "the silent killer" but that didn't mean it wasn't brutal, or so Maggie thought as she tossed and turned three hours later, utterly exhausted but totally unable to sleep. The clock read nine minutes to midnight when she finally climbed out of bed and stepped into the chilly corridor. The halls were dark and empty, but lights burned in the sconces like a trail of breadcrumbs in the night.

She was halfway down the stairs when—

"I told you not to sleep after a red-eye."

Maggie jumped and almost screamed. Her heart was beating a million miles an hour as she looked down at Ethan, who was sprawled across the bottom step like a sentry, standing guard but falling down on the job at the same time because Ethan always managed to be everything. All at once.

Cool but hot. Formal but relaxed. Intimidating but totally approachable. Even his smile managed to be self-deprecating but just a little bit smug at the same time.

"So what's your excuse, Mr. Post Red-Eye Protocol Man."

"Worst. Superhero. Ever."

She didn't smile. But he did. Just to spite her. She watched him look down at her T-shirt then mouth the words as he read NO, I DON'T PUT MY ENEMIES IN MY NOVELS. MY ENEMIES AREN'T THAT INTERESTING. When Ethan laughed, he got those little crinkles around his eyes that make hot guys even hotter and Maggie wished they were at the top of the stairs just so she could give him a push.

"Maybe I'm waiting for Santa," he told her.

"You're early."

She watched him sprawl across the steps like a cat in the sun, utterly at home in someone else's mansion. So comfortable in his skin and the world and his place. So sure that people would always adore him because people always had.

"Oh, I like to be prepared."

"Why? Are you a Boy Scout as well as a Navy SEAL and an Army Ranger and a CIA operative and . . . Oh yeah." *Seriously?* "International assassin?" Maggie stepped over his outstretched leg, then headed for the library, desperate for silence and solace and something to read. "Good night, Ethan."

"Why don't you like me?" Ethan's voice was flat in the dim, chilly air.

"I don't know you," Maggie tossed over her shoulder, not even slowing down and far too tired to argue.

"We've known each other for five years." He darted in front of her and forced her to stop.

"And for four and a half of them you couldn't have picked me out of a lineup."

"I . . ." It was like he heard the words but didn't understand them. "We've crossed paths a dozen times."

"And every one of those times *you thought my name was Marcie.*"

It should have felt victorious, the way the smile slid off his face. He looked like she'd just ripped off a mask and announced she was an alien. A hologram. A ghost. It was like he didn't know her at all. Which . . . he didn't know her! At all! But, evidently, that was news to Ethan, who tried to rally. "We've been together pretty much nonstop for twenty-four hours, so—"

"So I haven't been with a man! I've been with a social media feed." And then she couldn't help herself—she dropped her voice to a very Ethan-like tone. "Look at me, I'm charming on an airplane. Ooh. I'm hot in a limo. Hey! I'm quippy over . . . What?" she snapped when he gave her his cockiest grin.

"So what you're saying is . . . you think I'm hot?" He arched an eyebrow and Maggie couldn't stop herself. She burst through the library doors.

"Where is that sword?" The dagger would also do. "Oh, is that a crossbow?"

Someone had banked the fireplace and the flames flickered behind the screen, sending shadows dancing through the dark. Beyond the windows, falling snow filled the sky and even the stars had stopped shining. She was sleepy and a little hungry and the clock *dinged*. Midnight.

It was December twenty-third.

It was December twenty-third.

It was December—

"Maggie?"

She spun, but, in the darkness, the dark green and purple rug was hard to see and her foot caught on the upturned corner and Maggie felt herself falling, crashing, landing right in Ethan's arms.

She would have preferred the hard floor. Maybe a nice cliff? If only she could have broken a bone or two . . .

"Easy . . ." His voice sounded like chocolate tastes: dark and rich and like something you'd regret indulging in later. "I have you."

Maggie wanted to laugh. She was going to cry. Because, the truth was, no one had her and no one ever would. Maggie had herself. And that was enough. It was. It was—

December twenty-third.

"Hey." She was still in his stupid arms and he was still gazing down at her with his stupid face and stupid eyes, looking like he was worried—like he cared. Like—

A loud, crashing sound broke through the silence, reverberating down the stairs and through the library's open door.

At first, Maggie thought she might have dreamed it, but Ethan was already darting out of the library and up the stairs and into the long, main hall where Cece stood outside the closed door of Eleanor's office. There was a broken cup and saucer on the floor and she was struggling to balance a tray in her hands.

"Aunt Eleanor!" the girl called, kicking at the bottom of the door since her hands were full. "Aunt Eleanor, you locked me out again!" She waited a moment. "I found that tea you like in the back of the pantry. I told you no one else had been drinking it." Cece spotted Ethan and Maggie and lowered her voice. "Probably because it smells like the back end of an old donkey." She turned to the door again. "Aunt Eleanor?"

But no one called back and the door stayed closed and a moment later classical music came booming out of the room.

"I guess that's a no," Cece told them, sounding worried. "The doctor doesn't want her working all night anymore."

"Dr. Charles?" Ethan asked and Cece shook her head.

"No. The woman she saw after she fell." She shifted the heavy tray in her hands and moved to a small table a little way down the hall. "I'll leave your tea on the table. Don't work too late, okay?"

Down the hall, a door opened. "Would you keep it down out here?" Rupert snapped. "You're going to wake—" The baby began to cry and Rupert cringed as if he was the one who was going to have to put her back to sleep.

"Sorry, Rupert. Good night." Cece smiled at Ethan and Maggie, then gave a yawn and walked away.

There was a bookshelf on the wall across from the office door. It was covered with antique cameras and magnifying glasses and kaleidoscopes and crystals. Maggie could think of at least six Eleanor novels that were about prisms or looking glasses or seeing things in ways no one ever has before. There was a lesson there—Maggie knew it. But there was also a clock, nestled in the middle and blinking red: 12:03 a.m.

On December twenty-third.

And Maggie felt every ounce of fight drain from her body. Two minutes earlier she'd been full of steam, but now she was an old balloon, weak and sinking under the weight of too much string.

"Maggie?" She could feel Ethan's breath on the back of her neck, so close that, when she turned, she could actually feel the rise and fall of his chest, but she just stood there, caught in his gaze as he whispered, "I could always pick you out of a lineup."

He walked away and she went back to bed, and ten minutes later she fell into a deep, deep sleep.

CHAPTER *Eighteen*

One Year Ago

"Are you sitting down?" Deborah asked the moment Maggie picked up the phone.

It was two days before Christmas, but Deborah was a workaholic and Hanukkah was already over and she always said she liked the quiet of a nearly deserted office.

Maggie understood the appeal. She'd woken to the sound of Emily and Colin arguing about where to put the ice sculpture for their annual party. Maggie hadn't wanted an ice sculpture. Or a party. Or the big, fancy house the party was going to be held in—not far from where Colin's parents used to live, back before they ran out of money.

Maggie hadn't wanted any of it, but Maggie had been outvoted. So she'd retreated to a café to try to get two thousand words written because it's easy to zone out in a chaotic coffee shop but not in your own chaotic house and Maggie didn't even try to understand the difference.

"Please tell me you're sitting down," Deborah told her.

"Why?"

"Because this might be the phone call that changes your life."

It wasn't like Deborah to be hyperbolic, so Maggie was almost scared when she asked, "Change my life *how*?"

"You're a finalist"—Deborah gave a dramatic pause—"for Betty's Book Club."

"Betty's . . ."

"There's a fifty-fifty chance that you will be the Betty's Book Club pick for January. It's down to you and one other author, but . . . You know what this means, right?"

It meant millions of copies. It meant movie options. It meant that when strangers asked *Oh, have you written anything I might have heard of?* from that point forward the answer might actually be *yes*.

"Maggie? Did you hear me? This is big, but it's not a done deal yet, so *don't tell anyone*." Maggie swore she wouldn't and then she crammed her laptop in her bag and raced home to tell someone.

"Emily!" she'd called when she opened the door. "Colin!"

The house was full of flowers and chafing dishes and stacks of tables and chairs.

"Where are you two?" Maggie yelled, ignoring the ridiculous ice sculpture that someone had left dripping on the hardwood floor.

Then she heard the voices, hushed words, and frantic sounds from Maggie's bedroom. They were moving furniture, her tired brain thought as she threw open the door.

And . . .

And . . .

And . . .

Deborah was right, of course. That phone call had changed her life after all.

CHAPTER *Nineteen*

Two Days Before Christmas

Maggie came awake slowly in the unfamiliar bed in the unfamiliar room with an unfamiliar bright light shining all around her. She was half tempted to draw the old-fashioned bed-curtains and go back to sleep but then she remembered.

England. Eleanor. Ethan.

Not necessarily in that order. So she threw off the covers and squinted against the glare as she looked out the window and gasped because—

Snow. Feet of it. *Miles* of it. Clinging to every tree and bush, covering the rolling hills like a layer of thick, soft cotton. It was pure and bright and looked like Christmas—the kind in the movies. The kind that isn't real. But it *was* real. Maggie felt it in the cold that seeped through the glass and into her bones and made her whole body shiver. It was real, and Maggie didn't know whether to be excited or apprehensive as she pulled on an extra layer and made her way downstairs.

Sir Jasper, Mr. Banes, Dr. Charles, and the duke and duchess were already at the table, sipping tea and eating breakfast, but every eye turned when Maggie entered, as if, on some level, they knew she didn't belong there. And the problem was, on some level, Maggie knew they were right.

Of course, Ethan had never had that problem. "Good morning!" he boomed from the doorway. He must have been one of those people who can thrive on very little sleep because he practically bounded over to the sideboard and started piling food on his plate and, nervously, Maggie followed.

His hair was damp and he was wearing dark jeans and a plaid shirt and looked like an ad for a dating app that specialized in lumberjacks. Maggie gripped a warm plate in her cold hands and waited for the inevitable grin or smirk or wink, but nothing came. He didn't tease or cajole. He hadn't even glanced in her direction, and she thought about the look on his face the night before, the low soft words *I could always pick you out of a lineup.*

"Ethan?"

He kept his gaze on the sideboard, and when he spoke, the words were low and under his breath. "I'm hot while I'm pouring coffee. I'm charming while I'm dishing up eggs."

Maggie was trying to decide if she should feel irritated or relieved that he'd resumed his mocking ways when Kitty appeared at the door, exclaiming, "Good morning! Is everyone here?" She looked around the assembled group as if silently taking a head count. Aside from the children and Nanny Davis, only Eleanor and Cece were missing and, apparently, Kitty didn't feel the need to wait.

"I hope you don't mind, but I've worked up a little . . . agenda." She bit back a grin, like she didn't want to brag but she was *really* good at agenda-making. "Nothing formal. Just a few activities to make this"—*dramatic pause*—"the perfect Christmas."

Today's sweater was Seven Swans a Swimming, and Maggie wondered if Rupert's matched. She stared at him, mentally willing him to move so she could see.

"Item one!" Kitty went on. "Cut the Yule log. Now, Mr. Wyatt, you look like a man who can wield an axe."

Ha! Lumberjack! Maggie almost pumped her fist before she felt warm breath on the shell of her ear as someone (one guess who) whispered, "I'm hot while I wield an axe."

"When you're done, I have a few places you can stick it," she whispered back, but his only response was a chuckle.

"Item two! Decorate—"

But before Kitty could finish, Cece came bursting into the room.

"Miss Honeychurch!" Dr. Charles exclaimed. "What's wrong?"

But Cece was too busy to answer, scanning the faces, searching and desperate. "Is Aunt Eleanor here?"

"We haven't seen her," Rupert said, going back to his eggs. "Up writing half the night, blasted music blaring." He sounded more than a little annoyed.

But Cece . . . Cece looked distraught. "Has anyone seen Aunt Eleanor? Has anyone seen her *this morning*?"

A shiver went down Maggie's spine for reasons that had nothing to do with flannel-wearing men and chilly windows. "Why?"

"She's not in her bedroom," Cece said. "Or the library. She's nowhere. She's . . . gone."

CHAPTER Twenty

For a moment, the room was frozen, silent. It was like they had all misheard simultaneously. Like it was a joke and Cece was taking forever with the punch line.

"She's disappeared!" Cece blurted louder.

But the duke simply huffed from the place he'd assumed at the head of the table. "Ninety-year-old women—"

"She's eighty-one," Maggie cut in, but the man either didn't hear or didn't care.

"—do not simply disappear, young lady." He spat the words like it was somehow Cece's fault. Like Eleanor was a dog and Cece had let her off her leash.

"I know that," Cece implored. "But I can't find her."

"Well, did you check her office?" the duchess asked.

"It's locked. I knocked but—"

Rupert pushed his chair back and tossed his napkin on the table in a gesture that screamed *Do I have to do everything myself?* Then he stormed out of the room and up the stairs.

They must have made an odd little processional—Rupert in the lead with the rest of Eleanor's friends and family trailing behind him. Maggie shouldn't have been surprised to feel Ethan beside her, but there he was, expression oddly serious as they walked down the long hall toward Eleanor's office.

James was already there and knocking. "Ma'am? Ma'am, if you could open the door, please?"

"Give me the key," Rupert demanded, but James kept on knocking. "The key!" Rupert snapped at Cece this time, sounding a bit too haughty for a man who was currently wearing a sweater with a pear tree on it.

"I-I-I don't have it," Cece stammered.

"Then go get it," Rupert said, like that much should have been obvious.

"I don't have one!" Tears were in Cece's eyes then.

"You." Rupert pointed at the butler. "Get the key."

James didn't cry or whimper. He just looked at Rupert in the manner of a man who had been there long before Eleanor's ungrateful nephew showed up and who would be there long after. "There is only one key, sir. And Ms. Ashley keeps it with her at all times."

"Every old house in England has a master key." The duchess sounded annoyed. "Everyone knows that. So go get the master."

"That is true, ma'am, but—"

Ethan was squatting on the floor and looking at the lock, examining the door in a way the others hadn't noticed. "This lock is new. A master key wouldn't work on this door."

"Precisely," James said. "Ms. Ashley had this lock changed a year ago and was adamant that she keep possession of the only key."

"That's insane." Rupert turned to his sister. "I told you she was paranoid. Delusional. I was afraid something like this was going to happen."

The hall filled with bickering and shouts, but all Maggie could think was *What if something is wrong? What if she's hurt? What if, at this moment, Eleanor is on the other side of that door, and . . .*

Maggie turned and looked at Ethan. He didn't feel like a stranger anymore. They were the only silent people in the space but a whole conversation seemed to be taking place between them.

Can you believe these idiots? And *Priorities, people!* And, most of all, *This could be bad. This could be very, very bad and they either don't know or don't care and I honestly don't know which is worse and—*

She watched Ethan make up his mind. And spin. And kick. The door splintered, springing open, and the hall went suddenly silent.

"Oh, look. The door's open," Ethan said, then went inside.

CHAPTER Twenty-One

Maggie had probably spent a thousand hours imagining what the inside of Eleanor Ashley's mind would look like, but standing in her office had to be the next best thing.

The desk was the only clear surface in the room, with nothing but the tea tray Cece had been carrying the night before sitting near the edge. Everywhere else, there were stacks of mail and dog-eared paperbacks, empty water glasses, and crosswords done in ink. It was a room that was lived in. Used.

Three of the walls had built-in shelves full of nearly identical notebooks, but a large window seat covered most of the fourth. Soft, velvet pillows rested against the frosty glass, and, outside, the sill was piled high with fluffy fresh snow.

There was an old-fashioned turntable in the corner, and the low, steady scratching of a spinning record was almost ominous in the quiet room, but when Ethan picked up the needle, the silence was even louder. Because the most significant thing about Eleanor's office was simple: Eleanor wasn't in it.

"Maybe she went for a walk?" Kitty tried.

"It's freezing outside," the doctor said.

"Well, she's not in here!" Rupert grumbled as if this had all been someone else's idea and why were they wasting his time?

But that's when Maggie saw something on the floor beside the desk. She bent to pick it up. "She was."

"Oh, well spotted, Ms. Chase!" Sir Jasper said. "Look here, everyone, Ms. Chase has found the key!"

"There! Ha!" Rupert laughed. "Two keys! Clearly, Aunt Eleanor locked the room with the second when she left."

"Sorry, Roofus—"

"Rupert," Rupert corrected, but it was like Ethan didn't even hear.

"In no way does that prove there are two keys. And besides . . ." Ethan trailed off but angled the busted door so that everyone could see. There was a slide bolt on the back—the kind like you'd find in a bathroom stall—and it was latched. Ethan stood to his full, intimidating height. "She didn't lock that from the outside."

The moment stretched long and silent as they all stood there, doing the math in their heads. Two plus two suddenly equaled fifty and no one knew what to think—what to say.

"This is ridiculous!" The duke gave a huff. "A ninety-five-year-old—"

"She's eighty-one!" Maggie and Ethan said at the same time.

"—woman cannot simply disappear out of a locked room!"

Maggie was drifting closer to the window. Cold air radiated off the glass, and the world outside was soft and still, stretching for what felt like a thousand miles in all directions. But all she could say was "Eleanor Ashley can."

CHAPTER Twenty-Two

It didn't make sense. Except in all the ways it did. When Maggie stopped thinking about it as real life and started thinking of it like a story, it felt like the most obvious thing in the world. But the fact remained that Eleanor was an eighty-one-year-old woman with a bad leg and it was freezing outside. She could be lost or hurt or dying, and still Maggie couldn't bring herself to panic.

With only two exceptions, Maggie had always been cool in a crisis and calm under pressure. She never overcorrected the wheel or shouted fire or fainted at the sight of blood, so it shouldn't have been a surprise ten minutes later as she stood in the library with the others, trying to hear herself think over the sound of eight people talking at the same time.

"What do you know about it, Your Grace?" Rupert shouted at his brother-in-law.

"Oh, I have someplace you can shove your sweater, Kitty!" snapped the duchess.

"Say, when do you think they'll serve lunch?" (The lawyer.)

"Perhaps someone should call the police?" (The doctor.)

"I remember one time when I was consulting with Scotland Yard. Grizzly stuff. Blood everywhere." (Sir Jasper.)

"You think Aunt Eleanor is dead?" (Cece.)

A whistling sound pierced the air, sudden and quick, and the room went instantly silent. Ethan was always taller and stronger and more attractive than the vast majority of the world's population, but in that moment, he wasn't just the kind of person with their own gravity. He was someone who could control tides.

And he was all out of patience.

"Hi. Hello. Welcome back. Just . . . throwing this out there . . . But maybe we should *look* for Eleanor." It seemed like a perfectly logical next step but the others were staring at him like he'd just suggested they only have one course for dinner.

"James!" Ethan called.

"Yes, sir." James was right behind Ethan, and he jumped.

"Oh! Didn't see you there. How many rooms are there in the mansion?"

"A lot, sir." James's diction was precise, even if his answer was not, and Ethan gave a determined nod.

"*A lot*," he repeated. "So let's split up and search the house and—"

A whimper cut him off. Kitty was sitting in the corner, yarn and a half-finished something in her lap, but the knitting needles lay forgotten as she dabbed at her wet cheeks. Ethan's face fell.

"Ah, Kitty, it's okay," he said softly. "We'll find her."

Kitty wiped her eyes and blew her nose. "I'm sorry. It's just the baby didn't sleep and now Aunt Eleanor is missing and . . ." Her face screwed up. Her nose turned red. And the tears were just *right there*—they were getting ready to fall again. "No one is wearing their sweaters!"

"Uh . . . okay." Ethan straightened and turned back to the group. "Let's split up. Meet back here in an hour and—"

Kitty whimpered again and Maggie watched Ethan crumble. Then straighten.

"But first . . ."

Maggie didn't wait around to find out.

The hall was silent and empty as Maggie made her way back to the broken door near the top of the stairs.

It felt like she was doing something naughty as she stood on the threshold of Eleanor's office. She'd already been there, sure. But it was different, standing alone among the quiet shelves and splintered wood. The now-cold tea tray and old computer. The latched window and snow-covered sill outside.

"Heads up!" Ethan called from the doorway, and Maggie barely had time to turn before a soft, heavy weight landed on top of her head.

"Hey." She pulled it off and looked down at red yarn and fuzzy white birds.

"That's for you. We're turtledoves." He gestured to the sweater that covered his broad chest. "We match." He wriggled his eyebrows again, but Maggie just tossed the sweater on a chair and went back to the cold glass.

"This window is locked, and it swings out. The snow is undisturbed, so we know it hasn't been opened."

"One: I know," Ethan said calmly. "And two: Are we really entertaining the theory that an eighty-one-year-old woman jumped or flew or rappelled down the side of the building? During a blizzard?"

"I don't have a theory yet," Maggie shot back. "You shouldn't make theories until you have all the facts. Which you would know if you were a real mystery writer and not a . . ."

"Leather Jacket Guy?" he filled in as he leaned against the busted door and crossed his arms, biceps bulging beneath the yarn. "Oh, but now I'm an awesome sweater guy. Go ahead. Put yours on. Let's be twinsies."

Maggie's heart was beating faster than usual, probably because Eleanor was missing and Ethan was watching her and the result was a weird cocktail of adrenaline that hit her bloodstream like jet fuel. She wanted him to leave. Or tease. Or fight. She wanted him to do anything but stand there, watching her like she was the ultimate mystery and it was his job to solve her.

"You know, when I said we should look for Eleanor, I thought we might skip the one room we know she's not in." Ethan pushed off the doorframe and prowled closer.

"And I thought we might focus on the last place she was seen." They were chest-to-chest again, and Maggie felt suddenly hot inside the chilly room.

"Wait. *Was* she seen here?" Ethan challenged and Maggie thought back to the night before.

"Fine. The last place she was"—they both turned to the phonograph in the corner—"heard . . ."

But that wasn't true either. They didn't hear Eleanor's voice, just the music that had blasted through the doors, drowning out the sounds of Cece's shouting.

Ethan gave a shrug like *here goes nothing,* then picked up the needle and placed it on the record and soon the tune of "La Vie en Rose" filled the air. It sounded like Paris and cobblestone streets and warm, fresh bread and Maggie's stomach growled because she hadn't eaten breakfast.

"What I don't get is why you're *not* freaking out right now?" He tilted his head, eyes sharp. This wasn't Flirty Ethan or Charming Ethan or the Ethan who had probably been best man at two dozen different weddings. This was the Ethan who saw things—who saw *her*—and Maggie turned away, wishing she could go back to the days when he didn't even know her name.

"Maybe I'll freak out later. Maybe—" And then she realized what was wrong about that picture—about that scene and that moment and that place. "It wasn't this song."

"What?" Ethan asked, obviously confused. But there was something inside of Maggie, something moving and humming and coming to life. It was just right there. She just had to reach out and . . .

"It wasn't this song!" she said again, stronger now, but Ethan wasn't following.

"I don't—"

"Last night! When she put the record on, it wasn't this song!"

He nodded like *okay but you're missing the point.* "So she played more than one record. Why does it matter?"

Oh, she couldn't believe him. She was going to strangle him with his own sweater! How could anyone—anyone—sleep under Eleanor Ashley's roof and not know—

"It matters because, if you read Eleanor Ashley, you would know that this is the song that was playing when . . ."

And then the pieces started falling into place. Slowly. Maggie wasn't standing in Eleanor's office, she was in Deborah's, hearing her editor say, *Something is coming next year. Very big. Very hush-hush. And I think you're the person for the job.*

She was shivering in the cold wind, watching Eleanor wink and tell them, *I like a twist.*

I'm probably wrong, Maggie told herself. It had been so long since she'd been right. She could almost hear Colin's voice in her head, telling her that she was seeing things, hearing things, manufacturing mysteries out of thin air. But that didn't change the fact that Eleanor was missing. Eleanor was gone. And . . .

"Well . . ." Ethan prompted.

If she was right, then . . .

"It's nothing," Maggie said quickly. "You win."

"Wait. *I win?*" He sounded like that was the craziest part of their very crazy morning.

"Yeah. Let's split up. Search. I'll see you in an hour."

And then she pushed past his big, dumb body in his big, dumb sweater and set out to prove herself wrong. Trying to silence the little part of herself that was screaming she was totally right.

CHAPTER *Twenty-Three*

The house that had felt so large the day before flew by as Maggie darted into the hall and toward the stairs. She knew Ethan was at the threshold of Eleanor's office, watching her retreat, so she tried really, really hard not to run. It took every iota of Maggie's willpower not to scream as she moved down the stairs and through the foyer and into the library where she closed the double doors behind her and leaned against them like she might be able to keep Ethan and the world on the other side.

Flames flickered in the fireplace and, outside, the world was white and vast and cold, but she wasn't thinking about whether or not Eleanor was out there. No. Maggie was reaching for the key in the door and twisting—*click*. And then she was walking toward the shelves.

The song was fresh on her mind and coursing through her veins and, when she hummed, she remembered—

"What's that?" Colin asked as he lay on the twin bed in her dorm room.

"Nothing." Maggie blushed and turned her head.

"No. I want to know." He grabbed her by the waist and tugged her down beside him.

"Just my favorite song from my favorite book."

"What's that?"

Her hand was reaching for the shelves. Then? Now? Maggie couldn't tell. Past blended with present. With future? She wasn't sure. All she knew was that when she reached for the first edition of *Roses Are Dead, Violets Are Blue* she didn't even have to search for the page. There was something tucked inside already. A sprig of mistletoe. And just like that, Maggie knew. *She knew.*

She thought her heart might gallop right out of her chest as she held the mistletoe against her lips and read the novel's epigraph for the millionth time, "For a murder isn't a murder when there is no death. And a mystery isn't a mystery when"—she slammed the book shut—

"It's only a test."

For a moment, Maggie couldn't move. She could barely breathe as she stood there, thinking.

It's a test. It's a test. It's a test.

And then she heard Deborah's voice in her ear, saying, "*I think you're the person for the job. But I need you to get on that plane.*"

And she knew what Deborah hadn't been able to tell her: It wasn't just a test. It was a *contest*. And if it was a contest . . .

Then somebody had to win.

CHAPTER *Twenty-Four*

"I need to make a phone call."

"Excuse me?" James sounded confused.

"I need to call New York. Now. Can I use your phone, please? I can pay for the long-distance charges, and I wouldn't even ask except . . . I need to call New York. It's important."

This thing—if she was right—was the kind of thing that would change *every*thing. And Maggie needed to know. Not if she was right. No. She needed to know if it was okay to hope because Maggie had learned a long time ago that hope was the most dangerous emotion. It had been ripped from her and used against her. It had torn her to shreds a dozen times and she wasn't going to do that to herself if she could help it. She wouldn't survive it.

But if she was right . . .

"I need to call New York," she said again.

"The phones are down, miss. I presume the storm . . ."

Of course. The storm. Maggie was safe and warm inside those old stone walls, but, outside, the sky was angry. Snow swirled and the windows rattled. But it didn't matter. Nothing mattered except—

"James, I really need to call New York. Is there wi-fi? I can just FaceTime—"

"I'm afraid our internet is all satellite-based and with . . ." James motioned to the swirling white beyond the windows.

"The storm," Maggie filled in, hope and dread doing war inside her. "Where can I go to get a cell signal? Is there, like, a lookout point? Maybe a larger-than-average hill?"

"Ma'am, I cannot recommend leaving the house. The roads are impassable."

She saw it then—something in his eyes. He wasn't lying, but he didn't want her to know the whole truth either. "James . . . is there a place *inside* the house?"

James grimaced and looked guilty, like they were going to revoke his butler license for insufficient poker face. He gave a deep sigh but admitted, "One can occasionally get a signal in the old tower at the top of the east wing, but—"

"Thank you!"

"I do not suggest—"

"You're a lifesaver."

"But, ma'am, that part of the manor has not been properly maintained!"

"I'll be careful!" Maggie called but she never, ever looked back.

Ten minutes later, Maggie finally *did* have a signal. One tiny, precious bar, and as she paced at the top of the curving staircase that seemed straight out of a medieval romance, she didn't even feel the frigid wind that blew through the cracks in the stones and narrow, glassless windows. Snow gathered on the wooden floors that creaked beneath her feet and looked like they might collapse at any moment, but she couldn't bring herself to care as she brought the phone to her ear and waited.

"This is Deborah. Please leave a message. Unless this is Maggie Chase, then go enjoy your holiday, Maggie, and call me after the first of the year. I'm serious."

The floors creaked again. The phone beeped. And Maggie morphed into a veritable avalanche of words.

"Deborah, it's me. Maggie. Margaret. Chase. The one in your message. I . . . Uh, quick question. Is it possible that Eleanor Ashley is retiring and this whole trip is one big test to choose a writer to take over her ongoing series? Is it a test? Because, oh yeah, I'm here with Eleanor's family and two other writers and that doesn't make any sense—the writers, not the family. And then Eleanor disappeared out of a locked room last night and there are these clues—or at least I *think* they're clues and the whole thing feels very much like a . . ."

Three quick beeps told Maggie she'd lost the signal. Her tiny, precious bar was gone and Maggie was alone with her thoughts and the cold wind slicing through the arrowslits, stinging her face with icy pellets. The floors creaked again, but this time Maggie wasn't even moving. So either the floor was about to cave in or—

She glanced down the spiral stairs and that was when she saw him. "Ethan?"

"Whatcha doing, Margaret Abigail?"

"Looking for Eleanor." The lie practically rolled off Maggie's tongue. She even managed to add a little *isn't it obvious* lilt that she was especially proud of. "Why?" She sounded so innocent. So confused. "What are you doing?"

"Well, when a lady goes into a condemned tower—"

"I highly doubt this is *condemned*—"

"—all alone, a gentleman—"

"Are you supposed to be the gentleman in this scenario? Because I don't know if I'd go with *gentleman*." She made quote marks with her hands.

"—follows to make sure she doesn't fall and bust open her pretty little head."

"Awww. You think my head is pretty?" She gave him her best wide-eyed ingenue look. "You big softie."

"Maggie—"

"Should we go check on the others?"

"Margaret—"

"I'm going to go check on the others."

CHAPTER Twenty-Five

"Well?" Ethan asked five minutes later, but Eleanor's family barely looked up from their plates. The breakfast dishes were gone, replaced by trays full of sandwiches and tureens full of soup, and almost no one paid attention to Ethan. Which just proved there really is a first time for everything.

"Well, what?" The duke poured himself a fresh cup of coffee.

"Has anyone found Eleanor?"

"Obviously we haven't, Wyatt," Sir Jasper said. "She's not here."

"I can see that."

Maggie shouldn't have relished the way he looked at the ceiling and shook his head, frustration coming off him in waves. It was all she could do not to giggle.

"What?" He sounded more annoyed than offended.

"I didn't say a thing." But Maggie had to bite her lip as she went to the sideboard and started ladling herself soup, suddenly ravenous. Her stomach rumbled, reminding her that she'd been too nervous to eat the night before and she hadn't had anything for breakfast, and then she'd had a very busy morning of running up and down staircases, outsmarting Ethan Wyatt.

And Maggie was just getting started.

"What's going on with you?" Ethan whispered near her ear.

"Who? Me?" She took a tiny bite of a tiny sandwich, then added it to her plate.

"Yes. *You*. The president of the Eleanor Appreciation Society—"

"Oh, I'm only treasurer. The presidency has term limits."

"—is standing there with mustard on her mouth."

Maggie darted her tongue out and swiped at her lips. Ethan's gaze dipped and darkened and, for a moment, he looked like a man who couldn't quite remember why he was angry.

"You were saying?"

"I . . ."

She picked up another tiny sandwich and took an even tinier bite. "Ethan, are you unwell?" she asked with exaggerated patience.

"Me?" He shook off whatever he'd been thinking. "I'm fine. Unlike Eleanor. Who is *missing*."

Maggie slipped into a seat, unsurprised when he took the one beside her.

"I'm sure she'll show up. It is a big house, after all. Excuse me, Sir Jasper, would you pass the salt, please."

"It would be my pleasure, Ms. Chase!"

"Thank you." She gave him her brightest smile and Ethan made a sound that resembled a groan.

"Margaret Delphina Chase." Ethan kept his voice low. "What is going on?"

"I'm eating lunch. Want a bite?" Maggie held a sandwich out for him, then she turned her thoughts back to her meal and her mission.

She had almost forgotten about the sprig of mistletoe until he gently tugged it from behind her ear.

"You know, I think this has to be over your head, but I can make an exception," he teased. At least, she was 90 percent sure he was teasing as she snatched it back and laid it on the table.

"That's what I get for trying to be festive." There was a time when that little sprig of mistletoe would have reminded her of jingle bell earrings and red BMWs and a million other ways in which she'd never be Emily. But that was okay. Because Maggie was going to be someone infinitely better. Maggie was going to be Eleanor.

"Oh, you're trying *something*." Ethan narrowed his eyes, like a man who couldn't decide if he should be intrigued or annoyed. "And I'm going to figure out what it is."

She dipped her spoon into her soup, then oh-so-gently blew and his jaw ticked. Maggie wasn't sure what it meant, but she liked it— the uncertainty in his gaze. It was the first time in a year that she'd felt like she was playing a game. And she was winning. So she did it again.

THE MOST WONDERFUL CRIME OF THE YEAR   89

"Who was on the phone, Maggie Mae?"

Maggie's spoon froze halfway to her mouth. Had he heard her? Impossible. Not with the roaring wind and stone walls and creaking floorboards.

"Phone? I thought the phones were down?"

"So you just climbed to the top of the highest tower and had a conversation with yourself?"

"You know, hearing voices is a bad sign. You may want to see someone about that."

She reached for a roll, but Ethan's arms were longer and he tugged the basket away.

"No! No bread for you. Not until you tell me who you were talking to."

"I wasn't talking to anyone." She raised her right hand. "I swear." She wasn't even lying, which made her even happier. She was giddy. Bubbly. She was going to rise out of her chair and float away. She was even enjoying Ethan, the hard glint of his eyes and deep scowl on his face as he glanced around at the others and then lowered his voice.

"Listen up, buttercup. I don't know what kind of game you think you're playing, but you're not going to win."

"Oh yeah? And who's going to stop me?"

Maggie wasn't teasing anymore.

I'm not surprised he left her.

Ethan had said that. And he'd been right. Maggie had had a lifetime of being left. A lifetime of being alone and unwanted and unchosen. But Eleanor Ashley had invited three authors to her home for Christmas: Ethan, the best-selling juggernaut. Sir Jasper, a staple of the genre. And Maggie.

Three authors. One contest. But Maggie was the only one who'd found the clues.

Ethan was right about something: it *was* a game; but no one else even knew they were playing.

She glanced at Sir Jasper on the other side of the table—tweed jacket with an unlit pipe in his pocket—droning on to Dr. Charles, who appeared to be half asleep. "Well, I told those chaps at the Yard—that's what we call Scotland Yard when you're in the business. Just *the Yard*, you see . . ."

It almost wasn't fair.

"Just tell me this, Margaret Amelia—"

"That's cute." Maggie smiled over her sandwich. "How you decided that, even though you know my name now, you're still going to get it wrong every time because I'm so beneath you."

Maggie licked some mustard off her index finger and Ethan drew a ragged breath and closed his eyes for one long second. Then something in him seemed to snap and he shook off whatever he was thinking and asked, "Are you still going to feel like smiling if we find Eleanor at the bottom of a rotten staircase or in a snowy ditch or—"

"We won't," she said before she could stop herself and he pulled back. Just a little.

"What do you know?" The words were cold and hard and sounded like a dare and Maggie couldn't help herself, she looked at the sprig of mistletoe. It was pressed flat but still green—still fresh.

I know Eleanor.

Ethan was right beside her, putting off heat and pheromones and that omnipresent gravity that kept the whole world in his orbit. But Maggie was immune. She didn't need Ethan. She just needed a plan and a strategy and about five hundred Post-it notes. She needed whiteboards and reference materials and maps.

And time. What Maggie needed more than anything was time.

"I know . . ." The room was full of laughter and chatter, the scrape of forks and spoons. And Ethan—with his broad shoulders and even larger presence. For one brief moment, Maggie actually felt guilty because he did seem to be genuinely worried about Eleanor. But—

I'm not surprised he left her.

"Maggie . . ."

When she spoke again it was louder, and to the group. "I know they're making one of Ethan's books into a movie! Did you know that, Kitty? A movie!"

"They are?" Kitty squealed. "Which one?"

"Knight of the Living Idiot."

"*Dead of Knight*." Ethan shot Maggie a glare as the room turned into a madhouse.

Questions like "Well, who's going to star?" and "Do you have a role for me?" and "Who's writing the screenplay?" were flying around so quickly that no one seemed to notice when Maggie stood and walked back to the sideboard.

"Well, why don't *you* just play the lead?" Cece tittered and Maggie slipped out the door and across the empty foyer.

The little sprig of mistletoe was practically burning a hole in her fist and the collective works of Eleanor Ashley were ping-ponging around in her mind.

Roses Are Dead, Violets Are Blue took place in February, so there was only one reason for a sprig of fresh mistletoe to be in that particular book—on that particular page: it was a clue. Maggie was certain. Now all she had to do was follow it.

But follow it where?

Eleanor had written at least ten different stories set at Christmas, but *Murder Under the Mistletoe* had been her breakout hit. She'd even named her home Mistletoe Manor. So it all had to be connected. It had to matter. It had to . . .

Maggie was halfway up the stairs when she saw something out the window. The snow wasn't falling quite so hard, and something about the endless stretch of white that blanketed the grounds made her think about her fourteenth birthday. She'd only asked for one thing: a custom-order stamp that pressed words right into paper.

From the private library of Margaret Elizabeth Chase.

She'd spent all afternoon on her bedroom floor, sitting cross-legged and pressing those words into the title page of book after book, running her fingers over the letters. Wishing she could press them into her skin.

That was how the ground looked. *Embossed*. Like a pattern had been pressed into the earth. White on white, with long lines of shadows and bits of leafy green hedges standing out starkly against the pure white snow. A labyrinth.

"A maze."

It looked exactly how Maggie had always imagined it—exactly how Eleanor had written it in her very first bestseller. And for the first time in a long time, Maggie knew exactly what she had to do.

CHAPTER Twenty-Six

Maggie should have been freezing, but she wasn't. The hedges were thick and tall beneath their blanket of snow and ice, blocking out the wind and the world. From the window, the maze had seemed like Eleanor herself—complex and spiraling and too good to be true, but as Maggie turned down narrow path after narrow path, it felt more like Maggie's life. She didn't know where she was going or how she was going to get there. She just knew she was alone and she had no intention of giving up.

So she pinched that sprig of mistletoe between her fingers and she kept moving, using her own footprints as a cheat sheet to know which way she'd been.

Every time she hit a dead end, she marked it up as a path she didn't have to go down anymore, and she kept searching. Because the dead ends weren't setbacks. Not if she learned from them. Maggie had been backing up and changing directions her whole life. She could do this. She was *going* to do this. She just had to find—

Snow crunched behind her. Unfamiliar footprints laid ahead. And there was a deep voice on the wind, saying "Well, this is a funny place to look for Eleanor."

Maggie cursed beneath her breath but slowly turned and looked at Ethan, gave him her biggest, most innocent eyes. "Well, like you said, I'd feel awful if she'd wandered off and gotten lost in here. An almost ninety-year-old woman—"

"She's eighty-one."

"Well, you can never be too careful." Maggie pushed past him.

"So careful you ran out without a coat?" he called as she reached another dead end.

"You're right!" She spun on him. "Let's go—"

Ethan sidestepped and blocked her way. "I'm going to ask you one more time, Margaret Marie."

"Still not my name!" She pushed past him and headed down another path, then made a turn and—

Slammed right into Ethan.

"How did you get ahead of me?" Maggie asked, stumbling and a little unsteady.

"You sure seem awful busy out here. It's almost like you're . . . *looking for something.*" He flashed a knowing grin and, suddenly, Maggie couldn't meet his gaze.

"Just Eleanor. But you're right. She's not here. We should go."

She started back, but it was ridiculous how easily he kept pace beside her.

"So what's with the mistletoe? Is it because you want to make out? Because if you want to make out—"

"No, thank you."

"You'd have to hold it over your head first. Or I can hold it. Do you want me to hold it?"

"Nope." She made a turn and hit another dead end, and Maggie wanted to scream. It felt like the temperature had dropped ten degrees, but Ethan was standing there in his leather jacket, looking so hot the snow might melt. Meanwhile, Maggie's jeans were wet from the knees down and she'd lost feeling in at least four toes and her nose was starting to run.

"You're freezing." His voice was soft but slightly smug. "Lucky for you, I brought your sweater. Hands up."

That's when she noticed the bundle of items he held under one arm.

"You've got to be kidding me," Maggie said, but she was starting to shake as she stood there, arms wrapped around herself, hands balled up in her sleeves.

"You know, you're going to hurt Kitty's feelings. She knitted these herself."

"Really?"

Ethan shook his head. "I have no idea. Now up." Maggie didn't move. "Are you going to fight me, Margaret Jane?"

She felt like a petulant child but it was faster to stick her hands in the air and allow the world's most annoying man to tug a Christmas sweater over her head and gently work it down her arms. Her hair was standing on end and full of static by the time her head popped through. She felt ridiculous and he was looking at her like he would have given anything for a camera. A phone. Anything to immortalize her humiliation. But the worst part was that the smile Ethan gave her wasn't mocking. It was indulgent and kind and it made Maggie's fingers tingle. Either that or she was developing frostbite. Maggie hoped it was the latter.

"Thank you." She looked down at the snow.

"Any time." Then he draped a heavy coat around her shoulders like a cape. "James let me borrow these. They're Eleanor's favorites." He pulled a fuzzy wool hat with a pom-pom on top from his pocket and tugged it over her ears.

Maggie hated to admit it, but she really was warmer, maybe because of the clothes or, more likely, because Ethan was better than the hedges at blocking the wind.

"Great. Thank you."

But then he gripped the coat's lapel and pulled her closer.

"Now about that mistletoe . . ."

"Ugh." Maggie blew out a frustrated breath and headed back the way they'd come. "You're right. Let's go in."

"So why the maze?"

"No reason!"

Dead end. Darn it! And, of course, Ethan was right behind her. She was stuck, trapped. And she could feel him moving closer; the heat of his gaze was going to burn.

"You know, you're not a very good liar."

She wasn't, but that was hardly the time to start agreeing with him. "I don't know what you're talking—"

"What was in the book, Margaret?"

Oh no. "What book?"

"The one in the library."

"There are thousands of books in the library. *It's a library.*"

"See? You get a little line right"—he pointed to her forehead—"here when you lie."

"Hey!"

"So what was up with the phone call?" His gaze shifted from her eyes to her lips, then back again. Slowly. "Because it sounded to me like you think this is all some kind of . . . *test.*"

The word was low and crisp, little more than frosty breath, but Maggie watched it hang in the air like a snowflake. She thought it might not fall.

And, suddenly, she didn't care. It didn't matter if he knew they were running a race. It didn't matter if he sprinted ahead. It didn't matter.

Because Maggie was going to win.

"Why are you smiling right now?" He actually sounded afraid.

"Oh, Ethan, if you were an Eleanor Ashley fan, you'd already know the answer to that question. But you're not, Mr. Leather Jacket Guy, so it doesn't matter."

"It matters because either an eighty-one-year-old woman is lost and possibly injured, or she's not." Darn him and his perfectly reasonable point. "Margaret—"

"Of course it's a test!" She couldn't believe she had to say it. She couldn't believe he didn't know. "The greatest mystery writer the world has ever known disappeared out of a locked room two days before Christmas. Of course it's a test!"

"Why?" The word was flat and even, but there was tension in it, like a bowstring drawn tight and ready to fire.

"Because she's retiring." It didn't matter that it was just a guess. Maggie was right—she had to be. "Eleanor's retiring, but she wouldn't leave her legacy to just anyone. She'd pick a successor who is worthy and who appreciates her and who thinks like her. And . . ." She couldn't bring herself to say it.

"And you think you're that person?"

"I *know* I'm that person." Blame her Baptist upbringing or childhood poverty or the way that, according to Colin, her failures had always been hers but her successes had always been *theirs*, but Maggie had never had a lot of confidence. Not in her looks or her smarts or her talent. But she'd never doubted this. Not once. Not for a second.

"Why—"

"Because I'm the person out here with this!" She held up the mistletoe.

He gave another smirk. "So I guess we're back to kissing?"

"It's a clue, okay? It's a clue."

"How can you—"

"Because in *Murder Under the Mistletoe* the killer leaves a map in the middle of a maze. So . . . maze!" She threw out her arms, then huffed out a laugh. "But you wouldn't know that. Would you?"

Maggie had never felt so smug—so right. She hadn't won . . . yet, but the great Ethan Wyatt hadn't even realized they were playing.

Which was why it didn't make any sense when a slow smile started growing on his lips—when a predatory gleam filled his eyes as he said, "Oh, but I know now."

He plucked the mistletoe out of her hand and started spinning the little sprig between two fingers. Maggie lunged, but he held it high over his head like they were on a schoolyard, playing keep away with Maggie's future.

"Hey! That"—Maggie trailed off, realizing that, for the first time in her life, she could actually stop jumping— "doesn't matter."

"What?"

"It doesn't matter." Since she was eighteen years old there had been no room for error in Maggie's life, but right then—in that moment—she was free. "Oh, Ethan, don't you get it? That's just going to lead to another clue, but you won't know how to follow that one either. Or the one after that." She took a slow step toward him, cocky for the first time in her life. "Or the one after that."

She should have felt warm in her cloak of rage and satisfaction, but there was something in his eyes then, a calculating gleam. "See, that's where you're wrong."

Now Ethan was the one prowling closer and Maggie was the

one inching away. She felt something cold at her back. Little clumps of snow dislodged from the top of the hedge and landed on the nape of her neck, sliding, cold and liquid, down her spine as Ethan towered over her, bigger and brighter and blocking out the sky.

"I don't have to follow the clues." His breath was warm against her skin as he whispered, "*I just have to follow you.*"

The cold air in Maggie's lungs turned to fire. Her blood started pounding in her ears, and through it all, one sentence played over and over in her mind like a mantra. Or a curse.

I'm not surprised he left her.

I'm not surprised he left her.

I'm not surprised—

"Maggie?"

It was the pity in his eyes that did it—that lit the fuse and made her burn.

"Sometimes I lie in bed at night, thinking of ways to kill you and make it look like an accident."

His whole face changed. Pity turned to arrogance as his gaze dipped to her lips. And lingered. "So what you're saying is, you think about me in bed."

And then all Maggie could do was scream and storm away.

She could still hear his footsteps crunching behind her, but she didn't feel anything. Not anymore. Hopefully never again. And she walked faster, sinking in snow that was fresh and deep. It didn't matter that she was numb from her knees down. She had to keep moving forward. Then. Now. Always. If she stopped moving forward, she would die, so Maggie just walked faster.

"Why do you hate me so much?" he called.

She hated him because he was handsome and charming and they lived in a world where a man didn't have to be anything else.

She hated him because life was graded on a curve and he was the kind of guy for whom a seventy-six would always be an A.

She hated him because he was universally adored and even the people who were legally obligated to love Maggie had shrugged and said *maybe not.*

She hated him because she was alone and afraid and nothing. She was nothing.

And Ethan . . .

Ethan hadn't even known her name.

"Because we hate each other!" she shouted back. "We've spent years hating each other. It's kind of our thing."

Ethan darted out to block her path, but it was the look on his face that stopped her. His chest rose and fell in the chilly air, like he might start sweating despite the cold. Like he was in the fight of his life, and he was losing. "I don't hate you. I've never hated you. And so help me I tried," he mumbled as the snow started falling in a thick white wave—like they were inside a snow globe and fate had given them a good, hard shake.

For a moment, he was quiet. Pensive. And when he spoke again, the words were nothing but a whisper of frosty breath. "Just tell me. Please. What did I do?"

And Maggie tried very, very hard not to remember.

CHAPTER Twenty-Seven

Eleven Months Ago

"How are you doing, kiddo?" The call was bad news. It had to be, because Deborah was being nice. And Deborah was never nice. "Are you taking care of yourself?"

It was three in the afternoon, and Maggie looked down at her oldest, softest pajamas, terrified Deborah might be able to see through the line and know that Maggie couldn't remember the last time she'd washed her hair.

"I'm great!" Maggie lied. "So great. Just the perfect amount of greatness. If you're calling about the new draft, it's almost ready. So close. I'll have you something by the time I see you." Maggie laughed, but the sound turned to ash in her mouth. "I'm not getting on that train until it's finished, no sirree."

The loudest silence in the world is the one that fills the pause when something isn't actually funny, and, instantly, Maggie wanted to pull the words back, crawl in a hole—actually take that shower she'd been on the verge of taking for the last two days.

"That's not why I'm calling. And"—Deborah drew a heavy breath—"it also *is* why I'm calling. You know how I told you Betty's Book Club had it narrowed down to you and one other author . . ." Deborah trailed off, and, instantly, Maggie knew.

"No."

"It's probably for the best. You don't need this kind of pressure right now."

"Pressure is being an orphaned teenager, Deborah. Pressure is all your worldly possessions fitting into six cardboard boxes and not having a permanent address. Pressure is realizing the world is a high wire and you're the only person you know without a net. This isn't pressure," said the woman who had just found a piece of popcorn in her bra and she'd run out of popcorn three days ago.

But Deborah hadn't called to argue. "It's over, Maggie. It's decided. Betty's Book Club is going with the other Killhaven author—"

"Who?" Maggie demanded.

"I fought for you, kiddo. But you'll have other books, other chances."

"Who?"

"Your plate is full right now. Between the lawyers and the deadline and . . . Has he even moved out yet?"

"I moved out."

"Oh, Maggie . . ."

"I never wanted that house." Which was true.

"But you paid for it."

That was true, too, but Maggie wasn't going to let her change the subject. "What author did they pick, Deborah?"

"Have you gone a whole day without crying yet?" Deborah sounded stern and tired—like a mother—and Maggie wanted to cry again for all new reasons.

"Because I'm a woman, and everyone knows women are overly emotional and hysterical and—"

"Because you lost your husband and your best friend less than a month ago and it's okay to grieve that. Let yourself grieve that."

But Maggie didn't want to grieve. She wanted to win. "Who?" she snapped. "Who did they pick?"

"It doesn't matter."

"What book, Deborah?"

The silence was an ocean, dark and vast and deep enough to drown in. "*Thief in the Knight*. By Ethan Wyatt."

CHAPTER *Twenty-Eight*

Two Days Before Christmas

The snow was falling harder, and the world looked like static, blurry and out of focus and not quite right as Maggie blinked against the falling flakes. Even the wind had stopped howling.

"Why, Maggie?" Had he ever called her by her real name before? Maggie couldn't remember.

"I heard you," she said before she could stop herself.

"Heard me when?" His voice was so much closer than it should have been—softer and louder at the same time.

"At the party. You and Lance. I heard you."

"What—"

"*I'm not surprised he left her.*" She wiped snow from her eyes and saw the words land. They knocked him back like a punch. "Well, congratulations." She gave a joyless laugh. "Everyone leaves me, so it didn't exactly take a genius to see it coming, but that's okay. I guess you beat me there too."

"Maggie, please . . ."

This time she didn't slow down and she didn't turn back. It took her three false leads before she saw the exit up ahead, but, for once, Ethan wasn't following and that, to Maggie, felt like victory.

As soon as she got back to the house, she'd change out of her wet clothes and take a warm shower. She'd get something hot to drink and then call upon every word of every Eleanor book that had ever seeped into her soul. She would win this thing. She had to.

Because it was Eleanor.

Because it was something that Colin couldn't claim and Emily couldn't ruin.

Because, if she did this, then everything—everything—would have been worth it.

Everything would finally be okay.

She just had to follow the clues and find Eleanor and beat Ethan.

In that moment, Maggie wanted to beat Ethan most of all.

She was turning and heading out of the maze when she heard it—a bang on the air. Ice must have fallen off the roof, she thought. Somewhere, a car must have backfired. Or maybe it was the wind because, suddenly, the hedges rustled, big chunks of snow breaking free and landing at her feet with a *smack*.

And then the sound came again. A crack. A bang. And before Maggie knew what was happening, two strong arms came out of nowhere and grabbed her, pulling her backward through the snowy hedge. Arms flailing. Snow flying. Hair and sweater tangling and snagging on the branches.

And then there was nothing but the icy ground at her back and the warm weight of Ethan as he lay over her, pressing down. "Don't even think about moving."

"Get off me!"

"Not until the shooting stops."

CHAPTER *Twenty-Nine*

Maggie stopped fighting. She studied the face that loomed over her, eyes wide and alert and scanning the part of the maze he'd pulled her into. She was on her back in the too-soft snow and the air was full of falling flakes, but it wasn't the cold that froze her. It was the confusion. And the shock. And the fact that Ethan Wyatt's body was stretched on top of hers.

She should have felt crushed or smothered, but instead she just felt warm. Six feet two inches of muscle taking her anxiety away. It was the first time in a long time that Maggie hadn't felt like fighting.

But the strangest thing of all was the fact that Ethan wasn't teasing, wasn't taunting. He was the most serious man in the world when he looked down at her and whispered, "Are you hit?"

"Hit with what?" It wasn't making sense. Words didn't have meaning, not when Ethan's hands were running over her legs and down her sides—under her sweater and— "Hey!"

"Listen to me!" Warm hands cupped her cold cheeks. "I'm going to pull you up, and then I need you to stay close. Stay low. And run. Don't look back. And don't stop. If I get hit—"

"Get hit with *what*?"

"—just get to the house, barricade yourself in your room, and try to call for—"

"Ethan, what is going on?" *Shooting.* He'd used the word *shooting*, but no one was . . . "Ethan?"

Playful Ethan, Cocky Ethan, Life-of-the-Party Ethan . . . They were all gone, and the man who was left radiated efficiency and competency. And fear. He was afraid but a million miles from panicked as he cupped her cheek and breathed out the words, "I have you."

In the next moment, her cold hands were in his warm ones and she was almost weightless as he pulled her to her feet. Her legs felt like icicles, like they might snap off at any second, but that didn't matter as Ethan tucked her against his side and started to run out of the maze and toward the double glass doors of the library.

It was a strange sensation. Like flying. But that didn't make any sense at all because she was supposed to be terrified. Or annoyed. Or both. Really, Maggie should have felt both as they ran through snow so thick she could barely see the mansion's walls. But Ethan was the fortress then. Tall and impenetrable and carved from stone.

"You're being ridiculous," she said.

"Yes. Absolutely. Being used for target practice does that," he snapped as he threw open the library doors and herded Maggie inside. He turned the lock and pulled the curtains, but Maggie didn't move—couldn't move. She just stood there, staring up at him. He wasn't even out of breath.

"Come on." He reached for her hand. "We need to call the police."

And for some reason those were the words that broke her—that made a nervous laugh burst free.

"Because you heard a noise?"

He glared down. "Because someone shot at you." He tried to push her away from the doors, but she dug in.

"I told you." She was frustrated and annoyed and so tired she could cry. "It's a test. Eleanor's not missing. And she's not dead. She's retiring."

But Ethan just stood there, running a hand through his hair, white flakes melting and sliding across his skin. "Maggie—"

"It's a test," she said, stronger now. "And now I'm going to go find her." She was turning, she was leaving. She was *winning*. When she heard—

"It was a rifle."

The words were low and even, as flat and cold as the wind, and maybe that's why Maggie stood there, frozen. "A Remington 721—maybe a 722—if my guess is right and my guesses are usually right. But that means it's old, and someone hasn't been oiling it like they should, so three rounds from long range in high wind . . . That's a hard shot."

Slowly, Maggie turned. His eyes were on her then—only on her. And he felt like her only source of warmth when he said, "And that's why you're still breathing."

"You can't . . ." Maggie swallowed hard. "You can't possibly know that."

"Try me," he dared.

"How can you know that?"

He inched closer. "Because I'm the guy who takes the bullet."

What were they talking about? Maggie couldn't remember. She could only feel his stare and hear his breath and see the spark in his eyes, like a challenge and a dare and a promise, and right then Maggie wasn't sure why she hated the man in front of her. She didn't know if she should hit him or kiss him or kick him in the shins. She just knew she couldn't . . . shouldn't . . . wouldn't look away.

"Which is why"—he took a slow step closer—"we have to call the police."

And just like that the spell was broken. She shook her head and pushed away. "You may be an expert on rifles, but I'm an expert on Eleanor Ashley, and I'm telling you. *This is all a test.*"

He was opening his mouth to argue when a scream broke through the silence, vicious and shrill and coming from the second floor, and before Maggie knew what was happening, Ethan was turning and running and she had no choice but to follow—up the stairs and down the hall and to the door of Eleanor's office, where Cece was shaking and screaming and white as a ghost.

And Sir Jasper was lying, unmoving, on the floor.

Beside her, Ethan whispered, "You were saying?"

CHAPTER Thirty

Maggie had been imagining crimes most of her life. Hundreds of them. Thousands of them. She'd read them in other people's books and written them in her own. She'd listened to podcasts and watched movies and she knew what people always said.

It happened so fast . . .

It was all just a blur . . .

But right then, in that moment, for the first time in her life, she believed them.

Cece had stopped screaming and was standing, frozen, in the hall, but James and Dr. Charles were rushing up the stairs. Kitty came out of the bedroom—a crying baby on her shoulder, Rupert and Nanny Davis right behind her—as everything blended into a blur of shouts and cries and chaos.

"What is all this racket—"

"What's going on up—"

"Will you stop that screeching—"

"What is the meaning of—"

"Good god, is he dead?"

Suddenly, the hall went silent as all eyes turned to Ethan, who was already crouched over Sir Jasper and feeling for a pulse. It seemed to take an hour for him to look up. "*He's alive.*"

And then the world turned into a totally different kind of chaos.

"Rupert, take her." Kitty thrust the baby at her husband (who simply passed the child to the nanny) and tried to push through the crowd. "Let me through!" *Kitty's a nurse,* Maggie's frozen brain remembered.

"Get out of the way!" Dr. Charles cried before kneeling on the rug beside Sir Jasper and starting CPR.

They had a doctor there. And a nurse. And . . .

Maggie looked down at Sir Jasper, the way he was sprawled on the floor, lying half on top of the overturned tea tray, cookies and crumbs and pieces of shattered porcelain all around him.

"Oh, what have I— Crikey! Is that man dead?" Freddy Banes skidded to a stop in the doorway.

Maggie was turning to Ethan. "Ambulance," they said at the same time.

"Sir"—James was shaking his head—"I'm afraid the phones are—"

"I was able to make a call this morning. Just for a minute." Maggie felt guilty as she cut her eyes at Ethan, but he didn't react at all, no *I told you so*. No sarcastic reply or cocky grin. "In the east wing. The top floor of the tower . . ."

"I'll go." Freddy took off at a run.

"Now what are all of you doing standing out . . ." The duke was striding down the hall like a man who didn't have a care in the world, but he trailed off as soon as he saw Sir Jasper. "Good Lord. Is he—"

"He's not dead, but he will be if we can't get him to a hospital." Ethan ran a hand through his hair, dislodging tiny pieces of ice that hadn't had time to melt yet. Which seemed impossible. The maze had been an hour ago—a year. Everything was happening in slow motion and Maggie felt herself go numb. Like she was still out there, wet and disoriented and too cold to feel a thing, which was better than feeling everything. It was the only way she could think, and thinking trumped feeling any day.

She looked around Eleanor's office—at the notebooks on the shelves and the computer and the old record player that had seemed like such a clue a few hours before, but now Sir Jasper was unconscious and Eleanor was . . .

Eleanor was missing. Eleanor might be dead.

"Is he having a heart attack?" someone said.

"Well, it looks like a stroke—"

"Ew." Cece cringed. "Looks like he was kind of barf-y."

"It's poison." Maggie knew it. She just did. "Is his heart too slow or too fast?" she asked but no one answered. "Kitty? His heart rate! Is it—"

"Too . . . too slow," Kitty said.

"It could be foxglove?" Maggie tried to think. She was desperate to remember. "Maybe monkshood?"

"What's that?" the duchess asked.

"Wolfsbane. Some people call it . . ." Maggie was too busy racking her mind for anything she'd ever learned about poisons and antidotes and— Charcoal. "James, is there any activated charcoal in the mansion?"

"I'm not sure, but if it pertains to poisons, there is a good chance that Ms. Ashley has it. In fact . . ." There was a light in his eye, as if he'd just remembered something, and then he bolted for the stairs.

"Now see here," Rupert was saying. "I don't see any reason to jump to any conclusions. That man doesn't look poisoned to me. If you ask me—"

Maggie's gaze flew to Ethan's. She didn't know why. She didn't even want to *think* about why! But—

He was the guy who takes the bullet. And he was looking right at her.

"Everybody out. Now."

"See here, Wyatt." Rupert puffed his chest out. "I don't know what makes you think you're in charge, but I demand—"

"You want to make demands?" Ethan spun on him. "Go right ahead. But make them downstairs. Now out."

Maggie was aware, faintly, of people moving. Leaving. Heading downstairs or, in Nanny Davis's case, back to the children in their playroom. But Maggie was still glued to her spot by the door. She couldn't look at Sir Jasper. In fact, she was very pointedly looking anywhere *but* at Sir Jasper, but Maggie couldn't just walk away. Eleanor had last been seen in that room. Sir Jasper might still die there. And Maggie—

"That goes for you too." Ethan's hand was a sure, steady pressure on her waist. "We need to figure out how we're going to get him to a hospital if we can't call out."

"I know." But Maggie didn't move.

"Maggie?" He was so much bigger than she was, but it didn't make her feel small. It made her feel safe. "Maggie?"

"I know, all right? I know! It's just . . ." In the next second, she was airborne and the scene was upside down and the office was growing small behind her.

"Put me down!"

"No."

She banged her hands against the small of his back. "Put me down."

And then he did, tossing her off his shoulder and pressing her against the wall before glancing toward the stairs as if to make sure no one else could hear. "Listen to me." Hands were in her hair then, as gentle and as soft as his voice as he said, "You know what this means, don't you?"

"Sir Jasper was poisoned and someone shot at me and Eleanor is missing. Eleanor is missing and she's out there and . . ." Something about the sure, steady weight of his presence gave her the strength to say, "It's not a test."

Maybe it was the trauma or the jet lag or the cool, dim shadows of the hall, but Ethan's eyes turned the color of midnight. "It's not a test."

CHAPTER Thirty-One

They didn't go to the library or the kitchen or their rooms. No one ate or talked or moved. They just stood between the front door and the base of the stairs in that long, arching space that had felt like a cathedral when Maggie first saw it. Now it was as silent as a tomb.

It was exactly where she'd stood the night before, telling Ethan she didn't know him. But that wasn't true, she realized. She knew *an* Ethan—one who was easy calm and charming smiles, the human equivalent of sweet tea on a hot day, cool and just a touch too saccharine. The man beside her now was coffee, black.

"What about cyanide?" the duke's voice broke through the silence.

"Excuse me?" Ethan asked.

"Well." The duke pointed at Maggie. "How could she possibly know what poison it was? It could be cyanide. Did anyone smell almonds? Cyanide smells like—"

"It's not cyanide." Ethan blew out an exhausted breath.

"But how do you—"

"Because he'd already be dead," the duchess said flatly.

Cece shuddered and wrapped her arms around herself. *Shock*, a part of Maggie's brain filled in. Cece was wearing a headband with snowflakes on it and she'd just found a body. Of course she was going into shock.

But before Maggie could say a word there were footsteps at the top of the stairs.

"Well?" Ethan called up to Freddy Banes, who stopped on the landing.

"Nothing. No signal. I tried everywhere. Couldn't get . . ." the lawyer trailed off, a little out of breath. "Nothing."

"Okay." A hand was on Maggie's arm then, sliding past her wrist and into her palm. She felt a tug. "You all stay here. We're gonna go see if there's anything stouter than a Rolls-Royce in that garage."

The duke stepped forward. "I drove my Range Rover. Why?"

"Because if we can't call out, we're going to have to drive Sir Jasper to the hospital and get the police," Ethan explained as if he wished everyone would just keep up.

"Why on earth would we need the police?" Rupert asked.

"Because Sir Jasper was poisoned!" Ethan's grip on Maggie's hand tightened.

"Now I've had enough of that. You can't possibly know . . ." Rupert's face was turning red. "She thinks she's such a poison expert—"

"She *is* a poison expert."

Maggie didn't know whether to be grateful to Ethan or tell him to shut up. She really didn't want to explain that her poison bona fides came from writing books about a cat who could smell them. And the truth was, Maggie wanted to be wrong. She wanted Sir Jasper to be passed out drunk upstairs and not—

"I won't have that nonsense in my house," Rupert said, and Maggie heard ringing in her ears.

"This is *Eleanor's* house. And she's missing. Sir Jasper barely has a pulse—"

"Sir Jasper had a heart attack," Rupert declared.

"Maybe he did." Ethan gave a joyless laugh and inched a little closer to Rupert. "But someone took a shot at Maggie in the garden, so forgive me if I'm not willing to sit around and wait to be next."

No one had been expecting that part. Even Maggie had almost forgotten.

"Oh no!" Cece exclaimed. "Someone shot at you! Are you okay?"

"They're lying," Rupert said, dismissively. "If you expect us to believe—"

"Believe whatever you want," Ethan said, tugging Maggie toward the hallway that led to the kitchen and (presumably) the garage. "But we're driving out of here as soon as Sir Jasper can travel, and we're coming back with—"

The front doors flew open on a blast of blowing snow and icy wind. A flash of light sliced across the dim room and Maggie found herself squinting against the too-bright glare as a shadow filled the doorway. A great coat flapped in the wind. And a big voice boomed, "Merry Christmas!"

The shadow let out a low, deep laugh, and for a split second Maggie wondered if it might be Santa.

"Bloody lucky I got here . . ." The man took an awkward step inside and slammed the door. There was discomfort on his face and snow in his steely gray beard, but he was smiling, even as he said, "Hope you folks weren't planning on leaving any time soon—blasted bridge collapsed just as I cleared it. Then my car went in the ditch and I had to walk the last mile. Stepped in a hole . . . Landed on my arse . . ." He hobbled forward. "So, I'm sorry I'm late, Eleanor, my dear, but you couldn't have written it any better yourself!"

He searched the group for the face that wasn't there. "Well, what have I missed?"

CHAPTER *Thirty-Two*

Inspector William Dobson of the local police had taken off his great-coat and the snow and ice had melted in his beard, leaving him slightly damp and highly disheveled as he sat in front of the library's roaring fire. His pants legs were wet and covered in muck, and he'd propped his bad leg on an ottoman and pulled off one boot to reveal an ankle that was purple and blue and approximately twice its rightful size.

He was, in short, a man who was having a very bad day, and there was no doubt it had just gotten worse as he sat there, staring at Maggie and Ethan.

"Why do you think someone was shooting at you?"

That was it. No introductions or chitchat or easing in. It was like a bucket of cold water had been dumped over Maggie, and she glanced at Ethan, like the last twenty-four hours might have been a dream.

"Ms. Chase?" Inspector Dobson prompted.

"I'm sorry." She shook her head. "Do you mean *why was someone shooting* or why was someone shooting *at me*?" The man stayed quiet and Maggie rambled on. "Because I don't know about the first part but the second is pretty obvious? I think?"

She hated the uptick at the end of that sentence, the uncertainty in her voice. Maggie was an adult. Maggie was a professional. But, more than anything, Maggie was scared. And she needed someone to tell her it was real and not in her head and—

"It's incredibly obvious." Ethan's deep voice cut through the silence.

Dobson didn't like that one bit; Maggie could tell by the way he leaned back in his chair and folded his hands on his belly. He looked like the kind of man who would have retired five years ago if he wasn't afraid someone would make him get a hobby. "Humor me."

"It's just . . . I was wearing Eleanor's hat and coat," Maggie told him. "Snow was falling. Visibility wasn't great. From a distance, I would have looked like Eleanor." She glanced at Ethan, almost wishing he would talk about Remington rifles and being the guy who takes the bullet again, but Ethan never took his eyes off Dobson. "Someone shot at me because they're trying to kill Eleanor."

Dobson shifted his bad leg and tried to hide his discomfort. *Stubborn*, Maggie thought. He'd probably never stopped and asked for directions in his life. "At this point, Eleanor's just missing. What makes you think someone's trying to kill her?"

"Because Sir Jasper didn't poison himself?" Maggie felt like that much should have been obvious, but Inspector Dobson simply turned to the tray on the side table and began examining a container of tea like he was at a fancy restaurant—like a man's heart hadn't nearly stopped this afternoon with a tray almost exactly like that spread around him.

"What makes you think Sir Jasper was poisoned?" Dobson sounded almost distracted.

"Oh, just a . . ." Maggie watched Dobson add leaves to the pot of hot water and wait for it to steep. "Are you sure you want to drink that?"

"You say Eleanor was conducting some kind of . . ." Dobson flipped through an old-fashioned notebook. "Test."

Maggie had to look down at her hands. "I was wrong."

"What makes you say that?" Dobson turned his attention to the cookies but Maggie felt like the water in that pot—full of steam but not quite boiling.

"A test wouldn't leave Sir Jasper unconscious upstairs. A test wouldn't fire shots at me in the garden." That time her words didn't sound like a question. They were facts. Not opinions or theories or crazy, wild-eyed schemes. "Eleanor is missing, Inspector. And every minute we sit here is a minute we're not *looking* for Eleanor. Or for whoever is trying to *kill* Eleanor."

Dobson picked up the pot and poured. "Not whoever tried to kill Sir Jasper?"

"It's the same person," Maggie said with exaggerated patience. "No one has a motive to hurt Eleanor *and* kill Sir Jasper. That tea tray was in her office—"

"Why do you think the poison was on the tea tray?"

Maggie wanted to throw her hands up and scream.

"Maybe it wasn't," she agreed. "Maybe Sir Jasper just happened to be close enough to knock it over when he collapsed . . . Maybe he was poisoned some other place or time. Or maybe he wasn't poisoned at all? We won't know until we can get out of here and run a whole lot of tests. But, until then, I think we should work under the assumption that, maybe—just maybe—a deadly poison was delivered to the woman who is *currently missing* and who *someone has already tried to kill.*"

But Dobson was smiling at her over the top of his cup. He almost laughed when he said, "Funny."

"Is it?" Maggie's foot was starting to bounce, a *tap-tap-tap* on the hardwood floor. Her jeans were still wet from the snow, and the damp denim felt like a straitjacket on her calves. She wanted to change. To run. To vibrate right out of her own skin. And she might have done exactly that if a big, muscular leg hadn't started pressing against hers; she felt herself go still.

"You say it was a deadly poison, but Sir Jasper isn't dead at all." Dobson flashed a toothy grin, the human personification of *gotcha.* "What do you say to that, young lady?"

"I say the Latin name of foxglove is digitalis, did you know that, Inspector? It's *digitalis.* Have you heard of that? It's heart medicine. Sweet clover is a blood thinner. Henbane has been used to treat Parkinson's."

"I'm just a simple country copper, Ms. Chase. You'll have to—"

"The difference between a poison and a medicine is the size of the dose," Maggie finished, harder now. "I know that because when I was fourteen years old I read it. In *that* one." She pointed to a copy of *The Black Thumb Murders* high on Eleanor's shelf.

It should have been obvious, but Maggie said it anyway. "Sir Jasper is a giant, and, no, it didn't kill *him*, but . . ." Maggie was so cold—so cold and tired of carrying the weight of everything. All the time. She'd been carrying it since she was eighteen years old, and she wanted to put it down. She would. Just as soon as she made the inspector understand—

"It would have killed *Eleanor*," said the deep voice beside her.

Maggie jerked a little—surprised—by the voice and the calm resolve and the realization that at some point in the past ten minutes—or maybe the past two days—she had started leaning on Ethan Wyatt. Literally. Metaphorically. He had one arm draped across the back of the couch, not touching her—not exactly. But it made her feel shielded and safe and not alone.

She would need to unpack that later, maybe cry for a few hours or days, but now wasn't the time or place, not with Eleanor missing and Sir Jasper fighting for his life upstairs and Inspector Dobson sitting across from them, staring daggers.

Gone was the folksy gentleman warming himself by the fire as he said, "Oh, but I can think of *two* people who would benefit from the demise of both Eleanor Ashley and Sir Jasper Rhodes. And I'm looking right at them."

"Don't be ridiculous," Maggie said at the exact same moment Ethan uttered—

"Yeah, I can see that."

She spun, but Ethan just pressed his leg firmer against Maggie's.

Dobson cradled the tiny teacup in his big hands. "Taking over Eleanor's ongoing series . . . what would that be worth?"

"That's hardly the—" Maggie started just as Ethan said, "Millions."

Maggie wanted to kick him in the shin, but Dobson didn't notice. Didn't care. He was too busy sipping his tea and trying to decide whether or not to have another cookie. It was like this was a social call—a polite occasion. He wasn't even looking at them when he said, "Eleanor bought this house forty years ago—did you know that? Just a few months after I joined the force."

He looked around the room—at the towering shelves and roaring fire, the world's most beautiful Christmas tree and frosty windows—as if there was no place on Earth he'd rather spend Christmas.

"We don't get a lot of serious crime out here, thank goodness, but a young woman had gone missing. My father was the chief inspector at the time and he didn't think I could crack it, you see. But I wanted to show him, so one of the lads and I decided to pay a visit to our new author. Figured the great Eleanor Ashley had seen more crimes than the pair of us combined, even if hers were fictional. So we came out one day to ask Eleanor's advice."

He chuckled at the memory. "I can't imagine how we must have looked, the two of us still wet behind the ears. But Eleanor was a lady and she was kind, and she sat us down and helped us think through the case. We never did solve that one, but every so often she'd have us out for tea, and we'd talk about cases. Hers. Ours."

Then he put down his cup and leaned closer, and it was like the windows had all shattered, the room got so cold so quickly. "Eleanor Ashley is a friend of mine."

"So are you going to look for her or arrest us?" Maggie asked.

It took a moment for his face to change—for his lips to curve into something that wasn't quite a grin—it was a challenge. "Who's to say I won't do both?"

And then Maggie snapped. She was too tired and too cold and too worried. There were so many emotions running through her that she thought she might collapse before she reached the finish line.

"I'm telling you, we—"

"Are you finished with us?" Ethan asked.

"Actually—"

"You're finished with us." And then Ethan stood and pulled Maggie out of the room.

CHAPTER Thirty-Three

Maggie wasn't sure what to feel as Ethan dragged her into the tower-ing hall. "What was that?" she snapped, but Ethan didn't even slow down.

"Come on. We're going to go check on Sir Jasper and then—"

"Don't bother." At the sound of the voice, they turned to see Kitty sitting at the bottom of the stairs, slumping against the newel post like she'd started to climb but didn't have the strength so she just sank where she stood. Maggie looked from her tired eyes to her pushed-up sleeves. There was a deep black stain on her sweater.

"He's dead . . ." Maggie guessed. But Kitty laughed and shook her head.

"No." Then Kitty laughed louder. It was the sound relief makes when it collides with exhaustion. "He's stable. Breathing on his own."

"Is he awake?" Ethan asked.

"Not yet. But he's alive." Kitty rested the back of her head against the post, looking up at Maggie. "The charcoal saved him, you know? You saved him."

"No, Kitty. You did. You and Dr. Charles."

Kitty thought about it for a moment, then slowly climbed to her feet and gave her shoulders a sassy shake. "We rather did, didn't we?" Then she turned and started upstairs, shouting, "Rupert! I'm taking a nap!" And Maggie couldn't help but smile because if anyone in the world deserved a nap, it was Kitty. But also—

Sir Jasper was alive! He was alive and . . . Maggie realized some-thing else.

Ethan was still holding her hand.

"Come on." He tugged and started down a narrow hallway that led toward the kitchen.

"What was that?" Maggie said, remembering Dobson and the

library and the way Ethan hadn't even put up a fight. But Ethan didn't say a thing. He just kept dragging Maggie down the hall, then through the kitchen. It felt like walking back in time as he glanced into a laundry room and a pantry, opening old, creaky doors and peeking into shadows, searching, looking—

"What was that?" she said, swatting his arm as he peered into a room that smelled like lavender and was full of fresh linens.

"Ow!" He rubbed one beefy bicep but didn't even slow down. "You really are shockingly strong, you know that?"

She heard voices then. The duke and duchess were coming, so Maggie grabbed Ethan's arm and pulled him through the nearest open door.

"Wow. Seriously. Do you have a trainer or . . ." He looked around the dim, still space. Dying rays of hazy sunlight shone through leaded windows, illuminating the kind of room that probably hadn't been useful in decades.

There were worn wooden tables and shelves with tools for cleaning game, but Ethan's gaze caught on the cabinet filled with long, identical guns.

"Hey, you found it." He sounded . . . excited. Not at all like a man whose entire world had just turned upside down.

"Why did you tell the inspector we have a motive?"

Ethan glanced away from the gun case long enough to tell her, "Because we do."

"No! We don't. Eleanor can't choose a successor if she's . . ." The words almost tasted like almonds as they turned to poison on her tongue.

"Hey." He dipped down to look in her eyes. "We also have alibis."

"We do?"

He bit back a smile. "Someone shot at you, remember?"

She wanted to forget. "I remember. I just . . . I don't think Dobson believed us."

A chill reverberated off the windows as they rattled with the wind, but nothing was colder than the sound of Ethan's voice when he asked, "Do *you* believe me?"

No, she wanted to say. She wanted to fight and argue and bicker because that was what they did. In stressful situations, people revert to mean, and Maggie's mean was hating Ethan Wyatt because it was so much easier than hating herself. She wanted to tell him he was a big, cocky blowhard who didn't even recognize the sound of crashing ice when he heard it. She wanted to say anything but—

"I believe you."

She wanted to do anything but sway closer to him, shaking with shock and worry because things suddenly felt . . . real. This wasn't a novel or a contest or a game.

They were in the middle of twenty thousand acres with no phones and no internet and no help. The bridge was out and there was more than a foot of snow on the ground with possibly more on the way. A man was unconscious. A woman was missing. And—

"Someone Eleanor Ashley invited to Christmas is trying to kill her."

Maggie had only had two panic attacks in her life. The first was when she was eighteen and alone in a condo in Florida, surrounded by boxes and bills. The second was in a dark room that was so quiet she could actually hear the waves of the Atlantic breaking on the rocky shore. There would probably be a third someday, but not here. Not now. Not in front of him.

There was too much at stake. Eleanor's life. Their fate. Her self-respect. She couldn't risk it, but that didn't change the fact that—

"Dobson thinks *we* tried to kill Eleanor. But that's crazy. Isn't that crazy? I think that's crazy. Because you are *you*, and I am *me*, and we are not a *we*?"

"We could be a *we*," he muttered, but Maggie was having trouble forming coherent thoughts and words and conclusions.

"And even if we're not a *we*, we could . . . Wait. What did you say?"

"Nothing," he said as Maggie crept toward the frost-covered windows and fading light. That time of year and that far north, the sun set so very early, and the darkness was just one more thing stacked against them.

"What if she's hurt? What if she's . . ."

"Hey. They wouldn't be shooting at Eleanor if they'd already killed Eleanor." The room was warmer then. By a little. "Which reminds me, someone shot at you. It's okay to save a little of that pity for yourself, Margaret Elizabeth."

"That's . . ." she started to snap but trailed off, realizing . . . "*my name.*" And then she couldn't help herself. She laughed. "Well, I guess you were bound to get lucky eventually."

She waited for the quip, the tease, the wink that didn't come. But he was the most serious man in the world when he told her, "You're Margaret Elizabeth Chase. Born January fifteenth, which *does* make you a Capricorn. I don't know your rising sign, but I could look it up for you if you want. You've written twenty-eight novels under four different names—three of which you just started using in the last year. I don't know why, but I'm gonna find out."

He looked at her stunned expression but didn't smile. Didn't sneer.

"How . . ." She wanted to tell him it was a lucky guess, but there was something about him in that moment. Serious and . . . dangerous. He looked dangerous and yet for some reason that just made her feel safer.

"I've been paying attention."

Gulp.

"To the competition?"

He took a step closer. "To you."

Double gulp.

"Because I'm the competition?"

"Because you're the best."

He was so close then. Breath fogging on the cold glass, eyes looking down at her. Had he always been that tall? Had his shoulders always been that broad? Really, how were shoulders like that possible in nature? But the main thought she could pin down was simple: He'd noticed her not because she was Colin's wife or Emily's friend. He'd noticed her because he thought she was the best.

But she wasn't.

"Eleanor's the best," she reminded him. Herself. The world. Eleanor was the best and Eleanor was . . .

Maggie felt the tears come. She had to hold them back.

"Hey, it's okay."

She looked around the dim room, trying to understand, but mostly just wanting to look away. "Why are we in here?"

"Because of the Remington rifle that's missing from that case." Ethan pointed to the cabinet but never took his eyes off Maggie.

She made a sound that was something between a hiccup and a laugh. "You mean the case with the broken lock?"

"That would be the one."

There was something about the way he kept his eyes on her, about the warm timbre of his voice or the cold chill of the room that was now mostly shadow that made it all seem real.

"Because someone shot at me."

He nodded slowly, like *now she gets it*. "Because someone shot at you. Which means, right now, Maggie my dear, you and I are the only two people in this house that we can trust."

By the time the group was reassembled in the library, Maggie's heart rate was almost back to normal. Because Ethan was right. They wouldn't be trying to kill Eleanor if Eleanor were already dead. Which meant there was still a chance to stop them.

Whoever they were.

She looked around the room at Eleanor's guests. Rupert and Kitty, the duchess and duke, Cece, James, Dr. Charles, Freddy Banes. And, of course, there was Ethan. She was grateful for the sure, steady weight of him, for the heat. He didn't feel like the competition in that moment. It was the two of them against the world, which should have been terrifying, but something about the way he was looking at her made her feel calm and Maggie made a silent vow to chastise herself for that later.

James must have found Inspector Dobson a cane because he was leaning on one as he stood at the front of the assembled group like they were about to have a game of charades and it was his turn to draw a movie out of a hat.

"When the weather clears and the roads open, we'll get the contents of that tray to our lab. Don't you worry. We'll find out if Sir Jasper was poisoned."

"Which he was," Maggie muttered under her breath as Ethan slipped an arm over the back of the couch and gave her a little nudge.

Dobson glanced their way but kept on talking. "Dr. Charles and Kitty tell me he is resting comfortably in a guest room upstairs. In the meantime, I think we should proceed as if he were poisoned by someone or something in that office. It's a crime scene, ladies and gentlemen. And it's dangerous, so stay out."

The wind howled outside and the sky was dark. The whole world felt ominous and cold, but the strangest thing was how she felt herself leaning against Ethan, depending on Ethan, finding comfort in the very person who—twelve hours earlier—she might have fantasized about killing.

I'm the guy who takes the bullet, he'd said. And Maggie couldn't stop thinking that the person he would have taken one for was her.

"In the meantime, I'm afraid to say, you would all be wise to be careful," Dobson finished.

"Well, what does that mean?" Cece asked.

"It means he thinks Sir Jasper was poisoned," Victoria said shrewdly. "It means he thinks one of us . . ."

"Is a killer." Dobson nodded while looking at them all in turn.

For a long time, there was nothing but the crackling fire and howling wind and the too-heavy thoughts of strangers trapped together for the worst Christmas ever.

Then Freddy Banes looked around and asked, "Say, is it time for dinner?"

CHAPTER *Thirty-Four*

Maggie should have felt better after a warm meal and a hot shower, but if anything, she was colder now. She'd pulled on her thickest socks and softest pants and her second-favorite long-sleeve tee (JUST DREW IT! with a picture of Nancy holding a magnifying glass like a basketball high over her head).

But she couldn't get warm. And she couldn't get comfortable. And she couldn't stop thinking about everything long enough to think about anything, so she just lay on the giant bed, looking at her heavy door and its frankly inadequate lock.

Every time she closed her eyes, she heard a sharp sound on the wind; she saw the rustling hedges and felt the wet globs of falling snow. But, most of all, she remembered the way strong arms had grabbed her and tugged her through the hedges, the body that had pressed her down, shielding her. Protecting her.

I'm the guy who takes the bullet.

It was the first thing Ethan had ever told her that she'd one hundred percent believed. Then Maggie looked at the lock again, wishing she could make it stronger for whole new reasons.

The door opened in and there was an antique dresser beside it, so maybe it wouldn't be the silliest thing in the world to sort of . . . *shift* the dresser? Just a little?

She was being silly.

She was being foolish.

She was letting her imagination get the better of her, but her imagination had also paid the bills for the better part of a decade, so her imagination, frankly, deserved the benefit of the doubt. Or so Maggie told herself as she climbed off the too-tall bed and rushed across the cold floor and lifted. But the dresser didn't move. She went to the end and tried again, managing to swing it away from the wall just a little. Then a little more. And a little—

When the knock came, Maggie might have jumped. And screeched. It wasn't her proudest moment, in other words, as she inched toward the door and asked, "Who is it?"

There was a low chuckle on the other side. "Who do you think?" And Maggie didn't know if that was better or worse than the shooter.

"Are you here to kill me?"

She heard that quick, low laugh again. "Maybe. If you don't open the door."

She had to think about it for a moment, because right then she wasn't sure what was more dangerous—the killer she had to keep out or the man she didn't want to let in.

"Come on, Margaret Ann. Let me in." The dark wood was no match for Ethan's deep voice. "Please. Please. Please. Please. I can do this all night, you know. I've been complimented on my stamina many, many—"

He stumbled when she threw open the door, catching himself with the grace of a natural athlete, elbow on the doorjamb, smirk on his face. "I knew you liked me," he said, then looked her up and down—from her wet hair to her fuzzy socks—and gave a little growl. "*Sexy.*"

And Maggie wanted to kill him for all new reasons. She might have done exactly that if he hadn't started tossing things from the hall to the floor by her bed. Blankets and pillows and—

"Hey!" she snapped, but he was already dragging something heavy through the doorway. "What is that?"

It landed on the floor with a *thump*.

"My mattress."

For a moment, she just stood there, staring down. "I can see that. But why is it in *my* room?"

"Because I'm sleeping in here." Ethan started fanning out a bedsheet.

"Why?"

"Because even though I'm a sucker for an only-one-bed romance, I don't know if it counts if there's a second bed on the other side of the wall."

"But I *like* your bed being on that side of the wall. I like it even better when you're *in* that bed. And— Wait. You read romance?"

"Sweetheart"—Ethan lowered his voice and his eyes—"I absolutely read romance."

There was something about him in that moment. Boyish and charming and—

"Are you wearing glasses?"

That was it. It was too much. Really. It was. Dark frames rimmed eyes that were the color of sapphires, and somehow it made him look younger and less perfect. Nerdier, but in a way that was . . . *more*. More personality. More charm. More vulnerability. Which didn't make sense at all.

Ethan Wyatt was a persona. A mirage. A character born out of focus groups and case studies and every marketing department's wet dream. But the guy in front of her . . . he was different.

It was like a reverse Clark Kent. He'd put on his glasses and revealed his superpower, and Maggie couldn't help but like him just a little. Which, sadly, made her hate herself quite a lot.

But then he turned and she realized that his pajama bottoms had *Thief in the Knight* printed across the butt.

"Please tell me you're not wearing Ethan Wyatt swag?"

"Margaret!" He sounded scandalized. "Are you looking at my buttocks?"

"Your buttocks have the title of your third novel printed on them."

"Margaret! Are you trying to undress me?"

"No!"

"Because ordinarily I sleep in the nude, but given the circumstances—"

"Branded buttocks are fine!"

"I mean I'd rather not be totally naked if I'm called upon to protect you. Again."

"I don't need your protection," she shot back and waited for his reply, but that smug smile slid across his smug face again and he cut his gaze toward the heavy dresser that had obviously been dragged away from the wall.

"That's always been there," she said a little too quickly, and thankfully, Ethan didn't say a word. He just went to the dresser and lifted it as if it weighed nothing before settling it in front of the door.

Maggie felt her cheeks go red. She couldn't face him, but she managed a sheepish "Thank you."

He probably wanted to brag about how strong he was or show off his biceps, but he didn't tease or gloat, and Maggie felt the whole room shift. He wasn't joking at all when he said, "Nothing's going to happen to you."

"I know." The loose thread on the cuff of her T-shirt was suddenly the most interesting thing in the world. "The hat thing was a fluke. I don't really think anyone would be after me. I mean, I'm nothing. I'm no one. I'm—"

"You're not no one. And I'm telling you I'm not going to let anything happen to you. Not tonight." He took a slow step closer. "Not tomorrow." Another step—another heartbeat, way too hard inside her chest. "Not ever."

She tried to tease. "Because you're the guy who takes the bullet?"

He didn't even grin. "Exactly."

Maggie felt hot all of a sudden. Awkward and clumsy and like maybe if the dresser wasn't in front of the door she'd run right out of that room. Of the mansion. She'd run into the night and not stop running until she hit water. So she did the next best thing and stepped toward the bathroom.

"Well, thank you, Mr. Boy-Scout-Assassin-Spy—"

"Secret Service."

She stopped at the bathroom door and turned, expecting to get the smirk again, that teasing grin and boyish charm, but the man in the glasses was the most serious version of Ethan Wyatt that she had ever seen.

"I was in the Secret Service," he said again.

In the years since Ethan burst onto the scene, Maggie had probably heard a hundred theories—about who he was and where he'd come from, but she'd never heard a whisper about the Secret Service. For a moment, she assumed he must be lying—teasing. *Ethan-ing.* But there was something on his face then. He was serious. It was true.

She remembered the scene on the plane, the scar on his back. She wanted to ask a million questions, but she was frozen in the headlights of a gaze that was too hot and too strong—like a beam in a sci-fi movie, it was going to suck her in.

But she must have been the only one to feel it because he looked at the pile on her bed.

"Wait. Are those . . ."

"Nothing," Maggie blurted, darting around him as if she could block his view, but Ethan had gone all Ethan-y again and he just picked her up and set her aside.

"*Margaret Elizabeth Chase,*" he said slowly, drawing out the words, but that just reminded her of how he'd gotten her name right in the gun room—of how he'd known it all along. Of how he'd said she was the best. "Did you steal Eleanor's new book?" He plucked a notebook from the top of the pile.

"No," she blurted. He gave her a look that said *oh really?* "Okay. Yes. Maybe? I borrowed them. I couldn't help it! It's book number one hundred! I had to."

Did she sound like a whiny child? Yes. Did she care? Not even a little bit.

"Inspector Dobson clearly told us not to go into the office. It's an active crime scene."

"Well, Inspector Dobson also told Kitty that he'd always wanted a sweater with a drummer drumming on it, so Inspector Dobson lies is what I'm saying."

"So you snuck in? Without me? I am wounded." He thumbed through one of the notebooks, way too fast to read. "How is it?"

Maggie's legs gave out and she dropped onto the bed. "I don't know. It's . . . different. And I can't really put my finger on why."

"Well, it's a first draft," he told her.

"Yeah. And there are only seven notebooks, so it's not finished."

"But that's not what's bothering you."

Oh, she hated it—how well this man could read her.

"No, it's . . ." She knew in her heart she shouldn't tell him. And then she told him anyway. "I just keep thinking . . . what if it's the last Eleanor Ashley I ever read for the first time?" She toyed with the loose thread again. Even the words hurt. "What if it's the last Eleanor Ashley?"

Maggie didn't cry, but when the bed dipped and an arm fell around her shoulders she actually savored the weight. And when he tugged her closer, she didn't fight.

Gravity and Ethan Wyatt: two incontrovertible forces of nature were conspiring against her and Maggie was just too tired to struggle.

She felt warm breath against her temple. A brush of lips in the tiny wisps of her hair. "Hey. We're going to find Eleanor. I promise. Okay?"

It was all she could do to nod and stammer out, "Okay."

When he clicked off the light, her eyelids grew heavy and the night grew still and yet she didn't even dream of sleeping. Maybe it was the silence or the stress or the jet lag—or maybe it had simply been too long since she had felt another heartbeat, keeping time beside her in the dark, but Maggie heard herself say, "When I was a kid, we didn't have a lot of money. Camps and sports were out of the question. Even birthday parties, because you have to take a gift and then, eventually, you have to host the party, and besides, my parents were at work, so . . . Summers were the worst. Or the best?" She honestly didn't know. "Because I had two things: a library card and time. And then I guess I had three things because I also had her. I've always had Eleanor."

Maggie's head had ended up on his shoulder somehow, and she tried to pull it back, but he just held her tighter. Like it was instinct. Like it was natural. Like he was—she felt the rise and fall of his chest—*asleep*? Maggie was trying to decide whether she should feel disappointed or relieved when she heard—

"My dad was in the army."

Instantly, Maggie wanted to bolt upright and ask a dozen questions, but there was a tension in his muscles, a tightness in his breath. It was like the words were painful. Like even the guy who takes the bullet was only brave enough to say them in the dark.

"So we moved. A lot. He was . . . ambitious. No." Ethan's chest rose and fell too quickly—the silent laugh you give when nothing is funny anymore. "If ambition is hunger, then my father was starving. Unfortunately, ambition meant promotions and promotions meant moving and . . . I went to ten schools in twelve years is what I'm saying. So I didn't go to birthday parties either."

It was the nicest thing he could have told her, and even though Maggie never would have used the words *warm* or *cozy* to describe the man beside her, she somehow found herself nestling in, eyelids getting heavy. When he settled a blanket over her, she knew she should tell him to get off her bed. To go back to his room. To leave her alone. But she felt warm and contented and . . . safe.

Maggie felt safe for the first time in years, and a part of her wanted to pick apart that feeling, peel back the pieces and lay it bare. But another—stronger—part of her just wanted it to last a little while longer.

"Maggie . . ." The voice was lower now. Like he'd been fighting a war within himself. Like he was losing. "About what you heard . . . in New York . . ."

And just like that the spell was broken.

"Don't." She didn't want to have this fight, but the fight had come looking for her and she was already up and scooting to the other side of the bed.

"Please. I want to explain."

"Not tonight, Ethan. I'm too tired to hear about how I misunderstood or how you didn't mean it or—"

"I *did* mean it. I meant every word."

Maggie's blood turned to ice and then she said, "Get out."

"He was always going to leave you, Maggie."

"I said get out."

She was almost out of the bed when the whole blanket started to move, dragging her backward with it like a conveyor belt. "Maggie, stop. Please. Listen. He was always going to leave you because you changed the rules."

She felt the words like a slap she should have seen coming. "Yeah. Of course it was my fault." Everything was always her fault.

"You were never supposed to outshine him!" Ethan blurted and Maggie froze. Even her heart stopped beating as his eyes went soft and his voice dropped. "You were never supposed to do more than he did. You weren't supposed to *be* more. You sure as hell weren't supposed to *earn* more. I know men like that. I come from a long line of men exactly like that, so believe me when I say he needed you to be less than him, and you were always going to be more."

He raised a hand like he didn't know what to do with it. It shook in the chilly air, and when she felt a warm finger brush across her cheek to wipe away a tear it almost broke her.

"There's no way, no universe, no reality in which you aren't the brightest star in the whole damn sky, and . . ." His cheeks flushed. His hand shook, and he looked away like, suddenly, he was the one who was embarrassed. "That's all I wanted to say."

He was already halfway off the bed when Maggie caught his wrist. She felt it tremble, but for a moment they just sat in the glow of stars-on-snow, feeling his pulse pound beneath her fingers.

"Stay where you are."

He was biting back a grin as she crawled beneath the covers and lifted one corner, waiting for him to join her.

"Stop smirking," she warned him.

"I'm not smirking."

"You're just warm."

"I'm hot," he said with his cockiest grin. "Say it. *I'm hot.*" The voice was low and close and . . . teasing. "Hey, wanna make out?"

And Maggie—sleepy Maggie—tried her hardest not to grin. "No, thank you."

"Okay. If you change your mind, let me know."

"Okay."

But as Maggie turned on her side and closed her eyes, she hated how much she was smiling.

**Excerpt from the Official Police Interrogation
of Margaret Chase and Ethan Wyatt**

December 25

Inspector Patel: When did it start?
Mr. Wyatt: Oh. It started—
Ms. Chase: In the elevator.
Mr. Wyatt: Yeah. The elevator.

CHAPTER Thirty-Five

Five Years Earlier

ETHAN

It wasn't until the elevator doors were sliding open that Ethan realized he'd made a terrible mistake. He never should have answered the phone, but the big office building in Midtown Manhattan was a tower of glass and steel and strangers, and Ethan wasn't thinking clearly as a security guard waved him through a turnstile and pointed toward the elevator that would take him where he had to go.

The ringing phone had felt like salvation—like a sign. He was looking for any excuse to turn around, go home. Hide. So he'd answered the phone on instinct, totally unprepared to hear—

"Where are you?" Ethan's father hadn't worn a uniform in more than a decade, but he still sounded like a commanding officer—like it was the whole world's job to salute and say *yes, sir*. "I told the board you'd be here. We're doing Maui. Did I tell you it's Maui?"

He probably hadn't, but that didn't matter. Ethan wasn't going— a fact he'd mentioned on more than one occasion. He had a laundry list of excuses and could have picked any one: He still had physical therapy twice a week. Long flights made him antsy. He'd lost forty pounds of muscle and his suits didn't fit him anymore. Plus, no one wants the family disappointment at Christmas dinner. But Ethan couldn't say a word of that to his father, so he pushed the button for the twenty-seventh floor with his left hand and adjusted the contraption that held his right.

He'd wanted to ditch the sling for the party—had started to leave it home a dozen times—but physical therapists are better than poker players: they can always tell when you're bluffing. So he'd thrown it on over a dark blue blazer and even darker jeans and hoped he'd gotten the dress code right.

"Thought you'd be happy about that" was his father's response to the silence. "I know Aspen's not your favorite, and you can golf, right? I put you in my foursome."

"Well, being that I can't use my right arm, Dad, no. I probably won't be golfing in the near future."

"Watch that tone, boy."

Ethan did watch his tone, but only because it was easier. "I'm not coming, Dad. I have rehab. You pulled a lot of strings to get me into that clinic."

"Damn right I did. I need you back in shooting shape. Say, when will they let you hit the range?"

"Listen, Dad . . ." he was saying as the doors started sliding closed—just before he heard someone running, calling—

"Hold the elevator, please!" A small hand reached inside and the doors sprang back in an instant.

He heard his father say, "Where are you? I'll send the jet." But the words were static in Ethan's head as the elevator opened to reveal a woman. Cashmere coat and snowflakes in her hair, a little out of breath because she'd been caught out in the storm. It felt like she'd been chasing him his whole life and had only now caught up. Ethan wished he'd stopped running a lot sooner.

"Son? Ethan?" The voice was a dull roar in his ears. He could barely hear it over the pounding of his heart.

"I gotta go, Dad. Bye."

And then it was just the two of them and the sliding doors and the knowledge that Ethan didn't believe in love at first sight, but that didn't mean he could make himself stop staring.

"Uh, can you push . . ." She shifted, trying to see around him, and when she spotted the illuminated button, she exhaled. "Oh. I guess we're going to the same . . ." But she trailed off as she spotted her own reflection in the elevator's shiny interior. Black half boots and tights. That long coat and (now damp) hair. "Please tell me I don't look like that."

"Like what?"

"Like a Victorian street urchin someone tried to drown in a rain barrel."

Okay, so the snowflakes had melted, and her long, dark hair was matted under the weight, clinging to ivory skin that was tinged pink from the cold.

But something about the picture that she'd painted made him smile. "Are you an author?"

She looked like an angel when she smiled. "What gave me away? The fact that I can't remember how to walk in these heels or the emergency paperback in my purse?" She tried to finger comb her hair but that just made it do other things she evidently hated because she groaned.

Ethan wanted to smile, to laugh, to ask her if they'd met before but that would sound like a line, and besides, it would also be a lie. If he'd met her, he'd remember.

She pulled off her right glove and kept working on her hair, but something in the reflection caught her eye and her whole demeanor changed.

"Are you kidding me?"

"What's wrong?" he asked, suddenly worried.

"My pass has the wrong name on it!" She pointed to the sticker building security had to give all visitors before they were allowed in. "Did you know Eleanor Ashley might be at this party? Eleanor Ashley is going to think my name is"—she squinted at the name tag—"Marcie."

"Oh no. What will you do?" he teased, but no one had ever been more serious than she was in that moment.

"I will legally change my name to Marcie."

She would have done it too. She had the look of a woman who would have done anything, and Ethan found himself smiling for the first time in a year.

"What if I act like that's always been your name?"

She brightened. "You'd do that?"

He leaned his good shoulder against the elevator wall and smiled. "Absolutely."

The last sixty seconds were officially the best Christmas he'd had in ages and he was just starting to wish the elevator ride would last forever when the lights went out and the car stopped moving.

It felt, to Ethan, like the luckiest break in the world, but the woman beside him obviously didn't agree because she started quietly chanting, "Oh no. Oh no. Oh—"

"It's okay."

"Oh no."

He could feel her trembling. She pressed against the wall and her breath grew ragged and too fast.

"Hey, it's okay," he told her. "It's fine. I promise."

"I don't . . ." She started but trailed off like there wasn't enough oxygen in her lungs—in the elevator. In the building. "I don't love the dark. Or small spaces." It was the kind of intensely private thing she probably hadn't meant to share, and he watched her take him in through the red glow of the emergency lights. He saw her shudder and swallow hard, then force a smile.

"Or tall, strange, bearded men who look like they live on a mountain and kill all their own meat?" He smiled back because Ethan knew how he looked those days. Ragged and burned out and practically feral. But that wasn't the weird part. The weird part was that, until that moment, he hadn't even cared.

For a moment, she just stood there, weighing her options. "Um, just out of curiosity, is there a not-rude way to answer that question?" Ethan's laugh was his answer, and he felt her relax, just a little. "So . . . uh . . . Killhaven?" she tried.

It took him a moment to remember the name of his publisher and where he was going. And why. "Yes. Yeah."

"Are you an author too?"

"Yeah. I mean no. I mean kind of?" He looked down at the floor, almost embarrassed to admit, "I just sold my first book. It won't even be out until next year."

Ethan realized with a pang that it was the first time he'd said those words aloud. He hadn't told his friends and former colleagues, and he sure as hell hadn't told his father. Even his sisters-in-law were in the dark because they would feel obligated to tell his brothers and once the brothers knew . . . Well, then a dozen guys would rappel out of a helicopter and break his other arm. His father would be that angry.

But this woman . . . He wanted to see what she would say, do. He wanted to hear her smile.

"Congratulations!"

"It's not a big deal."

"Yes, it is." Her voice was soft and low and somehow he knew he'd never forget it—knew he'd be able to recognize it in the dark for the rest of his life. "It's a big deal."

Ethan met her gaze through the glow of the emergency lights. "It's a big deal." Her smile didn't just brighten her face. It transformed it, so he asked, "Hey. How's that panic attack going?"

She made a sound that was part hiccup, part laugh. "Okay? Maybe? I think we might have cut it off at the pass."

"Good," he said just as the lights flickered on.

The elevator started to move, but Ethan wanted to go back to standing still because that was the first time in a long time that he had felt like moving forward.

"Thank you." She looked away. She sounded sheepish.

"You're very welcome . . ." He glanced back down at her security pass. Her fake name was a whisper on his lips. "Marcie."

She smiled. He laughed. And all he could think as the doors slid open was that they'd known each other for less than five minutes and they already had an inside joke.

He could hear the sounds of the party. Glasses and chatter and Christmas music playing low, and Ethan knew he was supposed to be out there, meeting people and making connections and starting his next act, but he couldn't shake the feeling that it had already begun, somewhere between the twenty-first and twenty-second floors.

"Hey, do you want to—"

"There you are!" It was like it happened in slow motion—the way she turned at the sound of the voice. And smiled. And took off her other glove—her *left* glove. It was like someone turned the volume down—on the party. On the world. Because Ethan didn't hear a thing as he stood there, staring at the diamond on her left hand.

"I'm sorry," she was saying even though the words were somehow muted. "I didn't get your name. This is my husband, Colin."

Husband. She had a husband.

And then the sound came back at ten times the volume, loud and almost violent in his ears as she asked, "Is Eleanor here?" There was so much hope in her voice, but the husband, Colin, just shook his head, bewildered.

"Who? How should I know? What did you do to your hair?"

Ethan had never seen someone shrink right in front of his eyes, but that's what happened as her husband looked her up and down.

She tried to smooth her hair again. "It's snowing, remember? You didn't want to get your shoes wet so I parked the car?"

He'd made her park the car, then walk in heels in a blizzard. *Her husband.*

"They're suede," the asshole said, and then the anger Ethan was feeling turned to rage.

It was the first time he'd ever really felt like murdering someone, and right then—right there—he knew he'd found his true profession.

"Maggie!" an older woman called and he could feel her getting swallowed up by the party; she was being swept away.

And all Ethan could do was watch her go. And whisper, "Take care, Marcie."

CHAPTER Thirty-Six

One Day Before Christmas

ETHAN

On the morning of Christmas Eve, the sun broke clear and bright and far too late, but Ethan couldn't bring himself to move. As a connoisseur of only-one-bed romance novels, he knew they were supposed to wake up tangled and twisted together, but Maggie was on the far side of the mattress, curled into a tiny ball. Like, even in her dreams, she wanted to take up as little space as possible, like she wasn't even entitled to half of her own bed.

He wasn't trying to be that creepy guy, watching her sleep. It would have been better for him in every way if he could put her out of his mind entirely. But he couldn't. So he just crept into his own room and changed his clothes and brushed his teeth and three minutes later he was slouched in the chair by her fireplace, trying to guess how many favors he was going to owe his old man if he ever got to make the call he'd need to make.

"You're still here." She was nestled down in the blankets, and Ethan couldn't even see her face. Just dark hair on white pillows, two pale hands reaching above her head and stretching like a cat. It was so freaking adorable it hurt.

Then Maggie poked her head out of the covers and stared at him.

"I'm not going anywhere." He hated how much he meant it.

"Does that mean the bridge is still out?" she asked, because she had no idea he wasn't talking about the roads.

"I don't know." He looked out the window. Too-bright sunlight bounced off too much snow. Maybe the storm was over. Or maybe it was just taking a break. "Probably."

"Are the phones working?" She sat up and swung her legs off the bed and he laughed again at her T-shirt.

"No."

"You didn't have to wait on me."

"I'm not leaving you alone, Maggie," he said and she looked at him.

"Because we're the only people we can trust?"

The moment stretched out, as cold and silent as the snow-covered hills, and he could feel his heart pounding—like a telegraph operator tapping out a message he couldn't quite read.

Ethan gave a slow nod. "We're the only people we can trust."

He watched her stretch again and pile her hair on the top of her head. It almost wasn't long enough and little wisps broke free and framed her face as she pulled her legs up and wrapped an arm around her knees.

"I keep asking myself: What would Eleanor do?"

He bit back a grin. "Eleanor would work the case. Find the killer."

He saw the mistake as soon as he made it. He'd been outmaneuvered and outplayed, because Maggie was smiling now, her face nothing but focus and light. "Exactly."

"No—"

"Come on, Ethan. You said it yourself: it's what Eleanor would do. So it's what *we* have to do. We have to work the case!"

But Ethan wasn't just leery. He was scared. Someone had already shot at her once, and if they started kicking hornet nests, she was bound to get stung.

"No."

"But—"

"Inspector Dobson already told us to stay out of it."

"Inspector Dobson thinks we did it!" she reminded him, and she wasn't wrong.

"Maggie . . ."

"She's missing, Ethan! She could be out there, freezing and hurt and . . . She's missing. And you and I are the only two people in this house that we can trust."

"You trust me?" he asked, and she looked at him with the absolute innocence of a woman who didn't know her words were knives.

"I trust you." She gave a jaunty shrug of her shoulder and a come-hither stare. "Besides, we solve murders all the time."

"We also plan murders."

"And we're so good at it!" Maggie climbed to her knees and bounced on the bed.

And all Ethan could do was look at her. And smile. And say, "So where do we start?"

CHAPTER Thirty-Seven

MAGGIE

They found James in the kitchen, carefully filling chafing dishes and scrambling eggs.

"I've worked at Mistletoe Manor for almost thirty years," he said with a not insignificant amount of pride. "I run the home, manage the staff, drive the Rolls, and polish the silver."

Ethan pulled a scone off a tray. "So is there anything that goes on around here that you don't know about?"

"I don't know if the tea tray was tampered with or by whom," James said shrewdly. "And I don't know where Eleanor is."

Maggie felt Ethan glancing at her, as if he'd noticed it, too, but neither asked when James had started calling Eleanor by her first name and not *Ms. Ashley*.

"There's a gun missing from the game room," Ethan said with the kind of calm that you can only have when there's never been a doubt that you're a badass.

"I saw that." James studied Ethan from over the top of his glasses. "I also noticed that at some point yesterday afternoon, someone removed the firing pins from the remaining rifles."

Ethan's grin was slow and slightly crooked. "Someone did."

James nodded slowly. "Can I assume that someone could replace one of the pins should the need arise for a working rifle?"

Now Ethan was serious. "Someone could."

"Good." James went back to his eggs.

"We have to ask, where were you when the shooting started?" Maggie said, and James nodded as if he'd asked himself that question at least a dozen times.

"I cannot say for certain, as I did not hear the shots, but I was clearing the morning room when I heard Miss Honeychurch scream because she'd found Sir Jasper."

Ethan glanced at Maggie, who nodded. That tracked. They'd both seen James rush up the stairs behind them.

"Can you think of anyone who might have had a reason to hurt Eleanor?" Maggie watched James turn off the stove, then move the eggs off the heat, buying time as he considered the question. He didn't look like a man who was trying to find a lie—it was more like he was trying to carefully word the truth.

"Eleanor Ashley is a strong and powerful woman. Wealthy. Independent. And there will always be those who resent that."

Maggie felt herself leaning closer.

"And . . ." Ethan prompted.

Even though they were the only people in the room, James lowered his voice. "A few months ago, she started making phone calls. To her attorneys. I believe she was considering changing her will."

Maggie had no idea what they might pay junior barristers at the firm of Proctor, Banes & Jones but clearly it wasn't enough, because Freddy Banes III was sitting alone in the breakfast room, scarfing down food like he hadn't eaten in weeks.

"This is good," he mumbled with his mouth full, pointing at the eggs. "Do you want some?"

"No—" Maggie started at the same moment Ethan said, "Yeah."

He grabbed a plate off the sideboard and started filling it, but Maggie just looked at the man she hadn't paid much attention to before then.

Freddy Banes was in his late twenties, she presumed, with the kind of unobtrusive face that might be called cute or nice-looking but would never be considered handsome. He had the look of a man who would always be a boy, and there wasn't a doubt in Maggie's mind that he would grow a little more forgettable every day as he slid toward middle age.

"So how long have you been Eleanor's attorney?" Maggie asked as he took a sip of coffee.

"Oh." He laughed. "I'm not. I mean I am. But I'm not. You know?"

Maggie looked at Ethan, who shrugged because they didn't know, actually. Which was why she'd asked the question.

"Ms. Ashley has been with the firm for ages. With my grandfather. And my father. But I'm just . . ."

"Baby Banes," both Ethan and Maggie filled in.

"Exactly. Say"—he eyed the food behind Maggie—"can you pass the bacon?"

Maggie turned to the sideboard. She saw something that looked like ham and a tray full of sausages but no . . .

"It's there. On the left," Baby Banes said.

Ethan's arm snaked around her and plucked the plate of ham from the table and handed it to the attorney, who took three pieces and handed the rest to Ethan.

"I miss American bacon," Freddy said longingly. Then he brightened. "You didn't happen to bring any, did you?"

"No. I left my travel bacon at home." Ethan looked at Maggie. "What about you?"

"Same," she said.

"Pity that." Freddy sounded remorseful. "Best thing about America. The bacon."

Ethan gave Maggie a look, then whispered, *"He's not wrong."*

"I miss bacon. Almost makes up for the shellfish thing. I can't have shellfish. Allergic, you see. But I get a lot of the good stuff." He crammed his mouth full but kept talking. "Like bacon."

"Of course." Ethan couldn't have sounded more serious.

"And dairy. Love good dairy. A nice, buttery Brie. A good cheddar. People turn their noses up at Stilton, but I always say—"

"Was Eleanor changing her will or wasn't she?" Maggie blurted and Freddy started to choke, nervous. He couldn't meet her gaze.

"I can't tell you that."

"She's missing," she reminded him. "She might be dead."

"Look," he said, forceful now. Then he glanced over his shoulder as if to make sure they were alone as he lowered his voice. "I've only been at the firm a few months. I'm just—"

"Baby Banes," Ethan filled in.

"Exactly. They don't take me seriously for some reason," said the man who had strawberry jam on his chin. "I went to Eaton. I studied at Oxford. I did a year at Georgetown Law; did you know that? But they don't care." Then something behind Maggie caught his eye. "Say, are those scones still warm?"

She passed him the whole basket.

"Excellent!" He took a big bite. "All I know is my father came into my office two mornings ago and said I had two hours to pack a bag and get on a train and go keep Eleanor happy, so I got on the train and now she's not happy—she's gone! Father didn't say *don't lose her*, but I've lost her just the same, now haven't I?"

Then he looked down at the plate as if remembering that he should have lost his appetite as well.

"And yesterday." Ethan reached for the scones and slid one to Maggie before taking the last for himself. "Where were you when the shooting started?"

Freddy shook his head, confused. "I don't understand. I was looking for Ms. Ashley. Wait. Wasn't I supposed to be looking for Ms. Ashley?"

James came into the room with a fresh basket of scones and the lawyer looked up from his plate. "Say, what time is luncheon?"

Dr. Charles sat on the library sofa, looking to all the world like a man who just wanted to go home and take a very, very, very long nap. Perhaps not in that order.

"How is Sir Jasper this morning?" Maggie asked and the man glanced toward the window. The sun was almost too bright as it reflected off all that icy stillness, but there were dark clouds on the horizon—like the storm wasn't really over yet.

"Fine. I think." He gave a shrug.

"You *think*?" Maggie asked.

"We're in the middle of the bloody wilderness," Dr. Charles snapped. "This isn't a hospital. This isn't what I do."

Maggie and Ethan shared a glance. "What do you do?" Ethan asked.

"I'm a psychiatrist!"

"Oh," Maggie muttered.

"Exactly." The doctor gave a decisive nod. "True, I went to medical school and I practice at a hospital, but if you're having a heart attack on an airplane, I'm not the bloke you want to come running, now am I?" There was a decanter of whiskey on one of the shelves, and he eyed it like a drowning man eyes land.

"Well, Sir Jasper is alive, so you must have done something right," Maggie tried, but the doctor shook his head.

"I didn't come here for this."

"Why did you come here?" Ethan's question sounded innocent enough, but Dr. Charles sat up straighter—alert.

"For Christmas," he said simply, then he climbed to his feet and dragged himself from the room, and Maggie and Ethan shared a look, not really sure what just happened.

CHAPTER Thirty-Eight

MAGGIE

As they started down the long main hall, neither Maggie nor Ethan knew where to find the duke and duchess, but as it turned out, they only had to follow the voices.

"Just when I think we've looked everywhere I remember another— Oh. Hello." The Duchess of Stratford had seemed like the most elegant woman in the world that first night, ageless in a way that naturally pretty women with money often are, suspended somewhere between thirty-five and fifty-five, frozen in time. But now she just looked tired.

"Still no sign of Eleanor?" Maggie couldn't help but feel guilty. This woman was Eleanor's niece. Of course the stress would be taking a toll. "Don't worry. We'll find her."

"I should hope so," the duke said. "Do you have any idea how long it takes to settle an estate when they can't find the body?" He gave the loutish huff and exaggerated nod of a fool who thinks he's a genius and Maggie just stood there, wondering if she'd misheard him.

"David, why don't you and Mr. Wyatt go check behind that one?" Victoria said, and the duke turned to Ethan.

"Help me move that armoire?" He sounded like a little boy with a brand-new tree house.

"Sure!" Ethan sounded like a little boy who wanted to go play in it.

Maggie watched the two of them head for a large armoire that sat against the wall twenty feet away.

"Ignore him." Victoria waved her hand, as if she'd been saying those words her whole marriage. "Ms. Chase, you may not believe it, but I like you—"

"You do?" Maggie did not, in fact, believe it.

"—so please do me the courtesy of asking what you'd really like to know."

Oh. Okay. Maggie could do direct. Probably. "Are you trying to kill your aunt?"

"No." The word was crisp and clean like a hundred-pound note that had never been in someone's wallet. "Furthermore . . ." The duchess ticked off the following on her fingers: "I don't know where my aunt is. I don't know how she got out of the room. I don't know what happened to Sir Jasper. And if someone is trying to kill her, I don't know who or why."

There wasn't a doubt in Maggie's mind that Victoria, the Duchess of Stratford, was a world-class liar. There also wasn't a doubt she was telling the truth. Probably because she wasn't the type of person who would deny she'd committed a crime; she was the type who would laugh and say *prove it.*

Twenty feet away, David and Ethan had the armoire away from the wall and were inspecting the wood floors underneath. "This isn't it!" the duke called and they started moving the armoire back into place as his wife stood watching, a little too silent and too still.

"She never gave us presents." The words were so soft that Maggie barely heard them.

"Excuse me?"

"For Christmas. Birthdays. She never gave us presents." Victoria gave a dry laugh. A subtle shake of her head. "She gave us *clues.* Which led to more clues and, eventually, to one of a million little hiding places. Behind paintings and—"

"Under armoires?" Maggie guessed. The duchess gave her a look that was almost like respect.

"If we found them, we got a prize. If we didn't, well . . ."

"Let me guess, you're the girl who always won?"

"No." Victoria looked Maggie dead in the eye. "I'm the girl who stopped playing."

The duchess actually looked like that little girl then—a child who resented being asked to outsmart a grown woman and tried to win the only way she could, by refusing to even try.

"My aunt plays games, Ms. Chase. And she *always* keeps score. The truth of the matter is, I can't image a better way to earn Eleanor Ashley's respect than to try to kill her. Honestly, I'm mad I didn't think of it first."

Then the Duchess of Stratford threw back her shoulders and took off down the hall, dragging her husband behind her.

"Oh, Your Grace!" Ethan called and the duke turned. "What are you looking for, exactly?"

The duke gave an *isn't-it-obvious* headshake. "The safe."

But the duchess . . . The duchess never even looked back.

And Ethan . . . Ethan looked at Maggie. And said, "I'm going to go out on a limb and say they know about the will."

CHAPTER *Thirty-Nine*

MAGGIE

Maggie had known chaos in her life. The New York subway at rush hour. San Diego Comic-Con. The signing tents at MurderFest when word broke that Ethan Wyatt got a new leather jacket and was willing to sign bras. Still, nothing compared to the absolute bedlam that was a house full of weapons in the middle of a blizzard with four children under six in residence.

"We're just blowing off some steam!" Kitty called over the shouts that filled the long, narrow sitting room on the second floor.

The shelves had been stripped bare and all the couch cushions were piled on the floor. The children were playing a game that was evidently called *Crash Bang* where the objective was to Crash and also occasionally Bang, and Maggie had never felt sorrier for anyone than she did for Kitty, who was standing there, bouncing a crying baby on her shoulder and forcing a smile while Nanny Davis dozed peacefully in the corner.

"Before Cece found Sir Jasper? Oh. Rupert and I were in our room. Nanny Davis had just brought the baby down," Kitty shouted over a particularly loud crash. "Little Ellie here needed a nap, but . . ." At the sound of her name, the baby began to wail, fat tears streaking down chubby cheeks. "Shh, sweetheart," Kitty cooed, then turned back to Maggie and Ethan. "I'm sorry. She's teething and—"

Bang!

More crying filled the air. The baby's face was so red it was practically purple, and Maggie felt her heart break a little. Poor Kitty looked on the verge of crying too.

"I can't believe this is happening. All I wanted was for us to have the perfect Christmas. Aunt Eleanor was recovering nicely from her fall, and she and Rupert had finally sorted out that mix-up with the accounts, and—"

Crash!

Kitty glanced over Maggie's shoulder and screamed, "Eloise, where did you get that gong?"

But Maggie just shared a look with Ethan. "Ooh, what mix-up?" she asked as innocently as possible.

"Just something with her bank." Kitty tried to wave it off because Kitty, frankly, had more pressing worries. *Bang!* "Aunt Eleanor thought her royalty checks were getting deposited into one account, but they were actually going somewhere else. Rupert had told her all about it, of course, but she forgot. Dear girl. Getting older, you know. It was nothing, just— Eli, do not cut your sister's hair!" Then she looked back at Maggie. "What was I saying?"

The baby's cries turned into wails and Maggie began to worry little Ellie might pass out because how was she possibly breathing? Kitty paced and patted and looked like she might pass out, too, but then Ethan stepped forward.

"May I?" He held up his hands.

"Oh. You don't have to . . ." But she trailed off as the baby practically hurled herself into Ethan's arms.

"Oh. Well . . . Support her bottom . . ." But Ethan was already tucking little Ellie against his shoulder with one hand and supporting her bottom with the other as the wails grew softer and softer, like a siren disappearing in the distance until the only sound was Maggie's heart pounding and Kitty's chin hitting the floor.

Well, it is a girl, Maggie remembered. She reminded herself that it wasn't the first time a willing female had launched herself at Ethan Wyatt and it certainly wouldn't be the last.

"I . . . uh . . . what was the question?" Kitty asked.

"I have no idea."

They watched him walk to the end of the room, calling, "Hey, RJ, bring me that box of dominoes, I want to show you a trick." And then he sank to the floor and the other children hovered around him, and Maggie felt an odd flutter in her chest.

"He is . . ." Kitty started.

"Yeah."

"I wasn't expecting . . ."

"Me either."

"How long have you and he been . . ."

And something in the words broke through Maggie's trance. "Oh no! He and I don't . . . We aren't . . . We *hate* each other," Maggie said, but the words felt hollow somehow—like a dress that no longer fit, but it was her favorite and she was going to wear it anyway.

"Really?" Kitty gave her a look that was somewhere between knowing and mischievous. "Because he seems smitten."

"Well," Maggie conceded, "she is a very cute baby."

But Kitty's grin turned sly. "I mean, *with you.*"

"Me? No. He hates me. And I hate him." She had to laugh. "It's the one thing we can agree on."

But Kitty didn't look so certain.

Twenty minutes later, Maggie and Ethan were walking down a long, empty hallway. A damp chill clung to the air, and she half expected her breath to turn to crystals as she looked at him.

"Okay." Ethan rubbed his hands together like he was working on some evil plan. "Let's say Rupert's little 'miscommunication' with the accounts wasn't so little . . ."

"And Eleanor caught his hand in the cookie jar . . ." Maggie filled in.

"That gives him motive. Not to mention . . ."

"If James was right, and Eleanor was changing her will . . ." Maggie prompted.

"Then *a lot* of people have *a lot* of motive . . ." Ethan raised an eyebrow.

"But only if they knew about it," Maggie said.

"Which the duke and duchess obviously do."

Ethan gave a grin like *that was fun*, but Maggie . . . All Maggie could think about was spring break of her freshman year. She'd decided she wanted to write her first novel and Colin had decided he'd help. They'd spent a whole week lying side by side on the pier at the beach house, ideas bouncing back and forth like Ping-Pong, chasing the plot like tag. They'd taken turns writing longhand in a notebook because that was the way Eleanor Ashley did it. His handwriting was terrible, and his ideas were worse, but it was the closest Maggie had felt to another person, maybe ever, so she'd smiled and laughed and gotten a sunburn on her shoulders.

She didn't do what she should have done, which was throw that notebook in the sea.

"Maggie?"

It had been a long time since she'd felt that kind of back-and-forth. The parry and thrust of possibilities. Her thoughts swirled like the chilly air and blowing snow, but one thought felt real and tangible and right there in the palm of her hand: *he's not Colin.*

"Hey . . ." It was a face she'd seen on the back of a million dust jackets, but the expression was one she didn't recognize. It was like she was looking at a stranger and an old friend at the same time when he asked, "Where'd you go?"

There was a gilt-framed mirror behind Maggie, and her first thought was that she almost didn't recognize what she saw in it: a woman who looked eager and excited and . . . hopeful? And a man who was leaning toward her like a flower leans toward the sun.

"Ethan?"

But then she saw something else in that mirror: Rupert, walking down the hall while glancing over his shoulder, looking very much like a man who hoped he wasn't being followed.

So Maggie did the only thing she could do. She followed him.

CHAPTER *Forty*

ETHAN

Ethan shouldn't have been enjoying this. He was a terrible person. A scoundrel. A rogue. He was a bad guy is what he told himself.

Because *he should not have been enjoying this.*

A man was fighting for his life. A woman was missing. A shooter was somewhere in their midst and there were children on the premises. And Maggie . . . So help him if he wasn't able to protect Maggie . . .

But Ethan *was* enjoying this, he had to admit as they followed Rupert through the shadowy halls. He enjoyed it even more when Rupert stopped suddenly and Maggie grabbed Ethan's arm and tugged him into a narrow alcove, shielded behind a pair of heavy drapes.

"Seriously. You are freakishly strong."

"Shhh." She was pressing against him, squeezing in close and he was the worst kind of villain in the world because he slipped his arms around her waist and pulled her closer.

"Are we doing the *make out so no one suspects us* thing?" Ethan whispered.

Her big, brown eyes and soft, full lips were just inches away. Even in the shadows, he could see her thinking. "Maybe?"

He swallowed hard. "Maybe? Or definitely?"

"If he catches us, yes," Maggie whispered, but she didn't look away.

"It's a staple of the genre."

"As tropes go . . ."

He felt her breath on his lips. "It's a classic."

They were all alone in a house full of people, and Ethan tried to remember that she hated him, but her fingers were in his hair and they were standing so close that he could feel her breathe and—

"Hey, Maggie?" Had her skin always been so soft? "Do you want to make—"

But before he could finish, she was going up on her toes and he was bending down. Maybe they met in the middle? Or maybe they collided? Maybe it was an accident, or maybe it was fate?

The only thing Ethan knew for certain was that their lips touched. Just a brush. A graze. A whisper. But it lingered. It lingered and then it deepened and then Ethan was drinking her in, her taste and touch and little sighs. He wanted to memorize this moment. And he wanted to forget it ever happened—burn it from his brain because something so deep and arterial would someday leave him bleeding out.

But then Maggie sighed his name and gave him more of her weight and Ethan's mind went blank. He forgot about Eleanor and Sir Jasper and even Christmas. Ethan forgot his own name.

"Damn it, Rupert!"

A voice broke through the silence and Maggie pulled away. There was something like horror on her face. Horror and panic and regret. She was going to spiral—

"Maggie," Ethan whispered. "Don't—"

She was going to run, but then the voice came again from the corridor. "When you asked me to spend the holidays away from my family, you said it was an emergency!"

Maggie froze. It was almost like the kiss hadn't happened when she whispered, "Dr. Charles . . ."

All Ethan could do was stare at her swollen lips.

"But now here we are"—the doctor gave a low, dry laugh— "trapped in the middle of nowhere with a killer on the loose. Kirk and the girls are going to be terrified when I don't get off that train tonight, and I can't even call them because I'm stuck *here*. With you and your awful sister and terrible cousin."

"Don't call that woman my cousin," Rupert snapped.

Cece? Maggie mouthed, and Ethan nodded. It was the only thing that made sense.

"I didn't sign up for this. I don't care what strings you can pull at the hospital. I didn't sign up for shootings and poisonings and . . . I didn't sign up for this!"

They heard footsteps coming closer and, on instinct, Ethan spun, pinning Maggie to the wall. Shielding her. Keeping her out of sight and out of harm.

"Gregory! Come now. My aunt is delusional. That's why you're here, remember?" Rupert laughed again but trailed off like a man who'd just realized nobody finds him funny.

"In light of everything that's happened, her fear seems quite justified to me," Dr. Charles shot back.

"Now, Gregory. We agreed. My aunt is no longer of sound mind. Someone needs to take over her affairs," Rupert prompted like a parent getting a child through a play. "*For her own good.*"

"You said I'd have a chance to examine her, see her paranoia for myself."

"Well." Rupert huffed. "I should think the fact that she's run away just before Christmas would prove my point quite nicely."

"Actually"—there was a challenge in the doctor's voice. It was lower, deeper, closer—"if you ask me, it proves hers."

The hall went silent then, nothing but footfalls on old rugs and the sound of an even older house settling beneath a heavy snow. Everything in Ethan's training told him it was over—they were alone. And Ethan knew he should step back, give Maggie space to move and room to breathe. But Ethan didn't move and Maggie didn't protest, so he decided to stay right where he was, one hand on the wall behind her head, another around her waist, chests rising and falling together like a dance.

"That's the second time I've heard him call Eleanor paranoid," she said.

"Which is exactly what you'd say if your aunt had just caught you with your hand in the cookie jar."

"Exactly." Her eyes twinkled. Her skin glowed. It was almost painful to look at her, so he found a point over her head and tried to look there instead. The alcove must have been home to a piece of art at some point—something fragile and precious and rare. There was delicate wallpaper and intricate trim and . . .

That was when he saw it.

"Which means, if Rupert *was* stealing . . . Excuse me. Earth to Ethan. What are you . . ." Maggie trailed off as she looked up and saw the little green bundle overhead. "Mistletoe."

He knew the instant she remembered the kiss because her body went tight and her eyes went wide and he expected her to pull away, threaten him with death or dismemberment or some other form of destruction if he ever mentioned it again, but instead her voice got a little higher and she shifted on her feet. "Oh. Well. It *is* Christmas."

"Maggie—"

"And Eleanor seems like someone who would be big on . . . traditions. Not to mention the name of the house and . . ."

"Margaret—"

"It's a parasite, you know. And a poison. And . . ."

She was rambling now, nervous and shy and turning the color of new skin—fresh and pink and fragile. So Ethan did the only thing he could think to do. He kissed her again, playful and quick.

Then he dipped down to meet her eyes and whispered, "Maggie, how sure were you?"

"What?"

He brushed aside a strand of soft, dark hair because he couldn't stop his traitorous fingers. "Yesterday. Before the gunshot . . . Before Sir Jasper . . . When it was you and me in the maze . . . When it was just us, how sure were you that it was a test?"

Suddenly, she jerked away. He'd seen her recoil a dozen times, a hundred. He used to think she was pulling herself together, but she wasn't. She was pulling herself back, taking up less space and making herself a smaller target. When this was over, he was going to track down her cheating ex and Ethan wouldn't be responsible for what happened.

"I was wrong." Maggie shook her head too quickly. "I was stupid. I—"

"Hey." Ethan couldn't stop himself from tucking that errant

strand of hair behind her ear and cupping her face. "Don't tell me how *wrong* you were. Tell me how *sure* you were."

He watched her summon her strength—put it on like armor. "I can't remember the last time I was that certain of anything."

Good. Goose bumps were rising on his arm. "Now . . . Eleanor's mistletoe book . . . are there secret passages in it?"

Her eyes went wide. "How did you . . ." But Ethan was already bending down to kiss her forehead. "What . . ."

And then he reached over her head and touched the sprig of mistletoe that was carved into the wood.

And pressed.

He heard the *click*. They felt the wall shift. And Maggie gave him a look like this would be the best Christmas ever if it weren't for all the almost dying. But before she could say a word, they were both stumbling, falling, tumbling into the dark.

CHAPTER Forty-One

MAGGIE

Maggie had never liked dark places or tight quarters. Anything underground or too confined. Maybe it was the experience Colin had dubbed *The Wine Cellar Incident*. Or maybe it was the result of a childhood spent in tornado alley and too many late spring afternoons in a root cellar that smelled like damp earth and old cobwebs. (And snakes. But Maggie tried very, very hard not to think about the snakes.)

So she wasn't sure what to expect when the door swung closed behind them and the air turned heavy with dust and the faint traces of something she had started thinking of as Essence of Ethan. It was dark and broody and disgustingly good. They could probably sell it at department stores. Spritzers would wear leather jackets and they'd sell out every Christmas.

She watched him turn back to the hidden entrance and try to force it open, but the door stayed closed and the corridor stayed dark and all Maggie could do was stand there, way too still in the silence.

"So assuming I wasn't wrong . . ." she started slowly.

"You weren't wrong."

"And Eleanor wanted us to find this . . ."

"She did."

"Why?"

There was a thin strip of light from the hallway, slicing over the face of a man who was looking at her like this was it. Like he was all in. Like he was all in . . . with her. And it was too much. This feeling that things were about to get good. Because things *weren't* good. A man was clinging to life and a woman was missing and if Maggie knew anything, it was that *good* didn't last and the best you could hope for was *okay.*

Okay was fine.

Okay was bearable.

Okay was a nice, slow ride around a flat, even track—no angst-ridden climbs or terrible falls. A high-free, low-free existence and it was all she wanted.

But she looked up at him. She breathed him in. And the words came again, ricocheting around the narrow space: *This is getting good . . .*

And when Ethan said "Do you trust me?" and held out his hand, Maggie didn't even have to think before she took it.

Excerpt from the Official Police Interrogation
of Margaret Chase and Ethan Wyatt

December 25

Inspector Patel: So you fell into a secret passageway? And you thought that was normal?

Ms. Chase: Of course it's not normal. None of this is normal! But . . .

Inspector Patel: But?

Ms. Chase: She's Eleanor Ashley.

Inspector Patel: And you just followed it?

Mr. Wyatt: What should we have done?

Inspector Patel: You could have told the police.

Mr. Wyatt: You mean Dobson? Ha. No. We weren't going to tell Inspector Dobson.

Inspector Patel: So you decided to impede an official police investigation instead?

Mr. Wyatt: Yup.

Ms. Chase: How?

Inspector Patel: Pardon me?

Ms. Chase: How did we impede an investigation, exactly?

Inspector Patel: Destruction of evidence? Of property?

Mr. Wyatt: Why do people keep blaming me for fires that could have happened to anyone?

Ms. Chase: Besides, that wasn't until later.

CHAPTER Forty-Two

ETHAN

Turns out, if it's dark enough, a cell phone flashlight can be surprisingly bright. Which was a good thing because the corridor stretched farther than Ethan had first realized. And they'd been in there longer than he'd hoped. And the situation was more perilous than he'd feared as he glanced over his shoulder at Maggie.

She had the back of his shirt in a death grip, but at least her breath was slow and steady. "You doing okay back there?"

"Yes. Why?" Her fingers twisted in his shirt and pressed into the small of his back.

"No reason." He didn't want her thinking about how long they'd been in that narrow space or that there wasn't an obvious way out.

"That's not your *no reason* voice," she shot back, which . . . good. He'd rather have her picking a fight than starting to panic.

"I know you don't like the dark. Or tight spaces, that's all."

"Who said I was afraid of the dark and tight spaces?" She sounded like a woman who was *very much* afraid of the dark and tight spaces but wasn't about to admit it.

"Nothing. No one. If you see a crack of light or something, let's check it out. I'll walk you back to the room and—"

"Who said?" Now she just sounded annoyed.

"You did," he admitted.

"When?"

Oh no. Ethan had spent years avoiding this conversation, but he'd stumbled right into it. He felt a tug on his shirt, and it took him a moment to realize it was because she'd stopped. She'd stopped but she hadn't let go.

"If this is about Tucson—" she started.

"I thought we weren't supposed to talk about Tucson?"

"Oh." She huffed. "We are *not* talking about Tucson."

Ethan shouldn't have been grateful for the darkness and the shadows, but he was. He didn't want to face Maggie—see her. But, more than anything, he didn't want her to see him when he said, "It was a long time ago. You probably don't remember"—he *hoped* she didn't remember—"but we were in an elevator once. It wasn't a big—"

"It was you." There was wonder in her voice, like all this time, she'd thought she'd dreamed it. "At the Christmas party. I got stuck in an elevator with . . . That was you." He tried to pull away, keep walking, find someplace to hide, but it was like she was seeing him for the first time, there in the dark. "I didn't recognize you. Why didn't I recognize you?"

Because he looked different. Because he *was* different. Her hand was a soft weight against his back and his scar and the skin he hadn't felt in years, and something about her touch soothed him. Burned him? He didn't even know anymore.

"Ethan? That morning? On the plane . . ." Her voice was small and soft and he wanted to play dumb, blow it off, act like he hadn't heard her. "I saw your scar."

He didn't want to have that conversation—not then, not there, not ever. But he wanted to lie to her even less. So he settled on "It's not a cool story, Maggie. I didn't leap in front of a bullet or—"

"I don't want a cool story. You're not Evan Knight, hitman-turned-bodyguard. I don't want you to be. I just want to know . . ."

"You're not going to let this go, are you?"

She laughed softly and said, "What do you think?" So Ethan turned and leaned against a wall that was little more than strips of crumbling plaster.

"We have a place in the mountains. Wow." He ran a hand over his face. "That makes me sound like a rich asshole. My father is a defense contractor now, by the way, so he really *is* a rich asshole. He has a place outside Aspen. And it was Christmas . . ." He smiled in spite of himself because irony really was a bitch. "I went because that's what good sons do. And on Christmas Eve, I unwrapped a bottle of scotch I didn't drink and a bunch of ties I didn't need and then I got the hell out of there."

His eyes followed the dust as it danced in the flashlight's beam. "I didn't know the roads had gotten bad. Or" —he shook his head— "maybe that's a lie? Maybe I did know and I just didn't care."

"Oh, Ethan." Maggie's voice was so soft he barely heard her.

"I was halfway down the mountain when I saw them. A car had gone off the road and a pair of headlights were pointing straight up, reflecting off the clouds, snow falling down through the beams. It looked like the Bat Signal or something. I remember climbing down, but"—his laugh was dry and joyless—"the car was empty. I climbed down an icy cliff to be some kind of hero, and the car was empty. The next thing I knew, the cliff gave out and . . . the last thing I remember is the sound. I woke up in the hospital. I don't know how long I was pinned or how I got out but . . ." He thought he might choke on the words. "I am never going to forget that sound."

"Oh, Ethan . . ." Her voice quivered and her lip shook. He wanted to still it with his own.

"For the record, the look on your face right now?" He brushed a thumb across her cheek. "That's why I don't talk about it with strangers."

"I'm so sorry." Her eyes were too big and too wet and he hated that he'd made her weepy. "I'm so sorry I asked."

Her hand was on his chest and Ethan held it against his pounding heart. "I'm not."

"But—"

"You're not a stranger." He gave her hand a squeeze and felt her sway in the small space, lean against him in the dark.

"I'm sorry I didn't recognize you. I'm—"

"Don't be. When we met, I was coming off eight months of surgeries and four months of rehab. I'd stopped eating. I couldn't shave or comb my hair. I'd lost my job, and my friends had stopped taking my calls. It got so bad that, one night, I finally opened that bottle of scotch. I got so drunk I . . . Never mind." He pushed off the wall. They needed to keep walking.

"You got so drunk you . . ." She sounded so worried that he had to tell her—

"In my job we used to travel. Constantly. My team used to give me a hard time about all the books I read, so one day I started writing this novel about a guy named Evan Knight. It was nothing. Just a way to kill time on a red-eye. It wasn't even finished, and it probably wasn't very good, but what it lacked in quality I made up for in drunkenness, so I started querying literary agents, chicken pecking with my left hand. I honestly thought I'd dreamed it until I started getting the rejections. Then I got one that wasn't a rejection and—" He gave a tired sigh. "That was *Dead of Knight*. I guess you know the rest."

"Wow." She sounded stunned. "I didn't know it was possible to hate you even more."

He would have been crushed if she hadn't been smiling.

"So, yeah. That's how I ended up at that party. And that's why it's okay if you didn't recognize me. To be honest, looking back, I don't even recognize myself."

Ethan started walking, pushing aside cobwebs and pointing out rotten boards. They were lost inside the narrow space and he could feel Maggie—her gaze and her hand and her questions swirling like the dust and thick enough to choke on.

"Do you miss it? The Secret Service?"

"Yes. No. I don't know."

"That's . . . specific," she teased. "Really eloquent. Very—"

"I'm not *him* anymore." It wasn't a snap. It was a confession. That's what people never understood—that the reason Ethan didn't talk about his old life wasn't because he was private. It was because his old life didn't even feel like his. "I would miss it if I were still that guy, but that was someone else's life. I don't . . . I can't . . . Yesterday was the first time I've even touched a gun in years." Ethan shook his head, but didn't look back. He never looked back.

"What?" She gasped. "Ethan? Slow down. Ethan." She gripped his shirt again, stopping him. "What happened?"

Maggie was a world-class writer. Of course she knew there was more to the story. But that didn't mean he had to tell her. He could always lie. Evade. Flirt. With anyone else, he would have. But with Maggie . . .

"I did the surgeries and the rehab, but . . ." He held his right hand in the beam of the light and—at the end of the corridor—the shadow shook. Because *his hand* shook. Because his hand would *always* shake—always for the rest of his life. "See that? That tremor?"

"Not really."

"It's there. Trust me." He gripped his hand so tightly his fingernails left half-moon indentions on his palms. Scars that only he could see. "It's always there."

They were silent for a long time, lost inside the dancing dust and swirling secrets, so he wasn't expecting the question—

"Do you have kids?"

His laugh was sharp and too loud in the stillness. "What?" He started walking again.

"Don't laugh. It's just . . . you were so good with the baby, I wondered . . ."

"No. No kids. But I do have four brothers and four sisters-in-law—who send me annoying texts when they find out I'm skipping Christmas, by the way." He gave her a look and heard her laugh. "And nieces and nephews. So many nieces and nephews."

"How many?"

"Seven. No, twelve. Maybe eighteen? I don't know. They keep popping them out."

"You sound very attentive. Involved."

"Hey. I give piggyback rides and buy candy. Those little monsters love me."

Eventually, they reached a set of stairs that spiraled down into a space that looked even tighter and darker, so he tried to usher Maggie back in the opposite direction.

"Okay. Let's turn around and—"

"No. Don't you want to know what's down there?"

"You don't have to go," he said simply.

"I'm not scared." She tried the top step. It creaked beneath her weight but didn't break. And then the look in her eyes slayed him. "I'm with you."

At the bottom of the stairs, the floor was dirt and the ceiling was lower and Ethan knew without being told that they were underground. He needed to get her out of there. But Maggie was right behind him. And when he took her hand in his, it didn't shake at all.

CHAPTER Forty-Three

MAGGIE

Maggie should have been terrified of the darkness. Ethan's cell phone flashlight was far better than nothing, but what if his battery ran out? What if there was a cave-in and they got separated? What if they couldn't find an exit and were destined to roam the tunnels beneath Eleanor Ashley's mansion until they died of starvation or old age?

She didn't know what was scarier: knowing that she should have been panicking or realizing that she wasn't. She didn't want to think about why. In fact, she didn't want to think about a lot of things—not the damp earth or how the ceiling was so low in places that Ethan had to hunch. But, mostly, Maggie wanted to ignore the little voice in the back of her head, whispering that it was probably coincidence, a folly, a lark.

Not everything's a plot twist, Colin had always said when she noticed things he didn't want her to see—clues or coincidences that couldn't point to anything besides "Maggie is a little bit crazy."

Of course I smell like Emily's perfume. Have you ever seen Emily apply perfume?

How should I know how Emily's earring ended up in our bed? She's your best friend.

Sometimes Maggie worried that if she hadn't caught them together she might still be telling herself that it was all in her head—that she'd read too much and fantasized too often and was just one step shy of madness. If it had happened a hundred years before, they would have locked her in the attic and thrown away the key. And the worst part—the scariest part—was the fact that Maggie would have let them.

But as she held Ethan's hand and walked through that dark and dreary tunnel, she could still hear Colin's voice in her head, telling her she'd dragged Ethan into that dusty, endless space for nothing and—

"Stop it." Ethan's voice cut through the black.

Maggie froze. "What?"

"Whatever you're overthinking back there."

"I'm not overthinking," she said a little too quickly.

"This morning I watched you take fifteen minutes to choose a pair of socks."

"I'm not spending another day with cold feet."

"You brought three different kinds of toothpaste."

"Oral health is very important and sometimes I'm not in the mood for spearmint."

"You're not wrong, Maggie," he snapped, and it sounded like he was agreeing with her and arguing with her at the same time, and Maggie didn't know whether to be mad or grateful. "If you think Eleanor left clues for us, then she did. You found them. And we're going to follow them. You're *not wrong*."

"But what if I am?" She hated how small and frail her voice sounded—that it was still too loud in the darkness—that in that narrow space it might just echo.

Then Ethan stopped and turned. Colin used to look at her like he could see through her, but Ethan looked at her like he had x-ray vision—like he could see right into the heart of her, like there was no use hiding anything. And, suddenly, it started getting hard to breathe. The tunnel walls moved in and—

"Maggie, sweetheart, are you going to have a panic attack? Because you need to let me know if—"

"No," she blurted. "I mean yes. I mean . . ."

"Why the new pen names, Maggie?"

At first, she thought she hadn't heard him. The question was so out of the blue that she had to blink through the pale glow of the flashlight and she forgot all about the low ceiling and narrow walls. She stopped telling herself to breathe.

"Maggie? Pen names. Talk."

"Oh. Well. I felt like diversifying. You know, the new e-book algorithms really—"

Ethan leaned against the filthy wall. He was going to get his shirt all dirty. "Come on, Margaret Elizabeth, I showed you mine . . ."

"I got divorced." It was the dumbest thing she could have said, because he already knew that. *Everybody* knew that. But there was more to the story, and Ethan must have known that, too, because the silence stretched out like the darkness.

"I was twenty-one when I got married. My parents were dead and I didn't have two cents to my name, and Colin's family was Old Money—or so everybody thought, but . . . *Fun fact*: even generational wealth can dry up if the later generations are morons. At the time, though . . ." She gave a sad smile and a sadder laugh. "They said I was the luckiest girl in the world when they didn't make me sign a prenup."

Maggie hadn't minded the whispers because, in her mind, they were shouts. Surely Colin deserved a wife who had more power? Shouldn't Emily want a best friend who had more poise?

But what no one—least of all twenty-one-year-old Maggie—had realized at the time was that Colin and Emily liked her exactly where she was: somewhere between charity case and mascot. Someone who had no other options. Who was equal parts needy and independent, who could go anywhere anytime but who could only do it with them. *Because* of them. She was the ultimate foil—only there to reflect their light.

But now the light was gone and, if possible, the passageway got even darker.

The filthy wall pressed against her back as a big hand cupped her cheek and a deep voice whispered, "Breathe." It was an order and she did it. And then it felt so good she did it again.

Her hands were on his hips, fingers hooked through his belt loops and desperate to hang on. "We would have split everything in half, but it turns out, he didn't have anything, and that just made him madder."

Ethan gave a low groan and closed his eyes and then pressed his forehead against hers. "I'm so sorry, sweetheart. That asshole didn't deserve half your money."

"*No.*" The word was so jagged it could have sliced her throat to shreds. "He got fifty percent of my *copyrights.*"

Ethan pulled back. "*What?*"

Maggie nodded slowly. "By law, he owned half of every word I'd ever written. Every book. Every character. He was going to get half of every royalty check I earned for the rest of my life."

"Oh, Maggie . . ."

"Even if he'd had money of his own at that point . . ." This was the hardest part in some ways. Maggie's secret shame. "He'd helped me brainstorm book one a million years ago. I didn't use any of his suggestions, but the more successful I got, the more *my little hobby* became *our books.* He told himself they were *his* ideas. To hear him tell it, I only got published in the first place because of his contacts. They could both live on Emily's trust fund for the rest of their lives. He doesn't need money. But this way, even after we divorced, he could still own half of . . ."

She couldn't say it. She couldn't . . .

"Half of *you.*" Ethan's voice was low, more growl than whisper, and just like that she was glad they were locked in a glorified hole in the ground, glad they were snowed in with no phones, no internet, and no way out. Because she was terrified of what Ethan might have done next. It didn't matter that he couldn't use a gun anymore. In that moment, he wouldn't have needed one.

"Maggie—"

"The only way I could get free was to buy back his half of my copyrights. But even once I let him have the house and the car and my savings . . . it wasn't enough. Even once he had everything, the copyrights were still worth more. Which meant I needed cash. And I needed it to have absolutely no connection to him."

She knew instantly the moment when he got it. "So you wrote under pseudonyms."

She nodded slowly. "I wrote under four new names until I could buy him out—which I did." She was proud of that part. She'd worked twelve hours a day, seven days a week, for nine months straight, but she'd done it. "In the end, he got my house and my savings and my best friend—did I mention that part?" Maggie laughed to keep from crying. "But I got to keep . . . myself."

"You got the best part," Ethan said without missing a beat. "You got the only thing that matters. Tell me you know that."

She nodded yes and swallowed hard, and his hand kept rubbing against the back of her neck and she wanted to lean into the pressure. She wanted to make herself forget. But there was a subtle *drip-drip-drip* of melting snow, too loud in the stillness, a steady reminder that the world was still out there. *Eleanor* was still out there. And, without a word, his hand slid down her arm and into hers.

They were twenty feet farther down the tunnel when he realized— "Wait. You said *four* pen names?" And Maggie froze.

"Oh." *Oh no.* "I *meant* three."

"*Nooooo*. There's a fourth one! Wait. Is the fourth one dirty?" She felt her face go scarlet and even in the shadows, Ethan must have seen it. "Oh, the fourth one is *really* dirty!" Maggie bit her lip and tried to make him move, but he was a load-bearing wall—solid and sure and, without him, the whole tunnel would cave in. "Come on. Give me a hint."

"No."

"I'm going to find it. You know I'm going to—"

"We have sleuthing to do." She tried to slip around him.

"Oh, I'm gonna find it. And I'm gonna read it. And . . ." He caught her and held her, and suddenly, Maggie's breath was coming hard for all new reasons. She was breathing out as he breathed in, chests rising and falling and—

"Hey, Maggie? You want to make out?" he asked. It took three whole seconds for her to slap him lightly on the arm. "Is that a yes? Because impact play is something both parties need to discuss—" She did it again. "There are safe words—mine will be Sherlock—"

She did it again, harder that time, and the look on his face morphed into a smile that was almost a dare.

"Fine. Then I guess we'll just have to go up there instead." He pointed the light toward the end of the tunnel. And the trapdoor in the ceiling. And the ladder that was rising up into the night.

CHAPTER Forty-Four

ETHAN

Ethan insisted on being the first one through the trapdoor. It should go without saying that Maggie disagreed.

"Is this because you're a man?"

"No."

"It's sexism, isn't it? And the patriarchy. And—"

"It's because I'm taller and it's my flashlight and, most of all, the first person through the creepy trapdoor should always be the person who knows seven different ways to kill a man with an ink pen."

"Oh." For once, she looked defeated. "I only know three."

"Ha! There. I get to go first. Now hold this."

"Do you even have an ink pen?"

But he was already handing the phone to Maggie, who pointed the light toward the top of the ladder. The hatch was solid metal and cold to the touch. At first, it barely budged, inching up slowly as something scraped against it overhead. Ethan could feel the weight shifting, changing. But whatever was up there was heavy and the angle wasn't doing Ethan any favors.

"I would have been in already," Maggie said from down below.

"Something's blocking the door," Ethan shot back and pushed harder and then, suddenly, the door opened with a bang as it flipped over and landed hard on the ground, and for a moment, the two of them froze, not sure who might come running from the racket.

A long, quiet moment later, Ethan peeked out and looked around.

Night had fallen, but moonlight filtered down through snow-covered glass, and after being underground for so long, even that seemed bright to Ethan. It was colder, too, and he couldn't help but feel the chill as he climbed out of the tunnel and hunched over on a dirty floor, listening to the sound of the wind and the too-heavy pounding of his heart until he was sure they were alone.

There was a broken table lying on its side, trowels and shattered pots and a bag of potting soil that must have fallen on the trapdoor when the table collapsed, blocking it shut.

"Some of us are still down here, you know!" Maggie's impatient voice echoed up from down below. "Oh, the heck with this . . ."

He heard her on the ladder, and a moment later her head popped through, wide-eyed and almost giddy. That's what Child Maggie must have looked like, high on too many cookies and Eleanor Ashley novels, filling up notebooks and spying on neighbors. He wanted to go back in time and be her very best friend.

"It's the greenhouse!" Maggie's voice was full of wonder as he helped her off the ladder. Their breath fogged in the air, and snow blew through holes in the glass.

"Not a very good one," Ethan said as she aimed the light on row after row of blackened plants that stood dead and covered with a fine layer of snow like trees too long after Christmas.

"Maybe I'm showing my ignorance, but aren't greenhouses supposed to be . . . not freezing?" He shivered and put his hands in his pockets as Maggie turned the cell phone's flashlight on the broken panes of glass that were somehow darker than the others.

"What's that?"

He rubbed a finger across the glass, and it came away black and gritty. "Soot." He turned to look at Maggie, and at the same time they both said, "Fire."

It was pitch-black and freezing, but, suddenly, something went on high alert inside of Ethan. There was a bag of fertilizer ten feet from where the flames had licked along the floor and across a shelf covered with chemicals. He could track the way the fire had shot up the glass walls and made them shatter with the heat.

"Maggie . . ." he started, but she was making her way down the long row of tables, looking at the blackened plants, brushing snow off nameplates as she passed them.

"Henbane. Foxglove. Catha edulis. Oleander." One was in a cage. "Ricinus communis." One had a red ribbon tied around the base like it might be the worst gift ever. "Nightshade." She looked up at him. "Ethan . . ." He'd never heard Maggie's voice sound like it sounded then, trembling and uncertain and afraid. "These are all poisonous. This is a poison garden."

Ethan couldn't keep from grinning, biting back a laugh. "Leave it to Eleanor . . ."

But Maggie wasn't smiling, wasn't beaming. Instead, she was shaking her head. "Do you know . . ." Her voice broke. She swallowed hard. "Do you know what happens when poisonous plants burn?"

Her hand trembled. The light shook. And then he got it—

"They turn into poisonous smoke."

There was only one door, and Ethan rushed to it and pushed. It shifted a little, but only an inch.

"It's jammed." He took a small step back and lowered his shoulder, took the door at something between a lunge and a run, but it still didn't budge and all he got for his trouble was a sharp pain in his bad shoulder. But Ethan had suddenly forgotten to care. He reared back and kicked. Nothing.

Maggie was standing behind him. "Maybe they locked it after the fire . . . Maybe . . ." She pressed against the glass, aiming the light and trying to see outside.

"Maggie—"

"There's got to be a lock or a latch or—"

"Maggie."

She stopped and looked up at him, but he was pointing through the glass, at the crowbar that was wedged between the doorknob and the ground.

"Maybe Eleanor or James put that there after the fire? Maybe they didn't want anyone to come in because it was dangerous? Maybe . . ." But as her voice trailed off she looked up at him, a gentle pleading in her eyes. It was like, just once, she wanted a man to tell her she was paranoid and wrong and crazy.

But she wasn't. She never had been.

"Or maybe someone set a fire and blocked the door and without that secret passageway Eleanor Ashley would already be dead?"

CHAPTER *Forty-Five*

MAGGIE

By the time they made it back through the passageway and into the main part of the house, Maggie was able to feel her fingers again, but that didn't mean she wasn't numb.

"Well, what happened to the two of you?" Cece exclaimed as they passed the library and headed toward the stairs. Maggie didn't know if she was talking about the time that they'd been missing or the fact that they were covered with dust and their hair was full of cobwebs. Frankly, Maggie didn't care.

"When did the greenhouse burn?" Maggie blurted and Cece took a step back because, well, Maggie did slightly resemble a ghost or maybe a serial killer. Or the ghost of a serial killer. Or all of the above. But it didn't matter. Nothing mattered except— "Cece! When was the fire in the greenhouse?"

"I don't know," Cece exclaimed, like *How am I supposed to keep track of these things?* "Maybe three weeks ago? A month? Something like that. It wasn't much of a fire. We'd just had a sprinkler installed, and it put it out. Why?"

Maggie felt Ethan shifting. Turning. And she knew the moment when he saw the staircase, with its mismatched pieces of wood, old and new, dark and light.

"What about that?" Nothing about Ethan sounded flirty any-more. "What happened on the stairs?"

"Eleanor fell." Cece looked around, confused.

"*Why* did she fall?" Maggie demanded and Cece spun on her. She didn't like it coming from both sides.

"I . . . I told you. The runner came loose." She was flustered and frantic and fumbling. "And the . . . the boards were old. They were old and the railing wobbled, and . . . she fell."

Suddenly, the whole world felt unsteady—like the deck of a ship in rough seas, and Maggie wasn't just worried she'd fall down. She was terrified she might go overboard, and in that moment, she wasn't just looking at Ethan. She felt tethered to him. And he looked back like he wasn't going to let anything happen to her—like the ocean was going to have to go through him first.

Cece threw out her arms. "Why are y'all asking about this?"

There were a dozen different answers to that question. *Because not everything is a coincidence. Because, sometimes, accidents don't just happen. Because Eleanor was rich and powerful but also frail and alone. Because . . .*

Ethan shook his head, slowly—a single time—and Maggie blinked and said, "No reason."

"Why do people go to kitchens when the shit hits the fan?" Maggie asked as she sat at the big island and rested her arms on the cool marble of the counter. "You'd think they'd want to keep the shit as far away from the kitchen as possible, but no . . . Trauma equals kitchen."

All she had to do was look around to remember why, though. The room was large and bright and it smelled like lemons and freshly made bread. And also heaven. Yes. That's exactly what Maggie had always imagined heaven would smell like.

But as she shifted on her barstool, she felt Ethan's hand at the small of her back, a sure, steady weight, and she wanted to lean against it. She didn't think she'd miss the dark, narrow passageway and even darker—even narrower—tunnel, but there she was, bracing against the glare of a world that was suddenly way too bright.

"What's wrong?" he asked.

"You mean besides the fact that, evidently"—she looked around, then dropped her voice—"someone has been trying to kill Eleanor for weeks now?" She wanted to rest her head on her arms and go to sleep but sleeping probably wasn't a great idea, what with all the not-quite murder.

"You're squinting."

"My head hurts. It's nothing." Maggie knew for a fact that her headaches were nothing because Colin had spent the better part of ten years telling her so. "It could be a migraine or tension or . . . You know? I don't think I've actually eaten . . ." She trailed off as a sandwich slid in front of her. "And I haven't had any . . ." A coffee joined it. "Caffeine. Thanks. I'll just get . . ." Two sugars and the milk appeared and for a moment Maggie just sat there, staring.

"How did you . . ." She started, but Ethan was turned away, rummaging through the massive refrigerator. "Ethan?"

She waited for the inevitable joke or flirty whisper. She would have given anything for a wink. But Ethan wasn't even looking at her. He was staring into that fridge as if Eleanor might be hiding in the cheese drawer.

"Ethan, how did you—"

"I pay attention."

He came out with an apple and took a crisp, quick bite and Maggie felt instantly silly. *Of course he pays attention*, she told herself. He was a professional attention-payer. The Secret Service probably had classes and courses and tests. He could probably close his eyes and name fifty things in that room at that moment, but it felt different somehow, in the silence and the stillness, after the last few days. *He* felt different. Like maybe, all this time, he'd been paying attention *to her*.

So Maggie cupped the coffee in her hands and breathed in the hot, sweet scent, but nothing felt right. Nothing tasted right. Nothing would ever be right because—

"Someone has tried to kill Eleanor three times now. Right? Is my math right?"

Ethan ticked them off on his fingers. "Burned greenhouse, rigged stairs, poisoned tea tray. Yeah. That sounds— No. Four. I forgot about the shooting."

"Of course." Maggie nodded slowly, like *how silly of me*. "I'd hate to forget about the shooting."

"That would be a pity."

He grabbed half the sandwich and took a bite and she didn't even bother to slap his hand away.

His arm pressed against hers as he leaned against the counter, a warm and steady weight, reminding her she wasn't alone. It was maybe the most perilous situation of her life, but Maggie wasn't afraid, and she didn't let herself think about how—without the man beside her—she would have been terrified.

She could only smile down into her cup and say, "You know how I take my coffee." She didn't have a clue about anything else, but that was evidence of something.

Ethan gave a slow nod, a silent sigh. "I know how you take your coffee."

"Since when?"

"We've been in a dozen greenrooms together, you know? I've seen you drink coffee."

"Which greenroom?" she asked again.

A soft sigh. A silent curse. And then— "Tucson."

Maggie didn't know who moved first. It was like the rotation of the earth, something you never felt but was always there. And then her face was in his hands and her hands were in his hair and Maggie might have flown right off that stool—off the globe—if he hadn't stepped between her legs and pulled her tight against him.

"Maggie."

Her name was a whisper. He was just right there, so close. So—

"I don't give a damn where they are!" There was shouting in the hall, curses flying like the snow outside. "Everyone in the library! Now!" Dobson's big voice boomed.

Ethan's forehead fell against hers and he closed his eyes as the kitchen door swung open and James cleared his throat.

"Excuse me, but I believe Inspector Dobson would like a word."

CHAPTER Forty-Six

MAGGIE

It was a scene they all knew well by that point. The same library. The same crackling fire and falling snow. The same cast of characters, with the hapless husband and tired wife, the snobby couple and bored physician. The overeager girl and the lawyer still wet-behind-the-ears and asking, "Say, where did you get that sandwich?"

But it wasn't the same. Not at all. Maggie and Ethan had spent all day poking and prodding and learning how very *not-the-same* it really was. So Maggie didn't care that Dobson was standing in front of the fire, red-faced and livid.

"Where have you two been?" He looked a little like a rabid dog. "I told you to stay out of this! But then you disappear all afternoon, and now I hear you've been asking questions—"

"Was that a piece of spit that flew out of his mouth?" Ethan whispered, but there wasn't a doubt in Maggie's mind that everybody heard it. She was even more certain they were supposed to.

"If we weren't stuck here, I'd have you both arrested for impeding an official investigation." Dobson was choosing to ignore the spit comment, evidently. "For contamination of evidence. For—"

"Did you know someone locked Eleanor in the greenhouse and set it on fire, Inspector?" Maggie didn't recognize her own voice. She didn't smile or soften the words or do any of a million things she'd been trained to do to keep a man from feeling threatened. No. She just stood there, feeling the heat from the fireplace and trying not to think about a room full of flames and smoky poison.

"Did you?" Maggie asked again, louder now, and Dobson

practically shivered. *Guilty*. He *did* know. Maggie could tell before he even opened his mouth.

"Of course Eleanor told me about the fire, but as I told her, those doors weren't blocked intentionally—or very thoroughly—or else she wouldn't have gotten out, would she?"

"So you examined the scene, then?" Ethan asked with his most deceptive, *don't mind me, I'm just the eye candy* drawl. "Conducted a thorough investigation?"

"Of course not!" Dobson looked ready to spit again. "It was a small fire in a room with its own sprinkler system, and no one but some flowers got hurt."

Dobson didn't mention the poisonous plants or flammable chemicals or the bag full of fertilizer. Even under the best of circumstances, it didn't take a genius to figure out that flames and greenhouses shouldn't mix.

"What about the stairs?" Maggie asked.

From the other side of the room, Rupert huffed. It was a sound Maggie knew well. She wasn't born to their money or their mansions. She wasn't born with *anything*. But she'd earned plenty, and that gave her something the Ruperts of the world didn't have. And that was why the Ruperts feared her.

"My aunt slipped and fell because she's a careless old woman," Rupert declared.

"So careless and old that she wouldn't notice if some money went missing? Is that what you're saying?" Maggie asked.

"Rupert?" Kitty turned to him. "What's she talking about?"

"I've had it up to here with the two of you," Dobson snapped. "I don't know what you think you're playing at—"

"Oh, we're not playing." Ethan leaned against the mantel, too calm, too cool, too competent to be real—but he *was* real. Maggie couldn't believe it, but Ethan Wyatt was more than the sum of his parts. He was more than the sum of theirs, too, and every last one of them knew it. "We're not playing at all. No, we're getting used for target practice. Sir Jasper has already been poisoned. And Eleanor is still missing, not that any of you care."

"Now see here," the duke started, so Ethan glanced down at him. Smirked.

"How's the will hunt going, Your Grace? Find out if she wrote you two out and put her in yet?" Ethan pointed at Cece, who shifted on her chair, trying not to grin.

"I don't know what you're talking about." The schoolgirl act was slipping.

"Oh, shove it, Cecilia," the duchess snapped. "Everyone knows you're trying to get your claws into her."

"Aunt E asked me to come help—" Rupert and his sister both groaned, and Cece talked on. "We have a special bond—"

"She didn't even know you existed until six months ago!" Rupert shouted.

Well, that was news, and Maggie couldn't help herself—she looked at Ethan, who took a step closer to Cece. "What does he mean by that?"

Cece looked down at her hands, a little sheepish when she said, "My father was Aunt Eleanor's baby brother and, well, I guess he was a little bit wild. And he . . . well . . . I guess you could say he . . ."

"*Ran away,*" Victoria said a little too precisely, like Cece was a moron who needed it all spelled out.

"He moved to the States and lived there for a long time and, well, eventually, he met my momma and she had me and . . ." This time, Cece looked guilty as she trailed off. A little embarrassed or ashamed. It was the expression of someone who doesn't know where they stand or how they fit, but who has no other options. Maggie knew the feeling. "Then he ran away from us, too, I guess. I don't even remember him, but Momma told me he was from England and I got to researching and we found Eleanor and wrote her a letter, and now I'm here." She gave a sigh, like the story was a heavy weight and it felt good to put it down.

"That's all true," the lawyer chimed in. "Our firm did the DNA testing and verified Miss Honeychurch's claim."

But Rupert looked like his infant daughter at that moment; his face was so red it was practically purple and he was close to tears.

"Mark my word, Inspector, if what they're saying is true and some-one has been trying to kill my aunt for months, there's only one person that could be, and there she is!" Rupert pointed at Cece, who threw a hand to her chest.

"If Aunt E put me in the will—"

"Don't use that ghastly nickname," Rupert sneered and Cece gasped and it didn't matter that the storm had started up again; the blowing snow was nothing compared to the swirl of curses that filled the air. Accusations were flying.

But Ethan was suspiciously quiet as he stood by the fire. Maggie thought he'd be looking back at her, but his gaze was locked on Dobson. And he wasn't smiling anymore.

"Now tell me again, Inspector, how Maggie and I are the only people here with motive." It was the low, solid voice of a man who was far too dangerous for shouting, but Dobson wasn't going down without a fight.

"I know someone has been in her office. And I know it was the two of you."

"Why, Inspector . . ." Maggie gave him her big, innocent eyes. She sounded almost like Cece. "We've all been in her office. That's where we found Sir Jasper, remember?"

"I don't know what the two of you are playing at—"

"*We're not playing!*" Maggie never shouted. She'd been condi-tioned and trained and she knew better than to be loud because the loud girl doesn't get invited back. But the words were an avalanche that had started in the maze. They'd been chasing Maggie for two days, and she was tired of trying to outrun them.

The room went silent, and all eyes turned to her, but Maggie didn't care if they stared. Let them hear her voice crack. Let them decide, right then and there, that she wouldn't be invited to Easter. Maggie didn't care about anything.

Except Eleanor.

And Ethan.

"We're not playing, Inspector. We got on a jet with no idea where we were going or what was waiting for us when we got here. We flew to another country because a stranger asked. We weren't after her money. We weren't trying to be her successors or her saviors. We didn't want anything from her. We just wanted . . . *Christmas*."

Maggie felt her throat burn. She heard her voice crack. And she realized it was true. "We just wanted Christmas, and instead, we got all of you. You're Eleanor Ashley's family—*you're her family!* And not one of you cares that she's missing. Not one of you is worried that she's dead. Someone has been trying to kill Eleanor *for weeks*. They've been trying to kill her, and she's been telling you . . ." Maggie looked around at the faces that stared back. "And not one of you believed her."

It was like the last piece of a puzzle clicking into place—the tumblers of a lock falling home—because, right then, Maggie got it. For the first time, she understood. No one believed her, but Eleanor had never stopped believing in herself, and something about it made Maggie smile. And sigh. Braver now for knowing—

"That's not totally true. Of course one of you believed her. Because one of you has been trying to kill her."

And then the lights went out.

CHAPTER Forty-Seven

ETHAN

It was too early for bed, but it also felt like the middle of the night and Ethan didn't try to make sense of the math. The sun had been down for hours and the days were starting to bleed together. Christmas was coming, but Christmas had been coming for days now. It was like they were stuck in a time loop. Like they might never get out. So when Kitty started serving eggnog and asking if anyone knew any carols, Ethan looked at Maggie and jerked his head silently toward the door.

That was how they found themselves walking down a cold, empty hallway that felt even longer in the dark. Maggie was carrying a candelabra, and six flickering tapers framed her face in a kind of golden glow; she looked ethereal but also filthy, covered in cobwebs and dust. And she was the most beautiful thing he'd ever seen. Ethan was suddenly grateful for time loops and blizzards and bridges that fall down under the weight of too much snow.

Maggie, on the other hand, was all business.

"Okay. Assuming one person is responsible for shooting at us, poisoning the tea tray, and burning down the greenhouse . . ."

"Don't forget the stairs," he put in.

"Right." Tiny flames danced as she nodded. "And possibly the stairs."

"Which is a lot of assuming," he conceded and she spun on him. The candles flickered.

"Is it wrong?" She was honestly asking. "I mean, I may be wrong. I probably am. I could be—"

"Hey. We're not wrong."

It was the *we* that did it. Ethan watched Maggie start to speak—to argue. She could have fired off a dozen pithy comebacks, but her eyes went soft and warm and she inhaled a rushed little breath before letting it out, slowly. "We're not wrong."

Someday he was going to crush the people who had crushed her spirit. He was going to grind them into dust and not give it a second thought.

"I don't suppose you could tell where the shots were fired from?" Her tone was hopeful but her eyes had doubts.

"Not without checking the grounds. But they didn't come from the house. I know that much."

"Okay! Good. That means we can probably cross Cece off the list. I doubt she could have fired the shots and then made it upstairs in time to scream as we came through the doors."

"Agreed." Ethan nodded. "Which leaves the inspector—"

"Who wasn't here." Maggie sounded disappointed.

"The lawyer, the butler, and the doctor." He cut a look at her. "Hey, I think I know a joke that starts that way."

She gave him an indulgent smile, but told him, "None of them have any kind of motive."

"That we know of," he said and she cocked her head as if to say *touché*.

"We know Rupert and Kitty were in their room with the baby and the nanny," Maggie said.

"Which leaves David and Veronica."

"Victoria," she corrected.

"Whatever. The duke and dukette."

"Duchess."

"Whatever. But what would their motive be? Aren't dukes loaded?" Even though it was an excellent question, he watched Maggie look away. Like she was almost afraid to admit that—

"Sometimes money makes people careless, and careless people never realize that, eventually, money runs out." But what Ethan heard was *Sometimes careless people hurt careful people.* "Besides, they both seemed really worried about . . ."

"Finding that will," they said in unison and she looked down at her toes.

Ethan wanted to kiss the lip she was biting, but he settled for saying, "So all the people who have motive don't have opportunity."

"And the people with opportunity don't have motive. Ooh." The light was coming back in her eyes. "They could be *Strangers on a Train*-ing us."

"Or *Orient Express*-ing."

"Or *One-Eye Dog in a Snowstorm*-ing . . ." she started, then cocked her head at his vacant expression. "It's a novella Eleanor published in 1982." But then, suddenly, her face fell. She looked like a little girl at a carnival who had come *this close* to winning a prize. "But no one is a triplet."

"That we know of," he consoled and she beamed, and Ethan thought he might spend the rest of his life chasing the rush of making Maggie smile in that long, dark hallway, with the drafts and (possible) ghosts and cold wind howling right outside.

As they turned the corner and started toward their rooms, Ethan let his gaze drift to the window, frosty glass and inky black sky. Millions of stars and thousands of acres and the reflection of two people who had crawled and climbed and searched all day and yet had nothing to show for it.

Maggie made a sound and grimaced. "I look like I'm one long white nightgown away from being killed in a gothic novel."

But Ethan simply said, "I'll protect you."

She laughed softly. "From a ghost?"

"From everything."

And, suddenly, nothing was funny anymore. The drafty corridor was cold and still and even the wind stopped howling. Ethan forgot about murders and bullets and poison, about cruel fathers and feckless husbands and the fact that he probably didn't deserve her, but he was going to have her, anyway—if she was foolish enough to want him. And it was looking—right there—in that moment—like maybe she did.

"Maggie . . ." He stepped closer and raised his candle. She had to see—she had to know. "Sweetheart . . ."

But Maggie's gaze was sliding away. He could feel her swaying. Then slipping. Then freezing. And then she trembled.

"What is it?" Ethan spun, but there was nothing behind him but bedrooms and shadows.

She pointed to her half-closed door. "I thought I closed that."

"Stay here," he ordered, but Maggie was shaking her head.

"I don't know. I could be wrong. I'm probably—"

He cupped her cheek with his free hand. "Maggie. Did you close it?"

She shook her head like she didn't know what to say—what to think. Like she'd been told black was white and up was down so many times that she couldn't trust her own eyes, much less her memory. Like she'd been taught to live by two simple rules: (1) When in doubt, assume you're the problem. And (2) Always be in doubt.

"It's okay." He pressed a kiss to her forehead. "Wait here."

"I don't know. It might be in my head. Ethan—"

But the door was already swinging open, hitting Ethan with a wave of colder air as he braced for an attacker or maybe a baby ghost, but what he saw was somehow worse.

Maggie was at his back, pressing softly, saying, "Well?"

"It's definitely *not* in your head."

For once, he wished it had been because Maggie made a sound he never wanted to hear again as she stepped around him, taking in the rumpled bedsheets and tossed clothes, overturned chairs and overflowing suitcases. No part of the room was left untouched, and Maggie went rigid at the sight.

Someone had been there, among her private things—in the place where she slept. Someone had been there, and Ethan wanted to throw her over his shoulder and run, but he couldn't do that, so he settled for finding the bright side.

"Well, I guess there's one more thing we can add to the list: someone is looking for something."

Maggie gasped, then bolted to the bed, tossing covers and pillows and clothes until she turned. Her face was ghostly white. "They found it. Eleanor's new book—the notebooks. They're gone."

CHAPTER Forty-Eight

MAGGIE

Maggie was torn. She should have felt scared. Violated. Outraged. But as she stood in the middle of the room that had seemed so lovely two days before, all she could do was wonder how she'd turned into a woman who was looking at her watch, counting down the minutes she'd been apart from Ethan Wyatt.

Of course, it's easy to stay busy in a ransacked room, hanging up clothes and remaking the bed, stuffing cords and devices back in her bag. Only the sight of the laptop stopped her. She hadn't written a word since she'd boarded the jet, and Maggie didn't want to think about what it meant. Maggie didn't want to think about anything.

So she straightened the room and examined the fireplace. James had told them that the chimneys were safe to use and they should feel free to light a fire since the electricity would likely be off for the foreseeable future. So she balled up some notebook paper and stacked some wood; but every time she tried to light it, the paper would burn too quickly, leaving her with a tiny pile of ashes and the smell of smoke and no warmth of any kind. It reminded her of Colin.

When she heard a knock on the door, she threw it open, unsurprised to find Ethan standing there, taking up every ounce of space like his day job had been Door or Gate or Human Barricade.

"Margaret . . ." He looked like he couldn't decide if he should tease or scold. "Why did we go to the trouble of making a secret password if you're just going to—"

She slammed the door in his face and felt herself smiling at the wood for three solid seconds—right up until a fist rapped again, quick and light and almost . . . flirty?

She reached for the knob but said, "Password?"

"MacGuffin." He managed to sound stern and gleeful at the same time, so she opened the door just a crack—and there he was, hand on the doorframe, leaning down.

It was exactly how he'd stood on the jet. At the time, the pose had felt imposing and calculating, like some kind of big cat—a tiger or lion—stretching and getting ready to pounce. But this time it just made her feel . . . warm.

"Happy?" she asked, looking up at him.

"Getting there." His gaze dropped to her lips and he might have inched a little closer.

She knew, vaguely, that she was supposed to be doing something. Making fires or solving crimes or . . . moving. Yes. That was it. She was definitely supposed to be moving, but her feet were like lead and her body was weightless in the presence of a man who had always had his own gravity.

She felt a brush against her side, in the dip of her waist. *Fingertips*, her tired brain filled in. Ethan's fingers were grazing against a perfectly innocent part of her body—one you can reveal in swimsuits and crop tops and workout attire—but it felt almost indecent. It was the most naked a woman can feel while wearing a puffy coat. Her body was a live wire, and she was half afraid they'd start a fire. But then the hand pressed against her slightly and she remembered—

Door.

Room.

Electricity.

Eleanor.

Maggie stepped back, turning to the cold fireplace while Ethan closed and locked the door. She heard a scrape as he pushed the dresser into place, and then he slapped his hands together. "So, do you want the good news or the bad news or the I'm-not-sure-what-that-means-yet news?"

"Uh . . ." Maggie honestly didn't know. It felt like a very hard question. "Bad?"

"The generator's shot," Ethan said. "Looks like we are officially in the dark. Indefinitely. Or at least until the grid comes back on-line."

"Oh." She didn't know why she didn't feel more disappointed.

"The I'm-not-sure-what-that-means-yet news is that our room appears to be the only one that was searched."

"Okay." She took a deep breath, considering. Remembering. "What's the good news?"

Suddenly, his face morphed into what could best be described as Little Boy Performing a Magic Trick. He did everything but say abracadabra as he reached behind him with both hands and exclaimed, "I found flashlights!"

One was very large and silver and had to be at least fifty years old. The second was black and small enough to slip into a pocket, and that's the one he handed to her. "Here."

"Why do you get the big one?"

But he didn't answer. He just dropped to his knees and busied himself in front of the fire.

"That won't work. I think the wood must be wet or . . ." But she trailed off as a wisp of smoke began rising over Ethan's shoulder. A golden glow flickered across his jaw and in that moment, he looked like something painted on a cave wall a thousand years ago.

"How did you . . ."

"Man build fire," he said with a cocky grin. But then he almost blushed as he turned back to the flames. "And maybe I really was a Boy Scout."

"I knew it."

But when he looked up at her that time, the boyish grin was gone and the fire was burning brighter—hotter. Maggie couldn't shake the feeling that this was an Ethan she had never known before—had never met or seen—when he tugged her hand and said, "Come here."

Maggie sank to the floor, closer to him and the flames, trying not to think about how Christmas Eve was always the loneliest night of the year.

"Please tell me you read those notebooks." His voice was dark and even.

She came this close to blurting *What notebooks?* But then she remembered— "You mean Eleanor's new novel about a woman who fakes her death and runs away because someone is trying to kill her?"

She honestly hadn't been expecting him to laugh, but when the sound cut through the room it felt . . . right. "Eleanor is amazing. Can I be her when I grow up?"

"Can't." Maggie pulled her legs to her chest and rested her chin on her knees. "I called dibs."

"Yeah." He looked down at her. "You did."

She looked back at the flames, and when Ethan poked the fire and added more wood, little sparks flew up like fireflies. Like it was Christmas Eve and the Fourth of July rolled into one.

"Hey." He bumped his leg against hers. "Did she solve it for us?" He sounded almost hopeful. Like maybe this was going to be easier than he'd thought. Like maybe they could cut class, run away, play hooky until the holiday was over and the snow was gone and the villain was someone else's problem.

"No. The last notebook was missing, remember?"

"Right." He gestured toward the still-messy room. "Hence the search."

She nodded. "Hence the search. So I don't know how the book ends, and I don't know how *this* ends, and . . . Ugh." She took a deep breath and tried again. "I don't know how to do this. Or help her. Or . . ."

Be me.

The words fell into her head, unbidden, and Maggie didn't want to think about what they meant. She just knew she felt like crying. Like crying and screaming and sleeping. And when she felt herself start to shiver, she didn't try to stop it.

"Hey." Ethan's arm fell around her shoulders. "I can practically see your breath. Come on."

He tugged her to her feet and threw back the blankets on the remade bed and tucked her in like she was delicate and precious and that just made her shiver even harder. Because Ethan . . . cared. It was such a strange concept. An unfamiliar feeling. No wonder she didn't trust it. It was like a foreign cell and her body was fighting it, certain that it must be there to kill her.

But when he went to tuck the covers around her, she found herself reaching for his hand. It was warm while hers was cold, and maybe that's why he went still, suddenly uncertain.

"So am I sleeping on the floor tonight?" There was no cocky edge to the words, no teasing tone. He wasn't Ethan Freaking Wyatt anymore, and for the millionth time Maggie tried to reconcile this man with the one who had called her Marcie for the better part of five long years.

Ethan wasn't supposed to be warm and caring and kind. He was supposed to be a thin veneer with nothing at all beneath that glossy surface. He was supposed to be *less* but he was actually *more* and Maggie hated him for it. But mostly she hated herself for being disappointed that someone the world thought was amazing actually was.

He was also the only source of warmth in twenty thousand acres, and maybe her only ally for much, much farther. So Maggie held up the covers and said, "Get in. I need all the body heat I can get."

CHAPTER *Forty-Nine*

MAGGIE

When Ethan crawled in beside her and pulled her close, Maggie didn't let herself think about how perfectly they fit together—how their legs twisted and tangled and then clicked into place like her feet had always been the ice cream in the footsie sandwich. She didn't let herself wonder why she'd never felt that way with Colin. How she'd been so wrong before.

Ethan was just a space heater. A temporary ally. A friend? And soon the roads would thaw and the lights would come on and Christmas would be over. It might even be a dream. So she closed her eyes.

"You know"—something warm and soft brushed against her temple—"to do the body heat thing properly we really should be naked."

She hit him with a pillow, but he just laughed and pulled her closer, and Maggie sighed, marveling at the fact that it was her least favorite night of the year and she was in bed with her least favorite person in the world. And she didn't want to be anywhere else.

"What?" Ethan's chest rose and fell with the word.

"Nothing."

"That wasn't a *nothing* sigh. That was an *I'm freaking out, but I don't know why, and Ethan is the last person I'd ever tell anyway* sigh."

"Wow. That's a very intense sigh."

"Magg—"

"Do you think Eleanor's okay?" Maggie hadn't actually meant to say the words, but they were out there now and she couldn't pull them back, so she focused on the slow sweep of his fingers through her hair, the rise and fall of his chest.

"I think"—his words were careful, measured—"that Eleanor Ashley has proved very hard to kill."

It was true. She'd survived falls and fires, poison and poverty. If anyone could see the whole picture and spot the twist, it was Eleanor. But Eleanor wasn't there.

The wind howled and the fire crackled, and Maggie shivered from the sound.

"I'm sorry," he said softly. "This probably wasn't the Christmas you wanted."

"Oh." She couldn't help but laugh. "This isn't my worst Christmas. This isn't even my coldest." He pulled back and looked down as she explained, "My senior year of high school the entire state lost power in an ice storm and we ended up having to burn the fence."

It was the humblest of brags, but she couldn't help but giggle when he said, "*Nice.*" Those fingers were in her hair again, with their slow, steady sweep and Maggie had to bite her cheek to keep herself from sighing.

"When I was ten, we moved from Germany to Oklahoma and every single dish we owned got broken in transit so we ate Christmas dinner off a bunch of old Frisbees."

"When I was seven, our garage caught fire and burned all our presents."

"When I was nine, our living room caught fire because my mom's cat chewed through the Christmas tree lights. No," he added before she could ask, "the cat didn't die, but it did spend the rest of its life afraid of the color green."

"When I was fourteen, my whole family got food poisoning from eggnog."

"When I was twelve, two of my brothers had a fight with a Nativity set and one of them choked on the baby Jesus and had to have an emergency tracheotomy."

She smiled into his chest. "When I was twenty-one, my fiancé and my best friend sent me to get more wine, but the cellar door slammed shut behind me and I got locked in for a day and a half."

Suddenly, his chest was too still beneath her cheek. He wasn't laughing. She wasn't even entirely sure he was breathing.

"Maggie . . ."

"It wasn't a big deal. They just thought I went to bed, I think."

"You *think*?"

"I mean, I was always going to bed before them or reading by myself. It was my fault—"

"Says who?"

"What?" She pushed up a little just to look at him.

"Who said it was your fault?" His voice was dark and low and colder than the wind.

"It wasn't a big deal. The worst part was that the lights were on a timer and . . ." Sometimes Maggie could still hear the sound of the waves breaking on the rocky shore that was just beyond a window that was far too high and far too small to crawl through. She'd screamed herself hoarse and then she'd screamed so hard she didn't make any sound at all. And, it turned out, panic attacks weren't something a person got better at with practice.

Ethan moved slowly as he looked at her. The room wasn't totally dark, not with the fire. It was plenty bright enough to see him—to watch a coldness fill his eyes as he realized—

"That's why you don't like small spaces."

"It wasn't a big deal." Maggie was furious. Not with Ethan or even Colin. Maggie was mad at herself. It was a slip she knew better than to make, so she tried to pull away, to turn, to change the subject or the day of the year or anything. "It wasn't that bad. I got dehydrated or something and passed out eventually so—"

"What do you mean 'or something'? Didn't they take you to the hospital?"

"Of course not." She had to laugh. "Ethan, I was a twenty-one-year-old aspiring author. I didn't exactly have insurance."

"Any douchebag rich enough to have a wine cellar can cover

the hospital bills of the girl who got locked inside it and almost died."

"I didn't almost die."

But she *could* have, and that's the part Maggie never let herself think about. She could have died—not because she got locked in but because no one had bothered to come looking.

"Maggie—"

But she couldn't face him anymore. He saw too much, knew too much. She wanted to go back to being Marcie to him. Because that was so much better than having him see her as she really was.

"Listen to me." He was rolling toward her, eyes burning through the dark. "It wasn't your fault. They should have come looking for you. They should have taken you to the hospital. They should have . . . cared. They shouldn't have blamed you, and they sure as hell shouldn't have let you blame yourself. If you were missing, I'd find you. I'd tear the house down stone by stone. I'd rip apart every room and scour every field and I wouldn't stop. I would *never* stop."

He closed his eyes and rolled away, and she couldn't decide if he was hating himself because he'd gone too far or because he hadn't gone nearly far enough.

"So yeah." He blew out a tired breath. "This isn't my worst Christmas either."

And then Maggie remembered—the tunnel and the story and the scar. She was the idiot who was lying with her head on his bad shoulder, and instantly, she pulled away.

"I'm so sorry. Did I hurt your arm or—"

"Oh, no, you don't."

He pulled her back, and for a moment there was silence beneath the howling wind and crackling fire. She could almost hear his thoughts and would have given anything to know what they were saying. But the fingers were back in her hair and her limbs were heavy and finally warm, and Maggie thought she might actually drift off to sleep. And maybe she did because when the words came they were almost from a dream.

"When I was thirteen, my mom left for wrapping paper and didn't come back."

Maggie's eyes sprang open but she willed her body not to move and the words went on, low and dark in the stillness.

"We were getting ready to move, packing up. But there were still boxes in the garage from the *last* move, and she couldn't find the wrapping paper. That was it. My brothers were roughhousing and knocked over the tree, and my dad . . ." The words trailed off, and his chest stopped moving. "She couldn't find the wrapping paper, so she went to buy some. She should have been back in an hour, but I guess she just kept driving because we got a letter a week later. She was through. She couldn't take it anymore."

"I'm so sorry," Maggie whispered.

"I don't blame her. It wasn't her fault. My father was—*is*—a hard man to live with. And there were five of us boys, and . . . It wasn't her fault. She loved Eleanor Ashley."

It took a moment for Maggie to hear the words, they'd been so unexpected. "Wait. What?" She pushed up onto an elbow and looked down at him. And, amazingly, he was smiling—not at her. At a memory.

"They were the first grown-up books she ever let me read."

"But you said . . ."

The little boy grin was back on his hot guy face again. "I lied."

She pinched his side, but he just smiled. "They were our thing. Just my mom and me. She called it *book club* and my father . . ." The words turned cold and raw. "The week after she left, he burned them. They were all I had of her, and . . ."

"Oh, Ethan . . ."

"No. Shh. Don't cry for me, sweetheart." His fingers were in her hair again, the slow steady sweep and Maggie realized it was for him as much as it was for her. "A week later, I was in a new school in a new town, and it was like she never existed. It was easier that way, honestly. Move on. Be someone new."

Be. Someone. New. Maggie felt the words rattling around in her head. Like bells beginning to chime. Ringing out because, suddenly, the world made sense. *Ethan* made sense.

He wasn't some hot guy breezing through life with no worries and no burdens. He was the kid who had gone to ten schools in twelve years. He was the boy who had looked at the parts of himself that were just like his mother; and then he'd watched his father set those parts on fire.

Ethan wasn't who people wanted him to be. He was who he needed to be to survive: someone charming and easy and cool. Someone who makes friends and keeps the peace. The life of the party. The guy who gets invited back.

She'd heard at least a hundred theories about where Ethan Wyatt came from and who he really was, but in that moment Maggie knew the only version of him that really mattered: he was the guy who takes the bullet and a warm and steady presence in the dark.

"Ethan?"

His voice was groggy when he answered. "Yeah?"

"I want to make out."

CHAPTER Fifty

MAGGIE

For a moment, Maggie wondered if he hadn't heard her. Or if he'd *mis*heard her? Or changed his mind? Or maybe the offers hadn't been offers? Maybe they'd been meant to tease or mock or annoy or—

She hadn't known a man could fly while lying down, but in the next moment, Ethan was springing on top of her, the long, heavy line of his body pressing into hers as the too-cold room turned way too warm. It felt like all the air had left Maggie's lungs and, worse, she didn't want it back. Because Ethan was looking down at her like she was the prize, the gift—the only thing that mattered.

But when he moved next, it was slow and cautious—a careful, halting pace that seemed to ask *Is this okay?* and *Are you sure?* and *Am I still dreaming?* But if he was dreaming so was she.

And, suddenly, Maggie couldn't wait anymore. She surged up and found his mouth with hers, and every cell in her body came alive. She felt everything. She *heard* everything—from the crackling fire to the moaning wind and even the little voice that had spent the last year telling Maggie she wasn't smart enough, pretty enough, or sexy enough to keep a man like Colin, so what kind of fool would she have to be to think she might find somebody better?

But she had. Hadn't she? She'd found Ethan. And Ethan was a million times more. But if she wasn't good enough for Colin, then . . .

"Hey." The lips were gone, and she missed them. She reached up and tried to draw them back, but he held her face in his hands. "We don't have to do this."

"I want to do this. I'm sorry. I'm just not very . . . I want to." And then she kissed him again, and he made a sound that was low and dark and feral, and something inside of Maggie went silent. The words and worries went away. Like someone turning the music down until Maggie, a world-class overthinker, wasn't able to think at all.

Not about Colin and the first kiss he'd ever given her because that would have been like comparing a candle to a campfire.

Ethan's hands moved from her face to the delicate skin of her neck, sliding lower. Slower. And Maggie changed her mind.

It would be like comparing a campfire to the sun.

Suddenly, she couldn't silence all the sounds she wanted to make and she wanted to cringe with shame, but Ethan gave that low growl again and whispered, "There you go, sweetheart. Let me know what you like."

"I like you," Maggie blurted and, instantly, he froze.

As in he didn't move. *At all.*

No more kisses or wandering hands, just the heavy weight of him and she wondered for a split second if maybe he was a robot and she'd said the emergency kill code that made him power down because Ethan was completely, utterly motionless until . . .

The head came up. And she watched him morph into an Ethan she'd never seen before, boyish charm mixed with lethal intensity as he said, *"Finally."*

And then he kissed her again, harder this time, taking her in his arms and rolling until she was on top, and for a moment she pulled back to study the face that was too rugged to be pretty and too beautiful to be anything but gorgeous. Like an angel who liked to bend the rules but was still, deep down, one of the good guys and everybody knew it.

A beam of moonlight sliced through the curtains and fell across his face like a spotlight, and a little voice inside of Maggie whispered, *Blue*, as she looked into eyes that had been a different color almost every time she'd ever seen him—changing, morphing, blending—just like the man himself.

But this was a color she'd seen before. A color she'd seen recently.

"Sweetheart?" Ethan's hands were still and his gaze was burning as he looked at her through the dark. "We can stop. We don't have to—"

Blue. Something blue.

And Maggie remembered. "We have to search her office."

"What?"

She was already climbing out of bed, looking for her shoes, and reaching for the flashlight. "We have to search her office. Right now."

"You searched it already. The notebook wasn't in there."

"Not for the notebook! The envelope!" Oh, she was almost giddy. It was the same way she felt right before a plot came together, stars aligning and pieces clicking. "The blue envelope!" She gestured with one shoe and pushed her hair out of her face and tried not to think about how—or why—it was suddenly wild and free. "The day we got here, James brought in the mail, remember? There was a blue envelope in the stack. I just remembered it because it was the same color as . . ."

Oops. Maggie trailed off.

"As what?" Ethan asked, and she knew it was far too late to change the subject.

"Your eyes," she admitted, and he gave her his cockiest grin.

"I'm going to tease you about that so hard later, but for now"—he threw off the covers—"let's go."

CHAPTER Fifty-One

ETHAN

Flashlight beams sliced through the darkness as Maggie raced the shadows, trying to get to Eleanor's office before . . .

Well, Ethan didn't know what—or who—Maggie was trying to outrun. He just knew he couldn't let her go alone. She was like a ghost, floating down halls and around corners, toward the door that probably should have been locked at some point, but Ethan had already kicked it open once and, let's face it, that wouldn't have stopped Maggie anyway.

Nothing was going to stop Maggie.

Ethan smiled a little in spite of the hour and the circumstances and the fact that this mission had pulled him from a very warm, very pleasant bed.

He couldn't shake the feeling that he was standing on a ledge now, not sure if he was about to fall or jump—and no longer sure of the difference. He just knew that when he looked at her, his stomach dropped. It was like skydiving on the ground, and Ethan was half afraid to pull his chute.

By the time they reached the office, Maggie wasn't running anymore. She stood in the center of the room, flashlight like a searchlight sweeping over mountains of clutter and piles of books and then settling on the little table with its stack of mail.

"There!" Maggie exclaimed, pointing. "See? No envelope."

"You mean the envelope *the color of my eyes*?" His favorite thing in the world was teasing this woman, but she was too excited to even notice.

"It was right there . . . It was . . ." She was turning, searching. Desperate.

"I think it was from a doctor's office or lab or something. It had the swirly-snaky-logo thing." Maggie's voice turned soft and almost fragile. "That's why I noticed it. I was worried . . ."

"You think Eleanor might be sick?"

She kept her gaze turned down but shrugged. "Maybe? I mean it could have just been about her fall, but . . . I don't know. It's just that, looking back, Cece seemed especially eager to take the mail but Eleanor seemed just as insistent about keeping it."

"Not to mention, if Eleanor *is* sick and the new niece isn't in the will yet, the new niece would want to know."

"Exactly."

"Let's ask James in the morning, okay? Maybe he knows where it went. At the very least, he should know if Eleanor's health is failing. Okay?" He tucked that rebellious piece of hair behind her ear again.

"Okay."

He let go of her shoulders and slipped his hand into hers and was just starting to lead her from the room when she stopped moving.

For a long time, Maggie just stood there, frozen—the beam of her flashlight shining through the doorway, a spotlight on those shelves full of prisms and magnifying glasses and crystals of every shape and size—catching the light and sending it splitting and bending until rainbows and spots that looked like diamonds filled the darkness. It was like standing in a kaleidoscope, watching the light turn colors and change shapes. Seeing everything differently.

Even the one little light that didn't change at all.

"Maggie?"

"*The Nursery Crimes.*" She took a slow step forward, trancelike as she inched toward the shelves and the one dot of light that was tiny and blue and invisible until that moment. That little dot wasn't the way light looked when refracted through a prism—it was the way light looks when reflected *through a camera.*

"Maggie—"

"Don't tell me you never read *The Nursery Crimes*." She spun on him like that was the real tragedy of the last few days. "A woman catches her own killer using a nanny cam just"—she reached for the digital clock on the shelf—"like"—she turned it over to reveal the USB drive in the back—"this."

CHAPTER *Fifty-Two*

MAGGIE

"Eleanor hid a camera!" Maggie whisper-shouted in the hall. Ethan was practically dragging her away from the office and the family bedrooms but, to Maggie, it felt more like floating.

"I see that." He bit his lip like he was trying very, very hard not to smile. And failing. Like she was adorable and sweet and his favorite kind of candy.

"This *looks* like a clock! But it's not!" She pointed to the little lens in the center. "That's a camera!"

"So you've said."

"Eleanor hid it!" Maggie whisper-shouted again. "And I found it!"

"I know. I was there when it happened." He wore a patient, put-upon expression, like someone trying to get a drunk friend home from a bar or a three-year-old out of a bounce house. Which tracked. At that moment, Maggie felt like a combination of both.

"Eleanor just blew this case wide open!"

Ethan stopped walking. "Actually . . ."

In Maggie's experience, there was a high correlation between men who use the word *actually* and men who deserve to be hit in the ear with a snowball, but there was a warmth in Ethan's eyes when he told her, "I'd say *you* just blew the case wide open."

Not *we. You.* And it was all she could do not to jump up and down, maybe do a dance. Spike a ball of indeterminate purpose. At that moment, Maggie was high on adrenaline and kissing and the all-consuming rush of being right. Not to mention a steady dose of Ethan Wyatt pheromones, which should probably come with a warning from the FDA.

So she kissed him again because she was going on instinct and didn't allow herself to second-guess it. But there was something in the set of his shoulders, the feel of his hands on her waist, that made her pull back and look down at the nanny cam that was smushed between them. "What?"

"Nothing."

"That's not your *nothing* face. That's your *we might want to bury that before it explodes* face."

"I didn't realize I had one of those," he said, and Maggie tried not to roll her eyes.

"Oh, you totally have one of those."

"No." He was shaking his head. "I was just thinking . . . We can't play it."

"Of course we can play it!" she whisper-shouted again, gesturing wildly with her flashlight. But then she remembered . . . Flashlight. Darkness. Electricity. "Oh my gosh, we can't play it."

Then his tall body pressed against hers in a way that would have driven her crazy three days before. It would have felt intimidating and toxic but now it felt warm and safe as his fingers went to the back of her neck, massaging gently and making her moan. "Which means, we can't say a word about that." He cut his eyes down at the camera sandwiched between them. "To anyone."

He was right. Someone in that house was a murderer who just hadn't gotten the job done yet. If anyone knew about that camera . . .

Ethan pushed back and reached for it. "Here. You go back to the room and I'll go put that someplace no one will look."

"No." She held it to her chest. It was the closest she had ever come to uttering the phrase *my precious*.

"Maggie."

"I'm not letting it out of my sight." She sounded strong. She sounded sure. It was the way she always felt right before Colin made her regret it; when, actually, what she should have been regretting was him.

"Maggie."

"No one knows it exists, right? And they already searched our room, so when you think about it . . ." Maggie trailed off when she saw Ethan smirking. "What?"

"You called it our room."

She had. And she hadn't even realized it. "I meant *my* room."

"Oh, but you said *our* room."

"I misspoke."

"You—"

A low growl filled the air, but it wasn't a sexy growl. No. It was worse. So, so, so much worse, because it was a *hungry* growl. And it was coming from her.

"That wasn't me," she blurted. But then her traitorous stomach did it again.

"Okay." Ethan pointed to the door ten feet away. "You go to *our* room and lock the door, and I'll go raid the kitchen. And then we'll decide what to do. When I get back. *To our room.*"

She opened her mouth to argue, but her stomach growled again, so she darted for the bedroom and closed the door and turned the key, but she could hear him laughing as his footsteps faded down the hall.

CHAPTER Fifty-Three

MAGGIE

Maggie meant to stoke the fire—maybe fluff her hair—but as soon as she was safely inside the room she started to pace.

She needed to hide the clock, someplace dark and secret.

She needed to put it on a shelf, right out in the open and hidden in plain sight.

She needed to brush her teeth and put on fancy underwear and also go back in time and become the kind of person who owns fancy underwear.

There were a hundred and one things that Maggie needed to be doing, but she couldn't pick a single one, so Maggie kept on pacing.

Until she stopped.

The tiny flashlight was already back in her pocket, but the fire was going strong by that point, and in the bright orange glow she saw her laptop and a bundle of cords sticking out of her bag. And she remembered: laptops run on batteries.

"Come on, come on, come on," she was chanting two minutes later as she waited for the laptop to turn on. She found the right cord and adapter and plugged the nanny cam in and, suddenly, she was back in the hallway, looking at Eleanor's office door in black and white.

She hit rewind on the recording and watched the clock turn back. Literally. Figuratively. She saw herself walking the halls with Ethan in reverse and way too quickly. Night turned into day, then night again. She watched Sir Jasper enter the room, and part of her wanted to cry out, to stop him. But it was too late. You can never change the past.

She was so lost in thought that it took her a moment to realize that she'd let it go too far, so she hit play and watched as she stood there on the first night, arguing with Ethan. She could almost feel his breath on the back of her neck and hear the whisper. *I could always pick you out of a lineup.* Her arms were covered with goose bumps by the time she watched herself walk away.

For a while, the hall stayed dark and empty. She could see the corner of the tray on the screen. It was right there. All alone until—

A shadow passed in front of the camera, too close and too fast to see clearly, and Maggie remembered that she'd never really liked scary movies. She knew she should wait for Ethan, but the shadow on the screen told her someone was leaning over the tray. They were barely out of sight. If only they'd move a foot or two. If only . . .

The knob turned. The door opened. And then there was Eleanor, backlit by the light and haloed in the glow. She was smiling and laughing and happy. And . . . there. Eleanor was still there, and Maggie hit pause. Not because she wanted to freeze the image. No. She wanted to freeze time.

Maggie had never known a world without an Eleanor, but now she was gone—she was gone and she might never come back and—

Maggie's eyes turned hot and liquid—tears ran down her cheeks, but she didn't even wipe them with her sleeve. She was too busy looking at the last known picture of Eleanor Ashley, trying to burn the image into her brain. The picture of her smiling and laughing and—

Maggie hit play.

Taking a tray from someone whose back was to the camera.

And then that person was shifting. And turning. And that time, when Maggie hit pause, it stopped on the smirking face of Ethan Wyatt.

It didn't make sense. It had to be a mistake. She was determined to stand there until she could find some rational explanation because—

The floor creaked. A searing pain sliced through Maggie's head, and in the next moment, she was falling. She was sleeping.

She was gone.

CHAPTER Fifty-Four

ETHAN

She was gone.

Ethan stood in the empty bedroom, getting ready to scold her for leaving the door open. He'd been about to ask her if she wanted mystery cheese and crackers or mystery chocolates—he'd brought all three because he wasn't sure which would make her happiest, and he desperately wanted to make her happy. Probably because he got the feeling no one had ever tried. But . . .

She was gone.

He was leery as he inched toward the bathroom, calling, "Maggie? You forgot to lock the door, young lady. I may have to . . ." The bathroom door swung open with the slightest nudge. And it was empty.

She was gone.

Then Ethan felt his heart change rhythms. Training kicking in. Years of distrust and practice taking over. Because—

She was gone.

Fear was rising. Swelling. "Maggie!" And then it crested, carrying him out of the room and into the hall, flashlight sweeping through the dark as a feeling rose up inside of Ethan, a certainty that something was different—something was wrong—as he looked back at her room one last time. *Their* room.

And that was when he saw the pale green light that was blinking in the dark.

"Shit." He raced back to the bed and woke the laptop with the tap of a key. A moment later, he was staring down at his own face, scowling and skulking in the shadows.

"Shit!" he shouted louder as he raced out the door and down the hall.

His mind filled with a million thoughts and fears. She had to be hating him. She *should* be hating him. He looked guilty as hell. He *felt* guilty as hell. And now she was somewhere in that dark mansion all alone.

He couldn't decide what was scarier—that Maggie was running from him or who she might be running to, so Ethan stopped thinking and just ran harder, dashing toward Eleanor's office, shouting, "Maggie!"

A door behind him opened and Rupert's red face peeked out. "Keep it down out here!"

"Where's Maggie?"

"Who?" Rupert asked because Rupert was both very dumb and very selfish, but at that moment Ethan was in the mood to break something, so that was damned convenient.

He lunged and Rupert jerked back, banging against the door. "Where is she?"

"Ethan?" Kitty came into view. "What's wrong?"

"Have you seen Maggie?"

"No," Kitty said. "Why?"

"Nothing." He forced a smile. "I'll find her."

"Do you need us to help you—"

But before Kitty could get the words out, Ethan was already gone.

"Maggie!" He was going to wake up the whole house, and he didn't even care. "Maggie!"

"Can I help you, sir?" James asked as he reached the bottom of the stairs.

"Have you seen Maggie?"

"No, sir. Perhaps—"

Ethan wheeled and headed toward the library. It wasn't that late. Maybe she wanted a book to read. A fireplace poker to bang him over the head with. Something. He didn't care. The only thing that mattered was that he find her. Because the little voice in the back of Ethan's mind kept whispering that she hadn't stayed in the room.

She hadn't confronted him, fought with him. And his Maggie was a fighter.

But the worst part—the part he didn't even want to think about—was that she'd walked off and left the nanny cam just sitting there. Which Maggie wouldn't have done in a million years. Not willingly.

So Ethan threw open the library doors and shouted, "Where's Maggie?"

"How should we know?" The duke didn't even look up from the cards in his hand as he sat at a table with his wife and Cece and Freddy.

"What's wrong?" Cece asked.

Ethan took in the room: four people at the card table. James entering behind him and Dr. Charles dozing by the fire. Absolutely no one was concerned, because they didn't know—didn't care—that his life was falling apart.

"I can't find Maggie." He couldn't find Maggie, and she was out there. Somewhere.

"What's the meaning of all this shouting?" Dobson pushed into the library. He was already in his bathrobe with a towel around his shoulders, looking like a man who had never stayed up past ten thirty in his life.

"Where's Maggie?" Ethan demanded.

"Upstairs," Dobson told him. "In her room, I'd presume. Which is exactly where you all should—"

And then Ethan couldn't take it anymore. He stomped up to Dobson, forcing the older man back a step, reminding him without words that he was taller, stronger, and meaner than anyone had a right to be. That dangerous people had spent a lot of time and money turning Ethan into a dangerous man. Starting with his own father. Oh, how his dad had hated it when his middle son had chosen the only gun-toting profession that was entirely about playing defense, but whatever little voice had led Ethan to make that decision a decade ago was silent then, drowned out by warning bells and the pounding of Ethan's own heart.

"Listen to me, Inspector." Ethan's voice was dark and low. "I don't know where Maggie is at the moment, but I'm going to find her. And you're either going to help me or get out of my way because I'm getting ready to start breaking things. Lamps. Dishes." He cocked an eyebrow. "Heads."

To Dobson's credit, he didn't even flinch. "I could arrest you for that, you know?"

"Oh." Ethan didn't even try not to smirk. "You're more than welcome to try."

Excerpt from the Official Police Interrogation
of Margaret Chase and Ethan Wyatt

December 25

Inspector Patel: So you threatened a police
  inspector?
Mr. Wyatt: Oh. That? That wasn't a threat.
Inspector Patel: Oh really? Then what would you call it?
Mr. Wyatt: A warning.

CHAPTER Fifty-Five

MAGGIE

Maggie came awake slowly. Head pounding. Body aching. Mouth tasting like pennies and bad decisions. For a moment, she just lay there, shaking from the cold or the shock or maybe both.

Who was she kidding? It was totally both.

She couldn't quite remember where she was or why her mattress felt like cold concrete. But then she realized . . . that's because she was lying on cold concrete.

She needed to get up, but the room was spinning slightly, a swirl of grays and blues that kept coming in and out of focus. It looked like the galaxy through a high-powered telescope. Like the universe, big and mysterious and all around you—and also incredibly far away. She wanted to tell Ethan about it. She wanted to . . .

Ethan.

Another picture filled her mind then: Ethan's face in black and white, making Eleanor laugh before handing her a tray full of poison. Ethan smirking and glaring as he turned and walked away from the scene of the crime. Ethan staring down at the nanny cam in Maggie's arms like it was a land mine, like it was going to blow his life to smithereens.

Ethan.

That one word was enough to make the world stop spinning, rooting Maggie to the spot as her head cleared and the room came into focus. Concrete floor. Long tables. Dead plants. And the eerie silver shadows of moonlight shining through frosty glass.

Maggie had to get out of here. She had to get warm and stop shaking. She had to . . . Well, she actually didn't know everything she had to do, but step one seemed pretty obvious, so she tried to push herself upright and look around the greenhouse—she tried to scoot away—but her hands were bound behind her back. And that was the fact that broke her.

Even Maggie couldn't convince herself that this was her fault. She hadn't had an accident or gone sleepwalking or gotten blackout drunk. She hadn't tied her own hands behind her back because Maggie couldn't even zip her own dresses. So she couldn't blame herself for this one. She could only blame—

She saw Ethan's face on the laptop's screen and closed her eyes, forcing out a single tear even though crying wouldn't help. She'd cried in the wine cellar. She'd screamed and clawed and no one had heard her. No one had cared because Maggie had picked the wrong friend and the wrong guy and . . .

Some things never change. But Maggie had.

She was going to get out of here. She was going to get help. And she was going to start by rolling over because her arms were killing her and something sharp was piercing into her backside and . . .

Maggie stopped wiggling. She reached into her back pocket and pulled out something hard and plastic. She flicked a switch, then watched as a bright, white beam swept across glass and snow and plants made out of poison.

Well, Maggie had to say this for Ethan Freaking Wyatt: at least he'd given her a flashlight.

CHAPTER *Fifty-Six*

ETHAN

The fear that Ethan had felt ten minutes before was slowly—rapidly—turning into panic. Because Maggie hadn't just run away from him. *She'd disappeared.* She wasn't just mad. She was missing.

He knew it like he knew his own name, his own hands, his own ghosts. He knew she'd never forgive him and, worse, he'd never forgive himself if he couldn't find her. It had taken months of surgeries and rehab to regain the use of his right arm, but this . . . He would never recover from this.

So Ethan ran faster, toward the stairs at the back of the house, praying she'd gone to the tower to try to make a call. But as he passed a window, something made him slow and look outside, praying she wasn't out there. There was nothing but ice and snow and freezing wind. Nothing but—

Headlights shooting straight up into the sky like they were trying to summon a hero.

The flashlight shook in his hands. His breath fogged on the glass. But Ethan couldn't move. Because he wasn't on a staircase in England anymore. He was on a mountain just outside of Aspen.

The snow was blowing too hard and piling on the road. He should turn around, go back. But his mom wasn't coming back, so why should he?

So Ethan regripped the wheel and kept his gaze on the heavy snowflakes that were slicing through his high beams. They looked like stars and he'd just turned on his hyperdrive—like he was about to make the leap to light speed. His life was getting ready to change. He just didn't know how.

Not when the road curved. Not when he saw the beams of the headlights sticking straight up into the sky. Not even when he climbed down the icy cliff.

When he heard the sound, he thought his life was over, but it wasn't. It was just splitting in two. A clean break. A fresh start. And he'd been so much happier, there on the other side.

Or so he'd thought. Because, on the other side, there was Maggie.

Maggie.

Ethan blinked and cursed himself because he didn't have time to stand there, thinking about crashes and blizzards and a pair of headlights that were only in his mind. Except—

It wasn't a *pair* of headlights—just one shaky beam shining up from the greenhouse, and it was very, very real.

CHAPTER Fifty-Seven

ETHAN

The door wasn't wedged shut anymore, so at least she hadn't gone by herself through the tunnels. But as Ethan approached the greenhouse, he remembered that finding Maggie was only half the battle. He had a lot of explaining to do, so he threw open the door and didn't waste a single breath.

"Maggie, I know how it looks—"

But Maggie was nowhere to be seen. There was just the narrow beam of the flashlight, shaking and jerking around the room, as unsteady as the voice that said, "Go away."

Ethan started around the row of tables, but stumbled to a stop when he saw her lying on the cold, hard floor. She was bleeding and shaking and—

The flashlight was behind her back. Because *her hands were tied* behind her back. She was scooting away, a look of absolute terror in her eyes.

"Stay back. Stay back. Stay . . ." Her voice was rough, like she hadn't used it in ages. Like that was where she stored her tears and she was getting ready to make a whole new batch.

"Who did this to you?"

"Stay back!" she warned again, and Ethan swallowed down the bile that filled his throat.

He had to keep his voice calm. He had to make her see— "It's okay. You're safe now." Even when she winced against the glare of his flashlight. Even when he saw the blood on her temple and the crooked squint of her eyes like she had a concussion. Because of course she had a concussion. Someone had hit her on the head and bound her hands and carried her there. Someone was going to come back. "Don't freak out. It's me. Ethan."

"That's *why* I'm freaking out!" she shouted and in spite of everything Ethan bit back a grin because she was still the funniest, smartest, most challenging woman he'd ever known. And he loved her.

Ethan had never used that word before. He'd never even thought it. But somehow, he'd always known that it was true. Just like, right then, he knew he had to get her out of there.

"I'm going to untie you, okay?" She winced but looked away. "Please, sweetheart. Can you turn? Please?"

She'd scooted as far as she could and sat, huddled in a corner, on a bed of dirt and snow. Someone must have knocked the nightshade plant off the table because it was lying on the ground beside her. The ribbon was gone, though. The ribbon was—

She turned, and he saw it.

The ribbon was wrapped around Maggie's wrists and forearms— around and around like pointe shoes on a dancer's legs. Was this some kind of sick joke? Was she supposed to be some kind of present? Ethan didn't know and he didn't have time to find out, so he searched the cabinet until he found a knife. He held it loosely in his hands as he inched toward her.

"I'm going to cut you free. Can you turn a little more for me?" She did. "Good girl."

"Are you calling me a dog?"

"Not even a little bit." He bit back a smile and, with a deft flick of his wrist, she was free.

The red ribbon fell away and she climbed to her feet, still a little too unsteady. Still bleeding. Still the most beautiful thing he'd ever seen.

He bent down and picked up the wrinkled ribbon and shoved it in his pocket.

"If you make a joke about how I'm your present . . ." she started.

"Oh, I'm not in a joking mood." Not with her scanning the room like she'd never been there before—looking at him like he was a stranger. She was going into shock, but he had to know—

"What happened?"

"I played the video, that's what happened! You were on the video," she said, softer now. Like she was trying to do a puzzle in her mind. She was trying to make the pieces fit.

"It's not what it looks like."

"Really? Because it looks to me like you handed Eleanor Ashley a poisoned tea tray, then lied about it."

"Well," he had to concede, "when you put it that way, it's exactly what it—"

She grabbed a long-handled trowel from a table and held it like a sword. "Stay back."

"Okay." He put his hands up. "But just so you know, you're holding that . . ." She changed her grip and brandished it. "So well. Seriously. Did you take a class or—"

"You lied," Maggie said again, like that was the only thing that mattered, and maybe it was.

"I did. And I'm sorry. I know how it looks, but I didn't poison anyone. I couldn't sleep that night, so I was going to the library and then I saw Eleanor. I handed her the tray just as it was. You know me, Maggie."

"No, I don't!" she snapped.

"Yes, you—"

"I know the guy in the leather jacket."

Ethan didn't think it was possible for it to get even colder, but it did. The moon had disappeared behind the clouds and snow fell through broken panes of glass. But none of it mattered. Nothing except—

"You do know me." He had to make her believe him. He had to make her see. "You know . . ." And then he remembered. "Someone shot at us!"

"I never saw a shooter." She was shaking her head. "I heard a bang."

"How did I set fire to the greenhouse, then? I wasn't even in the country. When did I sabotage the stairs?"

"That's not . . . no."

"You know all this, Maggie. But right now, you're going into shock and I need to get you out of here. Someone brought you out here for a reason. Someone *kept you alive* for a reason."

"I . . . I don't know."

She did know. And given time and a warm blanket and maybe some mystery chocolate, she'd understand. But at the moment, Maggie was cold and shaking and her hair was full of snow and blood.

"Please, Maggie. What did I have to gain? You said it yourself: Eleanor hasn't chosen a successor yet."

"I was wrong." Even in the dim light he could see her enlarged pupils and too-white skin. She was in the middle of a nightmare and a flashback and a concussion all wrapped up in a literal bow and Ethan was going to do murder.

"Maggie—"

"I was wrong. I'm always wrong."

It was the *always* that broke him.

"Listen to me." He had to make her see. "*I'm not him.* I'm not going to cheat on you. Or steal from you. Or—"

"Hit me on the head and tie me up? Or poison me? Because, right now, I'm more concerned about the poison."

"Which is valid. But I'm not going to do that either." Her face was changing in the shadows, anger fading and fatigue taking over. She was so tired of that battle. She'd been fighting it for years, and the only thing Ethan wanted was to finish it for her. "It's okay if you don't trust me, Maggie. I get it. You weren't married to a man. You were married to an *Am I the Asshole* Reddit come to life. Just know— just please believe me. I'm not him."

He watched her struggling to think, to reason. Blood trickled down her forehead and into her eyes and Ethan saw red for lots of reasons. "Sweetheart, I need to get you out of here. I need to get you someplace safe."

"You lied," she said again. "And don't say lying by omission isn't lying because—"

"I did. I lied because I knew that, no matter what, my finger-prints were going to be on that tray, and the best way to clear my name was to find whoever did this. And I knew that to do that . . ."

"You'd need my help," she filled in.

"No. I knew I'd need *you*." He inched closer because he couldn't stay away. "I'm better when I'm with you, Maggie. Everything is better when I'm with you."

She was wavering, teetering. And he wanted nothing more than to kiss her tears and kill her demons. He'd kill every last one if she'd only let him.

"Is this the part where you say I should trust you?" Her voice broke, and Ethan shook his head.

"No. It's the part where I say you should trust yourself."

The trowel clanged to the floor and her eyes closed. It was like someone had just taken a thousand pounds off her shoulders and she was going to stumble because she'd gotten so used to the weight.

"I'm not crazy." Her voice was faint and frail and breaking.

"I know." And then she was in his arms and all Ethan wanted to do was hold her, but—

A streak of light caught his eye—another flashlight and a dim silhouette beyond the frosty glass, and he knew. He knew but he rushed for the door anyway, pressing and cursing when it didn't move.

"Maggie, watch—"

A shatter cut off the words. Glass rained down as the smell of gasoline filled the air. Gasoline. And fire.

Flames leapt across the floor and up the tables, but the sprinklers overhead did nothing. Maybe they'd been tampered with. Or maybe they just didn't work when the power was out. He didn't know, and it didn't matter. The only thing that mattered was Maggie, who stood between Ethan and the flames that were spreading across the tables, racing toward the cold, dead plants.

"Ethan!"

Do you know what happens when poisonous plants burn?

They turn into poisonous smoke.

Ethan forgot about the door and dove, crawling to the place where Maggie was already clawing at the floor, pulling up the trapdoor, and disappearing into the dark.

CHAPTER Fifty-Eight

MAGGIE

Maggie's eyes were blurry and her head was throbbing. Her legs hurt from the short fall and hard stop, but the thing she was most aware of was the dense, heavy weight on top of her, pressing her down and not letting her move.

Ethan.

"Get off me," she said just as a *boom* echoed overhead and there was nothing but heat and the sound of shattering glass. And Ethan. Pressing himself against her as the trapdoor rattled and dirt rained down. Covering her. Protecting her.

And, so help her, when he pulled back and muttered, "Chemicals," it was the sweetest thing any man had ever said, and for a moment, she wasn't sure where the heat was coming from, the fire or the man on top of her, worry and fear all over his face.

Sweat beaded on his brow, sliding over hot skin. "We have to get out of here. Are you hurt? Can you walk?"

"I . . . I'm fine." As she climbed to her feet, she felt steady enough, but the beam of her flashlight was shaking, vibrating in the dark, and once they were far away from the fire, she felt him stop and turn her.

"Let me look at you." He directed the light in her direction.

"I'm okay." But his hands were in her hair—which usually felt really good, but he touched a place that felt really *not* good, and she couldn't help but wince. "Ow."

She watched Ethan go cold. "I'm going to kill someone."

He sounded like a man making a to-do list. *Buy light bulbs. Gas up car. Slay your enemies and salt their fields.* It wasn't a threat or a promise or a dare. It was an inevitability, and for the life of her, Maggie couldn't bring herself to argue.

So she took his face in her hands and met his eyes. "I'm okay."

"You were gone." His forehead pressed against hers, and his breath was a whisper on her lips. "You hated me and you were gone."

"I'm okay."

"*You were gone.*" His eyes were full of pain and terror. Like this was a nightmare he'd had a thousand times and he'd just been forced to live it. Like he was going to be living it again and again for the rest of his life.

"I'm here." She pressed his hand against her pounding heart. "I'm okay."

"I couldn't find you."

"You did find me. And I'm okay. *We're* okay. Ethan—" She pushed onto her toes and pressed her lips to his, and she felt him shift against her, trance breaking, terror fading. And then he was the Ethan from the maze again, focused and calm—an impenetrable wall and human fortress as he looked into her eyes.

"I'm getting you out of here."

The tunnel was too hot, a reminder that the greenhouse was still burning and Maggie's mind filled with all the things they had to do.

"The snow should keep the fire from spreading to the main house, but we'll need to keep everyone away from the smoke. Not to mention . . . Ethan?" She glanced back at the ladder that rose to the passageway they'd found that afternoon. "We go up here."

He stopped but pointed his flashlight in the other direction, to where the tunnel stretched on and on, an unending string of shadows and cobwebs. It was exactly the kind of scene that should have terrified her, but she wasn't afraid of that dark, cramped space. She wasn't thinking about wine cellars or Colin or wondering if they'd find her body before spring. Not once. Not as long as she was with . . .

"Ethan?"

"What?" He gripped her hand and tugged, leading her toward . . . What exactly?

"We don't even know where this goes."

"It doesn't matter. We're not going back to the house."

"But we have to tell someone . . ."

"That the greenhouse is probably toast by now?" He huffed. "Either they won't notice or they won't care. And you're right—"

"I am?" She was never going to get used to someone saying that.

"The fire can't spread with all this snow. So . . ."

"So we're not going back," she filled in, but it still felt wrong. Like this was a play and she'd gotten her cue wrong. "They're going to be worried when they can't find us."

He let out a low, gruff laugh. "Good. Maybe then they'll stop trying to kill us."

Someone had tried to kill her. Not Eleanor. This wasn't a case of mistaken identity or wrong-place-wrong-time. They'd tried to kill Maggie. And suddenly her legs stopped working and she stumbled to a stop. The wall of the tunnel was rough on her back and her hair caught on something, tugging and breaking and she kept her eyes closed tight because the whole world felt like it was spinning so fast that she was going to be slung free, tossed out into the void.

"I have you." Soft lips pressed against her temple. "I have you."

"Ethan?" She looked up at him.

"Yeah?"

"No one has ever tried to kill me before."

"That's okay." He was biting back a smile. "People try to kill me all the time."

"Like who?"

"You." She swatted his arm and his grin grew wider. "Remember the Christmas party three years ago? You were wearing this green dress that showed your . . ." He made a gesture like he didn't know the word.

"Shoulder?" Her laugh was wet, full of tears she couldn't cry. "My shoulder tried to kill you?"

He gave a moan . . . "It slayed me. Killed me dead."

"What if I told you I also have it in black?"

She felt his lips on her cheek—a brush so quick and soft she almost missed it. "Then I'd say there's no better way to die."

The tunnel was close and warm in a way that had nothing to do with fires and killers at that point, but the smile slid off Ethan's face before he kissed her again, pressing and searching and pleading. A kiss like a promise—like a vow—saying *I have you*, and *I'm with you*, and—

"I'm getting you out of here."

Excerpt from the Official Police Interrogation
of Margaret Chase and Ethan Wyatt

December 25

Inspector Patel: There were several hours yesterday and last night where no one can account for your whereabouts.

Mr. Wyatt: We're accounting for them now.

Inspector Patel: It was well below freezing. There were blizzard conditions.

Ms. Chase: We are aware.

Inspector Patel: And you expect me to believe that the two of you just wandered down a dark tunnel with no idea where it led or what was waiting at the other end?

Mr. Wyatt: We were working on the assumption it couldn't be worse than what was waiting for us here.

Inspector Patel: How did you stay warm?

Ms. Chase: Uh . . .

Mr. Wyatt: Oh, we figured something out.

CHAPTER Fifty-Nine

ETHAN

Ethan didn't know how long they walked or how far they traveled. His training was failing him. His father would have killed him. He knew better than to lose himself in time and space and try to operate with imperfect intel, but Maggie made him crazy. *No.* Maggie made him brave.

She held his right hand—his bad hand—but it had never felt more steady as they made their way through the shadows of the passage and then finally up a steep slope toward a wooden door.

"Is there a knob?" she asked. "Do we knock? Can we—"

He kicked and the wood splintered as the door sprang open, ricocheting on its hinges.

"Oh look," she said. "The door's open."

It was exactly what he'd said outside Eleanor's office one day and a million years before, but Ethan didn't let himself smile at the fact that she'd remembered. He was too busy sweeping into a dark, cold room, trying to keep Maggie behind him while he cleared the space and scanned the walls.

"What is it? What is it? What . . ." She was like a little girl on Christmas morning as she took in the limestone walls and low ceiling. The rough, wooden floor and narrow bed. "Oh. It's a cottage!" she exclaimed like she'd always wanted to see one and wasn't this convenient.

Ethan drew back a curtain and peered into the dark and swirling white. It was snowing again, harder now. And the wind roared and moaned, but Ethan felt almost hopeful because—

"I think I can see the garage from here. Come on. Let's go see what the duke's Range Rover can do."

But Maggie pulled back. "Do you have the keys?"

He'd never been more insulted in his life. "I don't need keys."

"We can't drive," she told him. "The bridge is out."

"Damn it. Okay. I'll drive as far as I can, then walk for help."

He started for the door, but Maggie's hand was a soft weight on his arm. "Do you hear that?" She went quiet, pausing until there was no sound but the roar of the wind. "It's blowing like crazy."

"So?"

"So it's a whiteout out there. And even if you could see the road, it's buried under a foot of snow. It's pitch-black and we're in the middle of twenty thousand acres we know nothing about." Her voice was starting to shiver, to crack. "You could stumble off a cliff, fall down a ravine. You could die."

"I'm getting you out of here," Ethan snapped, but she was looking up at him and biting her lip. Nervous. Leery. Almost afraid, but the question was: Of what? The killer or the cold or the man she hadn't trusted at all until very, very recently? It didn't matter. Ethan didn't care, so he bent down to look in her eyes. "I'm going to walk until I find a cell signal and then I'm going to call for a helicopter and I'm going to get you out of here."

"You don't even have a hat. Or gloves. Or—"

"They're trying to kill you!" he shouted because that was the only part that mattered. "And I'm not going to let that happen, so you have two options. Buckle down in here and don't make a peep or walk through hell knows what out there and . . ." He shook his head. "Screw that. You have one option."

He pressed a quick kiss to her forehead. "It might be warmer in the tunnel. Wait there. I'll be back soon."

Maggie darted out in front of him before he could reach the door. "Where are you even going to get a helicopter?"

Should he pick her up and move her? He could pick her up and move her.

"Ethan? Where—"

"My father." He didn't want to say it, but he didn't have a choice.

About anything. "My father has contacts in the UK. I can ask him for a favor."

"The book burner does favors?" No one had ever sounded more aghast and that just made him love her more. "Ethan. No!"

He ran a hand through her hair. "He'll send it. I'll owe him, but he'll send it."

She shuddered and backed up until she was braced against the door. Her voice shook. "Owe him what?"

"It doesn't matter."

"Owe him what?" she demanded, and Ethan had to look away.

"He's been asking me to join the family business for a while now, and—"

"No."

It was the sharpness of that word that did it, cut his last thread of self-control and let him loose. He wasn't joking, wasn't teasing, wasn't charming anybody anymore. This was who he was—deep down. The man he'd never wanted to be: single-focused and determined and dangerous.

"If it means saving you, then yes. That's exactly what I'm going to do."

"You don't have to do that." She might as well have told him to stop breathing.

"Yes, I do."

"Why—"

"Because it's you!" The words were already out there, turning to ice in the frosty air, and Ethan couldn't bring them back. And worse, he didn't want to. "It's always been you, Maggie. Losing my job? It was nothing. I was glad to be rid of it. Losing my mom? It sucked but it was a long time ago and I've made my peace. But losing you? It would break me." He felt his pulse change rhythms, like his heart had found a gear he didn't even know it had. "It would break me in ways that would never, ever mend."

Her lip trembled. Her eyes were too big, and he didn't know what it meant that she'd never looked more terrified.

"We barely know each other."

"Yes." He took a small step forward. "We do."

"But . . . But . . . We hate each other."

"No." Another step. "We don't."

She was shaking her head but searching his eyes. It was like being at a drive-in movie, the way the last five years flashed across her features, a highlight reel of the best and worst moments of his life.

Then her eyes closed. Her voice trembled. "Is this about Tucson?"

Did she really not know? "It's about every time I've ever seen you. It's about the fact that you're nice to everyone but me. It's because you're the only person on the planet who's willing to call me on my bullshit. It's because you're the most amazing person I've ever met and yet you're the only person who doesn't get that. It's because I love you, Margaret Elizabeth Chase." He almost sounded angry. "Don't tell me I don't, and don't tell me to stop because, believe me, I've tried. I know you don't feel the same. But I love you. And so I'm going to get you out of here."

He'd been pinned down by a sniper the day before, but Ethan had never felt more exposed. The wind howled outside those old stone walls, blowing snow and turning the darkest night of the year pure white. And she was right, there were deep drifts and rocky cliffs and a hundred other ways to die out there. But it didn't matter. Because what was in here mattered more.

The big, silver flashlight picked that moment to flicker and go out. They'd already turned off the little one to save the battery, so all that was left was the darkness. Even the moon was hiding, so Ethan could do nothing but listen to the sound of her breath. The faint creak of someone taking a small, slow step on ancient floorboards. And then there were fingers, searching. Pressing against his chest, then sliding to his shoulders, his neck, the back of his head. And then he felt the soft brush of lips against his.

"Maggie . . ."

She sighed into his mouth as his hand slid beneath her seventeen T-shirts and touched the soft, warm skin of her back. "I have to keep you safe," he breathed against her neck, but the impossible woman just squeezed him tighter, like she was never going to let him go.

"I am safe." She sighed again, sinking against him, like she'd spent her whole life just trying to stay upright. Like it was the first time she'd ever been allowed to lean. "I'm always safe with you."

And that was the part that broke him. "No, you're not. If you knew the things I want to do to you . . ."

"What kinds of things?" Her voice was timid and bashful. Even in the shadows, he thought he saw her blush.

"I want to know what your hair feels like wrapped around my fist. I want to lift you up and press you against that wall until your lips get plump and your breath goes ragged and your legs wrap around my waist because, otherwise, you'd just melt away. I want to feel your hands on my shoulders and mine on your waist. On your ass. I want to feel you everywhere. I want to know you everywhere. I want to purge you from my system and I want to never let you go. I want you. And I want it to end.

"But I can handle those moments, painful as they are. The bad moments—the ones I really hate are the five hundred times a day I want to hold your hand. Or touch that little piece of hair that never stays behind your ear. Or walk just a little bit closer to you than I have to. I want to stop feeling like life is a game of tag and you're base. I want to forget that base hates me."

"I don't hate you." Her hands were on his shoulders then, almost like he'd willed them there. "And maybe . . ."

"Maybe?"

"Maybe I want those things too?"

It was like finding their way up a mountain in the dark, feeling along, trying to determine where the boundaries were and then realizing there were no boundaries. It was like realizing you can fly. And Ethan snapped.

In the next moment, Maggie was in his arms, and her legs were around his waist and he was pressing her back against the door. Even in that freezing room, his blood burned. His head spun. He wasn't strong enough to fight it anymore, and he never, ever wanted to fight it again because there was a *click*, the way she snapped into place, fitting herself into his arms and his body and his soul.

He didn't have to see her; he could feel her. The brush of her breasts and the squeeze of her thighs and the way she tilted and canted and ground as if trying to get closer, needing . . . more. They both needed more. He'd never felt so complete and so unfinished at the same time, so he turned and carried her to the bed and they fell together in a tangle of arms and legs and roaming hands, cold sheets and warm kisses that rose and fell and crested like the tide. He was never going to get enough of her. Of this. Of them.

She sighed and stretched and arched her back as he kissed the soft skin of her throat.

"Do you want this, sweetheart? You need to tell me."

"Yes. Yes, I've always wanted this." Her voice was small and shallow, like she'd forgotten how to breathe, and something about it jarred a laugh out of him.

"Since when?"

She stilled beneath him. Her hand rubbed across his cheek where he needed to shave. "Since Tucson."

CHAPTER *Sixty*

Nine Months Ago
Tucson, Arizona

This was a mistake.

Maggie had packed the wrong dress and she was wearing the wrong shoes and she'd ordered the wrong cocktail. It had only been three months, but she hadn't left her apartment in what felt like so much longer. She had never been very good at peopl*ing*, and then she'd up and lost her people—her only two—and so when Deborah emailed to ask if she still wanted to attend the Tucson Festival of Books, Maggie said she was totally planning on going! And was looking forward to it! And was absolutely up for the challenge! (*Three exclamation points! She'd used three!*)

In other words, she'd lied.

But her only other option had been curling up in a ball and thinking about the husband and best friend and big break that had all disappeared since December.

So that was how she ended up at a party she didn't want to be at, with a beverage she didn't want to drink, standing on shoes she didn't want to wear while sharing awkward smiles with people she didn't want to talk to.

Oh, everyone was nice enough, but Maggie heard her name in whispers; she read their thoughts in stares. She wasn't Maggie Chase, bestselling author at that point. She was the woman who'd been dumped by her husband and passed over by her publisher. She was the person whose whole life had fallen apart and paved the way for Ethan Wyatt, and no one in that ballroom knew whether to pity her or avoid her because that kind of bad luck might be contagious.

So she got another drink at the bar, then looked pointedly across the crowded party, smiling big and walking fast, the personification of *Oh, there you are!* and *Isn't this fun?* When a woman from her panel waved for her to join their group, Maggie was overjoyed to look down and realize that her phone was actually ringing, so she mimed *I've got to take this!* and headed for the doors.

It was either someone concerned about her car warranty or the attorney who was going to take all the money Colin hadn't claimed yet, but Maggie didn't care as she brought the phone to her ear and pushed her way outside.

"Maggie?" The screen had said UNKNOWN CALLER, but Maggie knew that voice. She knew it better than she knew her own. "Hello? Mags, are you there?"

Emily sounded nervous, which didn't make sense. Emily had been born pretty and wealthy and fun. Emily would have known the names of everybody at that party. She would have made eight funny videos for four different people and already be organizing an after-party at a great karaoke place nearby. Emily was *never* nervous. But Maggie always was. It was good to know at least one of them was capable of changing.

"I bought a prepaid cell phone," Emily explained. "I knew you wouldn't pick up if you saw my number."

"I'm not supposed to talk to you."

"I know. It's just . . ." Emily trailed off, like she was waiting for a click or a curse, but Maggie just stood in that empty courtyard outside that busy restaurant, phone against her ear, frozen.

People filled the busy sidewalk, rushing out to dinner or off to drinks. They crawled into cars and laughed with friends, and the desert turned cool with the fall of night while Maggie shivered, wishing she'd worn a heavier jacket, pretending she was only shaking from the chill.

"Maggie?"

"I'm not supposed to talk to you. Please contact my lawyer with any—"

"I'm pregnant." The silence was louder then, violent and pulsing in her ears. Even after Maggie closed her eyes, she could still see the strings of patio lights spinning behind her eyelids. "I know we're supposed to do the lawyer thing, but . . . I didn't want you to hear it from someone else."

"Who would I hear it from, Em?" Her voice didn't break at least. "You were my only friend, remember?"

"That's not true." Emily had the audacity to laugh, but it wasn't mocking. It was *don't be silly*. Which was almost worse. "Everyone adores you. You just don't see it, but that's okay." *It wasn't okay. Nothing was okay.* "I saw it enough for both of us."

Maggie wanted her to say something selfish and greedy and cruel. She wanted her first best friend to be Female Colin and not the girl who had "lost" a laptop, a cell phone, and two winter coats their sophomore year and then suddenly found them once she had replacements and *Oh well, Maggie, do you want the old ones?* because she knew Maggie would never take a handout.

Maggie's throat burned and her eyes were wet, and she would have given anything for her friend to be a lie. To be dead. To be anything but the voice on the phone, breaking her all over again.

Emily was still talking. About baby names? Baby classes? How lovely the guest room in Maggie's house would be for a nursery? Maggie didn't care until she heard a deeper voice in the background. Colin.

She'd know it anywhere, that accusatory tone. None of this was her fault, but when he told this story later it would be. It would be all her fault, and . . .

Maggie looked down at the active call and then she threw her phone in a trash can because she'd honestly forgotten that you can just hang up.

She forgot. And then she remembered.

It was fully dark by that point, those strings of multicolored lights shading everything in red and green. It might have been March in Arizona, but it felt like Christmas in upstate New York. She was homeless and alone with absolutely no place to go and no one to worry if she got there.

She was alone. And tears were running down her face while the phone she really couldn't afford to replace sank deeper in a glob of guacamole.

She was still standing there, trying to decide how to dig it out when a strip of bright light sliced across the patio.

She was practically standing on her head, reaching to the very bottom of the trash can when she heard the words—

"What happened?"

Maggie knew that voice. Maggie *loathed* that voice. He must have been drinking because it was pitched lower—darker—than usual. Or maybe he just didn't bother with his Mr. Charming act for her.

A foot scraped against the ground and she grabbed the phone and pushed herself upright because Ethan Freaking Wyatt was there, watching her dig in the garbage and cry. Ethan Freaking Wyatt was walking toward her so slowly that she barely registered the movement. She just knew that one moment he was on the other side of the patio, lost in shadows, and the next he was right there with his stupid leather jacket inches away from her stupid tearstained face.

"Who did this to you?" he asked.

She tried to hear the taunt in the words, the joke, the punch line. She tried to hear the Ethan she knew, but the words were as cold as the wind and his face . . . it was darker than the shadows. And Maggie felt herself crumbling, breaking into a million pieces and turning to dust. The wind blew across the patio. She was going to fly away.

"Tell me." The words were soft.

"No." It came out more petulant that defiant, but that was close enough. "It's nothing," she tried again, wiping the phone clean with a napkin. "I'm fine." She wasn't fine. "I'm . . ." She choked on the words but managed a pleasant "Good night, Ethan. Enjoy the festival."

And then she walked away, off the patio and down the sidewalk. She thought her hotel was that way, but it didn't matter. Maybe she'd end up in the desert. She really didn't care. And maybe that's why it took her two full blocks to feel the presence behind her.

"You're kind of annoying, you know that, right?" she called over her shoulder but kept walking.

"Now, Marcie, that might be the sweetest thing you've ever said to me." She laughed in spite of herself because it was no doubt true.

She glanced back again, then stopped. "If you're here to kill me, make it quick. My feet hurt."

But all Ethan did was smile, a little sheepish, like he was honestly embarrassed he'd been caught. "It's after dark in an unfamiliar city, and I'm not letting you walk home alone."

He was ten feet behind her then, hands in his pockets like the most harmless guy in the world. It was the posture of *oh shucks* and *gosh darn*, but the words echoing in her mind where different.

Who did this to you?

She watched him catch up, but she couldn't make herself move. And when she asked, "Aren't you going to mock me?" her voice cracked.

"Nope."

"Tease me?"

"Not tonight."

Maggie looked down at the sidewalk and the words slipped past her defenses. "Figure out my deepest, darkest fears and torture me with them until I'm driven slowly insane?"

But that time Ethan didn't even smile. "I'm going to walk a lady to her door and make sure she's okay."

Oh.

He took a step closer, slow enough that she could bolt if she wanted to, just run away, but Maggie was frozen, caught in his gravity—the slow, steady pull she couldn't feel and couldn't break. He was holding her, and he hadn't even touched her. "You *are* okay. You know that?"

His voice was too soft—too gentle and kind. She wanted him to chide or taunt or tease. Even one of Colin's mumbled insults or backhanded jabs she could have handled, but Maggie no longer knew what to do with kindness. She didn't trust it. She didn't trust *him*. But the streetlights were blurry overhead, and when she closed her eyes, the tears spilled over.

Her face was wet and her eyes were shut tight. She couldn't see.

Didn't want to. And when the strongest arms she'd ever felt wrapped around her, she let them. When his big hand cupped the back of her head, fingers weaving through her hair and pressing her cheek against soft, warm leather, she didn't try to pull away. She just cried harder. Gasping, ugly tears that were soundless and desperate and cruel.

It was the sound that hope makes when it leaves the human body, but Ethan didn't say a thing. He just held her tighter.

And tighter.

And tighter.

When she finally remembered to breathe, her throat was raw and his jacket was ruined, but she managed to croak out, "You will *never* speak of this."

"Okay," he whispered into her hair.

And true to his word, he never did.

CHAPTER Sixty-One

Two Hours Before Christmas

MAGGIE

Maggie didn't really sleep, but that didn't mean she didn't dream. About dorm rooms and deserts and being desperate to stay warm. About fires and red ribbons and women who disappear without a trace.

"Easy." Something soft brushed against the back of her neck. "It's okay. I have you." The arm draped across her was a heavy, unfamiliar weight that should have made her want to run, but she settled beneath it, burrowing in and coming fully awake in the darkness.

Looking around the tiny, frigid cottage, Maggie had to wonder if she'd always been destined to spend Christmas Eve in a small, unheated room. It was what that first year without her parents would have been like if it hadn't been for Emily, and part of her wondered if she would have been better off freezing in her dorm. *Yes*, she would have said three days ago. But now? A big, warm hand slid around her waist, and a little voice inside her whispered, *Maybe not.*

"I need to put more clothes on," Ethan grumbled, sounding more than a little bitter about it. "But then *you'll* put more clothes on, and I don't like that. But"—he pushed up and looked down at her—"I like you cold and shivering even less. So . . ."

They scrambled into their layers and then he padded toward the fireplace. "Hey. At least someone left some wood." He pointed to the stack in the corner.

The cabin clearly wasn't used very often, but it wasn't totally abandoned, either, and Maggie busied herself, opening cabinets and trying not to think about the last few hours. Or the last few days. Or the last few years. Maybe it would be better not to think about anything ever again?

"Hand me that old newspaper, will you?" Ethan squatted in front of the fireplace, and Maggie passed the paper, then watched him rip off the back page and light it with a match before nestling it into the wood.

Thirty seconds later, a small flame flickered and caught. And grew. And Maggie watched the glow take away the shadows. She felt the first little tendrils of heat taking away the chill. And she heard Ethan's words again: *It's the part where I say that you should trust yourself.* It was the first time anyone had ever tried to take away her doubts.

"Hey." The voice was soft and gentle. "What's wrong?"

She shook her head like *nothing*. But what she thought was *thank you*. What she said was "Whoever stocked this place didn't leave any snacks."

Then Ethan pulled something from his coat pocket. "You mean like this?" Maggie didn't recognize that brand of chocolate but she didn't exactly care when Ethan said, "Come here."

And that's how she found herself nestled in front of the fire in her archnemesis's arms on Christmas Eve, eating mystery chocolate and wondering exactly how her life had come to this and exactly why it felt like she might like it.

"Let me look at you." He tilted her head toward the orange glow of the flames and used the cuff of his shirt to wipe away a spot of blood.

"I'm okay," she reminded him.

But he only growled and kissed her again, and she looked down at the ground because looking at him was dangerous and she'd almost died enough already.

The newspaper was right there, something from the village—a headline about Christmas Eve service and the coming storm, but Maggie couldn't stop staring at the date: December twenty-second. Just two days before.

Two days.

Two days since they'd arrived. Two days since she'd met Eleanor. Two days since the man behind her had been her enemy. And then her friend. And now more. At least it felt like more? All in the matter of two days.

Maggie shouldn't have been surprised. Her whole life had changed in two seconds once. Two days could alter the universe.

"What?" He pulled the blanket off the bed and wrapped it around them both, making a cocoon that smelled like dust and snow and Ethan.

"I was thinking . . . this is only our third night here. It feels like a lifetime."

He made a noise, then interlaced their fingers. "Next year, let's go someplace warm for Christmas."

He said it like that was something people do—make plans a year in advance and keep them. They look forward to things and dates and dreams. They live life as if they're never going to stumble through a door one day and leave their whole world on the other side. He said it like he didn't know that plans are like hearts: they get broken.

His lips brushed against her temple and stayed there as he asked, "Did I just freak you out?" And Maggie tried not to cry. Or laugh. Or run out into the blizzard.

"Me? No. I'm not freaking out. I'm totally—" *Freaking out.*

"Hey—" The arms squeezed tighter. Like even Ethan was summoning his courage. Like it was the bravest thing he'd ever done. "I know the world hasn't given you a lot of reasons to believe this, but just so you know, if you were mine, I'd never make you park the car because my shoes are suede. If you were mine, I'd carry you through the storm. If you were mine, I'd fight the sky."

The wind still howled and the snow still fell, but Maggie couldn't even hear it over the roar of her own heart. She was supposed to say something. It was definitely her turn to say something! But the words got stuck, so she wrapped her arms around him. And her legs. And she squeezed tighter too.

"Ethan, I . . ." She couldn't get the words out, so she pressed her lips to his instead, and when she pulled back, her cheeks were wet and his hands were in her hair and—

"It's okay," he said. "You'll get there. I had a head start."

"Since when?" She felt herself blushing, suddenly obsessed with the loose thread on one of Ethan's buttons. "Since Tucson?"

His hands stilled. It was like he had to summon his courage to say, "Since the elevator."

But that didn't make any sense. They'd never even been in an elevator except—

"The one where we got stuck?"

He nodded like he'd forgotten how to speak. "It was snowing and your hair was . . ." He gestured to the top of his head like he, a best-selling novelist, had forgotten the word *damp*. "You said you looked like a Victorian street urchin."

She let out a silent laugh. "How did I really look?"

But Ethan grew serious, thinking . . . remembering . . . deciding. "I thought you looked like forever."

This wasn't happening. It wasn't real. There aren't actually men who *look* like that. And there aren't men who *say* things like that. And they definitely don't say them *to Maggie*. The Venn diagram of that moment was three very different circles of nonexistent men, and yet . . . Ethan Wyatt was . . . real.

Imagine that.

Guilt was doing war with butterflies in her stomach. "I'm sorry I didn't recognize you. I was—"

"It's okay.

She thought about snow and suede shoes and—

"I remember the panic attack. You were so nice, and I should have remembered—"

"It's okay. Really."

"Was that the year they told us Eleanor might be there? I was so mad because—you know how the security desk has to print those little stickers? Well, that year, mine had the wrong name on it and I spent the whole night thinking I was going to have to change my name to—"

She remembered the word but she forgot how to speak and the silence that followed was deafening, full of flying sparks and crackling logs and snow falling in clumps off the rooftop.

And then a deep voice whispered, "Marcie."

She covered her mouth but the gasp came out anyway, almost echoing in the silence.

He tucked her hair behind her ear. "All this time, I thought you knew. I thought we had an inside joke."

"Oh, Ethan—"

"If I'd known you didn't remember . . . I never meant to hurt you. The last thing I would ever do is hurt you." The words were almost as hard as the look in his eyes. "I will never hurt you."

"I know."

"And that's why . . ." He trailed off but looked out the window and she didn't even have to try to read his mind.

"No."

"You don't even know what I was going to—"

"I'm not letting you go for help."

"I could—"

She scooted off his lap, backing away. "No. I know you'd carry me through the storm and fight the sky and all the other really hero-y hot stuff—"

He flashed a small, slow grin. "Is that the technical term?"

"But if you tried to carry me through this storm, we'd probably both break our necks."

"Try me." He took it like a dare.

"Next Christmas," she blurted, feeling nervous and shy and terrifyingly optimistic. "If you still want me, we can do that next Christmas. Someplace warm."

"It's a date." And then all he could do was kiss her. And kiss her. And kiss her. Until he pulled back and breathed against her lips. "And next year, I'll get you a present."

Like a magnet, they both turned and looked at the narrow strip of satiny red ribbon that had fallen out of his pocket and onto the floor.

"At least they didn't strangle me with it."

Every muscle in Ethan's very muscly body went taut and Maggie knew she shouldn't have said it. Shouldn't have reminded him. Shouldn't have taken the kissing away.

"I'm going to find the person who hurt you, Maggie, and then, so help me, I'm not sure what I'll do."

He kissed her forehead and she leaned against his strength.

"It's a clue, at least." Maggie pointed to the ribbon. "If we can figure out where they got it—"

"We know where." He pulled back, remembering— "Oh. That's right. You were busy being concussed. Well, you know the plant that had the bow on it? It was on the ground beside you. Without the bow, so I'm guessing that's it."

"So it wasn't premeditated?" Maggie was thinking. "Someone knocked me on the head and got me to the greenhouse and grabbed the first thing they could find to tie me up with?"

"Right. Unless they gave Eleanor that plant for Christmas and are experts in forty-seven-dimensional chess, there's no way they'd even know—" Maggie bolted upright. "What? What did I say?"

"*Was* it a present?" Maggie was honestly asking.

"What?"

"The nightshade. When I saw it in the greenhouse, a part of me thought, yeah. Makes sense. That's the kind of thing someone would give Eleanor Ashley, but . . ." Maggie closed her eyes. She tried to remember. "It wasn't as dead as the others."

"No. It wasn't. Which means it wasn't in the fire." Ethan was catching on.

"But why would Eleanor put it in a burned-out greenhouse where it would definitely die from the cold unless . . ."

There was something inside of Maggie—a swirling, starry haze. Like she'd been hit on the head ninety minutes before and was only just now waking up—like the whole picture was slowly coming into focus. A kaleidoscope of Eleanor and mistletoe, old beat-up paperbacks and other people's presents. But, mostly, Maggie saw Ethan and the greenhouse and the way they could have died, surrounded by ice and fire and smoke made out of poison.

"We have to go back." Maggie bolted upright and started looking for her shoes.

"What?"

"Get your coat on. Hurry. We have to go back."

"Go back where?"

"To the house! We have to follow the last clue!"

It was filling her up then, like helium. Like hope. She was glad she was inside because she felt light enough to float away.

"What clue? Maggie!" Ethan was reaching for her, stopping her. But not like he wanted to hold her back; it was like he wanted to keep her safe, and she had never been more achingly aware of the difference. He said the words slowly: "*What clue?*"

"In *Deadly Shade of Night*, the killer left a nightshade plant tied with red ribbon on the porch of the victim. Now hear me out—what did you say this afternoon?"

"That you were right and Eleanor must have left us clues so that we'd find the greenhouse."

"Right! But what if that wasn't the end of it? What if—while we were in the greenhouse—we were supposed to find another clue?" She threw her hands in the air, furious with herself. "I can't believe I missed it!" She was looking, searching the room. "Did I have a pony-tail holder?"

"We can't go back."

Maggie froze. "Of course we can. We have to."

"There's a killer in that house, Maggie."

"I know." She pressed a hard, quick kiss to his lips. "And this is how we stop them."

CHAPTER Sixty-Two

ETHAN

Ethan was going to kill . . . someone. The killer, obviously. And maybe Eleanor for getting them both into this mess. Or Maggie. He was definitely going to kill Maggie, he decided, because in his tired, frozen, freaked-out brain it was the only way to keep her safe and wasn't that very serial killer of him? With a side of toxic masculinity? So he just shook his head and reached back for her hand.

She'd spent five years being not quite real to him. More idea than flesh and blood but now he knew the way she felt and tasted and sounded. He was never going to forget her sighs and gasps and moans. They were burned into his soul at that point. He couldn't forget them if he tried. And he had absolutely no intention of trying.

So he kept her hand tight in his as they traversed tunnels and ladders and passageways until they finally reached the dark, empty halls of the house. Someone must have banked the fires, but the coals glowed orange as they slipped into the library and closed the doors behind them and, reluctantly, Ethan let Maggie pull out of his grasp.

"Okay, so what is the game plan? Exactly?" he asked as she slipped through the dim light toward the shelves and ran one finger down the row of Eleanor's backlist, stopping when she came to—

"A *Deadly Shade of Night*." When Ethan saw the cover, he remembered— "That was my mother's favorite."

It was strange, thinking about his mom. In Ethan's family, it was like she never existed—like Ethan and his brothers had sprouted out of Zeus's head, fully formed. But they hadn't. Once upon a time, there had been a woman in his world. She'd made cookies from the dough you bought at the grocery store and she'd known all the words to every song ever sung by Dolly Parton and she'd loved Eleanor Ashley.

"Then you should do the honors."

The book felt too small in his hands, a physical reminder that he wasn't the little boy who had been left behind anymore—he was a man. And the only thing that mattered was the woman beside him. "What am I looking for exactly?"

"There may not be anything," Maggie admitted. "But Eleanor hid a piece of mistletoe in the last one, so . . . I don't know. Something stuck in the pages or highlighted passages or . . ."

They must have seen it at the same time because Ethan stopped flipping and Maggie stopped talking and they both stared down at the copyright page—at the numbers circled in a row. Too few digits to be coordinates or a phone number; too many to be a date or a time.

"Is it just me, or does that look like . . ."

"A combination?" Maggie guessed, and for a long time, they stood there, thoughts and theories flying like the snow until—

"We have to find the safe," he said.

She nodded. "We have to find the safe."

Maggie's cheeks were pink and her eyes were bright. She looked flushed with endorphins and energy and the high that comes when things start making sense. But then, just that quickly, her smile faded. "But the safe could be anywhere!" she whined. "The duke and duchess have been looking for it for days! It could be . . . Wait. Where are you . . ."

She must have missed the rattling of the doorknob, the low hum of the voices in the hall, because she made a small squeaking sound as Ethan half carried her toward the spiral staircase that led to the library's second story.

They had just reached the shadows of the upper deck when the library door opened and Kitty entered the room.

Or at least Ethan thought it must be Kitty. She was carrying a veritable mountain of boxes and presents and what looked like most of a whole bicycle. Rupert was tagging along behind her, carrying an old-fashioned lantern and one lone wheel.

"Rupert," Kitty called through the pile of presents in her arms. "Help."

"Help with what?" said the man holding approximately one-tenth of one present.

"We have to put the gifts under the tree."

His answer was to grumble about having to do everything himself as he took two presents from the top of the pile and dropped them near the windows. "There." He took the rest of the bicycle parts from Kitty and laid them beside the fireplace.

"We have to assemble it."

"Why?" he shot back.

"Because it's Christmas! And RJ didn't ask Santa for bicycle *parts*. He asked for a bicycle. And don't forget the train set."

"I am *not* setting up that blasted train set!"

"But—"

"Santa came, Kitty. He dropped off toys. He's a busy man and no one expects him to stick around for assembly. That's what servants are for. Besides, how are we going to get the blasted thing home if we had to disassemble it to get it here in the first place?"

They couldn't make out Kitty's answer because Rupert was already ushering her out the door.

And then Maggie and Ethan were alone. And together.

It was actually quite nice on the second floor with the heat rising from the still-glowing fire downstairs. It might have been romantic if it hadn't been for all the almost dying. They could have stayed there all night, her head on his shoulder, alternating between talking and laughing and making out like teenagers. It would have been the best Christmas ever. But then Ethan looked at the woman beside him, and a little voice said *it already is*.

They only needed one thing, and they were so, so close to finding it.

"Okay. The safe." Maggie studied the book that lay between them with a focus that could only be described as unrelenting, and Ethan knew he wanted to spend the rest of his life losing board games to this woman. "I think we should rule out all the usual places—behind paintings and mirrors—stuff like that. Because the duke and dukette—"

"Duchess." This time he was the one doing the correcting.

"—would have looked there already, and . . ."

She trailed off, and Ethan watched her gaze go a little hazy as she looked out over the library beneath them. They'd been in that room a dozen times. It was the heart of the house. The place someone like Eleanor—someone like *them*—would have felt most at home.

But Ethan had never really seen it until he looked at it in the dark. Until he watched Maggie's finger start to move—to point.

He had never—not once—given a second thought to the rug on the floor below. He remembered the corner being turned up that first night and Maggie almost tripping—the way she'd fallen into his arms. But he had never paid attention to the pattern of green leaves and purple flowers that looked like—

"Nightshade." Her voice sounded like victory.

It's a miracle neither of them fell in their race down the spiral stairs, but a few seconds later they were standing beside the over-turned rug, looking down at the library floor—the old wooden planks and new state-of-the-art safe.

"So do you want to do the honors or should I?" Maggie wiggled the book with the code for good measure, but Ethan didn't reach for it. He couldn't do anything but look at her. It wasn't the dash down the stairs that had his heart racing—not the clues or the mystery or the chase. It was her—it had always been her.

"Just so you know, whatever's in there . . . it doesn't change any-thing."

"What do you mean?"

"I mean . . ." He inched toward her, closer and closer. And closer. "Nothing in there matters more than you."

"Oh." She tucked her hair behind her ear and bit back a smile. "So, what you're saying is, I'm what you want for Christmas?" She was turning red. She was trying to tease.

"No." *Oh.* "You're what I want for always." He kissed her—slow and sweet and sure. Then he dropped to the floor and reached for the safe. "Now read me off those numbers."

CHAPTER Sixty-Three

Christmas

MAGGIE

There is a myth to Christmas mornings. Snowy lawns and garland-wrapped banisters. Trees and presents and the sound of feet running down staircases, little voices crying out, "*He came! He came!*"

So Maggie couldn't help but feel a little giddy as she stood in the dim hallway that led to the kitchen, watching the kids race down the stairs, then through the library doors. She heard their squeals and shouts and she felt her eyes go misty but she didn't know why. Then a hand slipped into hers and she remembered.

She didn't even mind that he'd made her put on a new matching sweater. (She was Rudolph; he was Vixen.) But somehow—looking up at Ethan, feeling the warmth of his hand in hers and seeing the clear, bright light reflecting off the snow outside—the sounds of "*What the hell is all of this?*" and "*Rupert! Language!*" Maggie couldn't help but shiver.

It wasn't the Christmas she would have written, but that didn't mean it wasn't the one she needed.

"You ready?" Ethan asked, and together they walked toward the library doors.

"This is bloody brilliant!"

"RJ! Language!" Kitty said. "Watch out for the—"

Too late. RJ had already knocked over a lamp with his bicycle. The train made a sound as it raced, fully assembled, around the room. There were streamers and wrapping paper and a room full of flabbergasted faces as Maggie and Ethan stood in the doorway and shouted, "Merry Christmas!"

The children were still playing and screaming, and James was laying out a tray with tea and scones, and the whole group looked at Maggie and Ethan as if they didn't understand what the fuss was about.

"Surprise!" Ethan tried again. "Look who isn't dead!"

"Why would we think you were dead?" Freddy Banes shoved a scone in his mouth, and Ethan cut a look at Maggie.

"Because . . . the greenhouse caught fire? Crashing glass? Poisonous smoke?" Ethan made it sound like a question, but only Dobson seemed to care.

"So you did that, did you?"

"Oh no. *We* didn't do that," Maggie told him.

"Then what have you been doing?" Dobson spat.

Ah. Finally. She looked up at Ethan and he grinned down at her, and Maggie couldn't help but beam as she turned back to the group and said, "We've been solving a murder."

Thirty minutes later, it actually did look like a crime scene, between the ripped paper and ragged ribbons, piles of mutilated boxes and Styrofoam packing peanuts and way too little sleep. But none of Eleanor's guests seemed to notice. Or maybe they just didn't care. The children and their new toys were upstairs with Nanny Davis, and all eyes were on Maggie as she stood at the front of the room, counting heads. They were only waiting on one person.

"Here he is!" Ethan called from the doorway, Sir Jasper leaning heavily on his arm. There had been a great deal of debate about whether or not he should try the stairs, but in the end, no one deserved to hear this more than he did.

"Thank you, my boy," Sir Jasper said, slipping into a chair by the fire.

"How are you feeling, Sir Jasper?" Maggie asked.

"Lucky, my dear. Extremely lucky. And ready to hear what you have to say." He gave Maggie a nod, and she felt her palms start to sweat. Her heart was a little off-rhythm.

She was nervous. But that didn't mean she was wrong.

"First of all, Merry Christmas!" Ethan stood at the front of the room and rubbed his hands together. "Did everybody get refreshments?" He pointed to the silver tray covered with tea and cakes.

"Say your piece, Wyatt. I suspect the phones will be working soon, and you'll likely be behind bars by nightfall." Dobson's words were tough, but he shifted a little, wincing. It was hard to be afraid of a man carrying a cane with rosebuds on the handle.

"Inspector, I appreciate you have a job to do, and I'm sure this isn't how anyone wanted to spend Christmas, so if you would please just bear with us," Maggie pleaded. Then she beamed. "I think you're going to be impressed by what we've found."

He must not have seen any choice because he took a seat next to Kitty, who reached for a bag of yarn and nervously started to knit. The rhythmic *clack-clack-clacking* was almost soothing in the suddenly quiet room.

"Do we have to sit through this?" the duke whispered to Dobson. "We should be—"

"Looking for the safe?" Maggie finished for him. She thought she saw him blanch. "Oh. We've already found that."

For the first time, she truly had their attention. Everyone sat up a little straighter as Ethan placed a large square box on the table. It was done up in beautiful wrapping paper with a big red bow attached to the lid. Maggie thought it might be the most beautiful present she'd ever seen, but all of Eleanor's guests just sat there, looking at it like it might be a bomb.

"This really is the gift that keeps on giving." Ethan flashed her a smile. "But let's not get ahead of ourselves."

"We're Eleanor's family!" The duke surged to his feet. "If that came out of her safe, then that box is our property. We have the right—"

"I'd sit back down if I were you." Ethan's tone was chipper but his eyes were dark, and the duke dropped onto the couch cushions like he wanted to turn into spare change and disappear. Then Ethan turned to Maggie, gave her a tip of an imaginary hat, and exhaled one single word: "Sweetheart."

The floor was hers, and Maggie felt her chest filling with something warm and lighter than air.

"Let's review, shall we? Several weeks ago, Eleanor was walking down the stairs . . . and slipped on a runner that was suddenly loose. She tried to cling to a railing that was suddenly wobbly . . . and she fell." Maggie looked over a group of people who had known that much for ages but hadn't been able to bring themselves to care.

"Now, it's an old house," Maggie went on. "Things fall apart. Maybe she thought it was an accident. Or maybe she had her suspicions."

"Suspicions about what?" Kitty asked, but Ethan made a gesture, as if to say *please hold all questions until the end.*

"We may never know what Eleanor thought. All we know is that a few weeks later, someone locked her in a greenhouse full of poisonous plants and started a fire. But you don't become Eleanor Ashley without having a few tricks up your sleeve, so she escaped. Now Eleanor had a problem. Either her luck had gotten very, very bad . . ."

"Or someone was trying to kill her," Ethan finished.

The room was silent except for the crackling of the fire. All eyes were on her. But Ethan's smile, his nod, the silent *go on, you're doing great,* was the only thing Maggie saw. The only thing she needed.

"Eleanor soon realized she had a second problem. You see, whenever she mentioned these incidents to anyone—her nieces and nephew, even her old friend the police officer . . ." For once, even Dobson looked guilty. "They told her it was all in her head. She was imagining it. She was getting older, after all. Maybe she'd spent too many years looking for mysteries that weren't there."

And, suddenly, Maggie wasn't talking about Eleanor anymore. "You know, if mankind has one universal superpower, it's gaslighting women into thinking they're the problem." It was actually a great comfort, knowing that if it could happen to Eleanor, then maybe Maggie could forgive herself for not realizing it was happening to her. "To the world, Eleanor was just an old woman who wasn't quite as sharp as she used to be. But even if that were true"—Maggie didn't even try not to grin—"half of Eleanor Ashley is still worth two of most people."

"So she summoned the best minds . . . The most brilliant detectives . . . The most elite—"

"Us," Maggie cut Ethan off. "She invited us. And Sir Jasper." She smiled at the man by the fire. "And Inspector Dobson." She gave him a deferential nod. "To join you all for Christmas."

"Why?" Kitty looked up from her knitting.

"I don't know," Maggie admitted. The truth was, she'd been asking herself the same question for days. "Maybe because most of us were strangers. Maybe because she trusted people who think like her. Eleanor's detectives were always outsiders, seeing things with fresh eyes. I think that's what she wanted from us. But whatever her reasons, she summoned her detectives—"

"And her suspects—" Ethan put in.

"And laid out a series of clues that only people devoted to her would see and follow. She didn't tell us what was happening. No." Maggie felt the pieces falling into place in her mind. "She let us figure it out for ourselves. And then sometime in the night . . . she vanished. She might have been wrong, after all. Maybe it was bad luck . . ."

"But bad luck didn't poison that tea tray," Ethan said. "Now the question is, who did?" He looked carefully around the room but his gaze landed on Rupert. "The ungrateful nephew with the sticky fingers?"

"Now see here!" Rupert started. "I don't know what you think you know—"

"Us?" Ethan looked at Maggie.

"Oh, we don't know anything," she told him.

"True. But Eleanor . . . Oh, Eleanor knew *everything*." Ethan was just a little bit dramatic as he carefully took the lid from Eleanor's present and retrieved a large manila folder. "For example, did you know that, according to London's premiere forensic accounting firm, two point six million dollars has gone missing from Eleanor's accounts in the past year alone?" Then he leaned close to Rupert and stage-whispered, "Don't answer that. That would be cheating." He looked at the others. "He already knows."

"Rupert!" Kitty exclaimed.

"I didn't kill her! I didn't even try." Rupert was looking up at Maggie and Ethan, a sick pallor to his skin and a desperate, pleading tone to his voice. "I swear, I never touched a hair on her head."

"Oh, we know you didn't kill her," Ethan went on.

"You do?" Rupert actually sounded surprised.

"Of course!" Maggie said brightly. "You, Kitty, and Nanny Davis all have alibis for when the shots were fired in the maze and, besides, why would you poison the tea tray when you'd already arranged to have Dr. Charles declare Eleanor incompetent so you could take over her affairs?"

"That's preposterous!" Rupert bellowed just as Kitty exclaimed, "Rupert!"

But Ethan was undisturbed. He just looked at a very sleepy, very bored Dr. Charles and asked, "Was that the plan, Doctor?"

"Absolutely it was," Dr. Charles said.

"I'd lean into that if I were you," Ethan whispered to Rupert. "It's a lot better than murder."

At which point Rupert had the good sense to shut up. Kitty's hands started flying again, needles thwacking together as Ethan looked over the other suspects in the room. "So if it wasn't the greedy nephew, maybe it was Eleanor's niece, the greedy duchess?"

Maggie waited for outrage, but all Victoria did was laugh. "Why would I do that? I am, as you say, a duchess."

"The duchess of a bankrupt dukedom," Ethan exclaimed, but Maggie lowered her voice.

"I think it's duchy."

"That can't be right," he whispered. "Dutch-y? That sounds like a pastry you can only buy in Amsterdam. I think it's dukedom. Maybe—"

"It's both!" the duke snapped and Ethan gave Maggie a look like *how about that?*

Maggie fought a grin as Ethan pulled a stack of papers out of the box and started riffling through them like he was about to deal a hand of cards.

"You had already come to Eleanor for money, hadn't you, Your Grace?" Maggie asked as Ethan laid the cards on the table. IOU after IOU. "Dozens of times. What happened?" Maggie honestly wanted to know. "Did she cut you off?"

The duke and duchess didn't say a word, but then again, they didn't have to. The answer was all over their faces.

"Unlike Rupert and Kitty," Ethan pointed out, "the two of you were off by yourselves when the shots were fired."

"That doesn't prove anything!" His Grace snapped.

"He's right." Ethan looked at Maggie. "I hate to say it, but Sir Dukes-a-Lot has a point."

"True. It could have been"—Maggie turned to Cece—"the mysterious new niece who, we should remember, actually delivered the deadly tray to Eleanor's office."

"I didn't poison it!" Cece sounded near tears. "I took it to her and left it in the hall and went to bed. You saw me!"

"We did," Maggie conceded. "But you could have poisoned it before you took it upstairs."

Cece was just opening her mouth to speak when Ethan put in, "What you could *not* have done is shoot at Maggie in the maze."

"But I . . ." Cece trailed off, processing the words. "Ooh. That's right! I was upstairs!"

"Exactly," Maggie said. "You couldn't have fired the shots. But your accomplice could have."

It was almost funny, the way the color drained from Cece's face. "I . . . I don't know what you're talking about."

Maggie could almost read Ethan's expressions by that point. They had their own language of little smiles and tiny touches, inside jokes and knowing looks. So it felt almost like a dance when they both said, "*Shrimp puffs.*"

"I . . . What?" Dobson exclaimed, but Maggie was looking right at Cece.

"When did you meet Freddy Banes?" she asked.

"I . . . uh . . . three days ago." Cece looked like it must be a trick question. "The same day I met you."

"And you, Mr. Banes?" Ethan asked. "You were new to Eleanor's legal team, didn't you say?"

"Well, of course," the man said.

"And you were a last-minute addition to the guest list, were you not? Weren't they expecting your father?"

"That's true, but I don't know what that has to do with—"

"So Cece"—Ethan flashed his most charming smile—"maybe you can tell us how you knew this man was allergic to shellfish?"

"I . . . uh . . . I *didn't* know."

"Really? Then why did you pull the tray of shrimp puffs away from him on his very first night here?"

"I . . . uh . . ." She crossed her arms. "That was a coincidence."

"See, we considered that. But then there was the case of . . . the blue envelope." Ethan pulled it from the box with a flourish.

"Recognize that?" Maggie asked. "You should. You saw James bring it in our first day here. But Eleanor didn't let you touch it, did she?"

"I don't see what some silly ol' envelope even matters."

But Ethan was already turning to the lawyer. "Your firm handled the DNA testing when Eleanor's mystery niece showed up, did you not?"

"Certainly. But—"

Maggie cut him off. "So it would have been simple enough to switch the samples or the results if you wanted to get your accomplice—maybe an old girlfriend from when you studied in the States—through the door?"

"That's ridiculous." The man jolted to his feet, but plopped right back down with one look from Ethan.

"Eleanor probably looked like an easy mark. She was old. She was rich. And for all intents and purposes"—this was the part that Maggie found most painful—"she was alone. But she was also savvy. And she wasn't going to do anything without being sure, so she ordered a new—and possibly secret—DNA test." Maggie pointed to the envelope. "And the results arrived three days ago."

Someone gasped as the group turned to Cece.

"You're not her niece," Ethan announced. "You're a con woman. And that man is your lover."

Maggie winced, then whispered, "I thought we agreed not to use that word."

"What's wrong with lover?" His voice was so low the others could have missed it.

"I don't know. I just don't like it."

"How about moist? How do you feel about—"

"Enough!" Dobson shouted. "I've seen enough."

"Oh, they didn't do it," Ethan said simply.

"But—"

"They're guilty of fraud, absolutely." Maggie nodded. "But they didn't try to kill me."

On the other side of the room, Dr. Charles raised his hand, annoyed with himself that he was actually paying attention. "But you just said he"—a gesture toward Freddy Banes—"didn't have an alibi."

"For when the shots were fired," Maggie said slowly. "They *do* have an alibi for when I was knocked unconscious and carried to the greenhouse last night after the electricity went out."

There were murmurs and looks and questions, but Maggie kept her gaze locked on Ethan.

"I came downstairs the moment I realized Maggie was missing, and I found the two of them in the library playing cards—"

"With us," the duchess pointed out.

"Yes!" the duke exclaimed. "We were there! So if they have an alibi, so do we!"

"Excellent point, Veronica!"

"Victoria," Maggie whispered.

"Whatever." Ethan shrugged.

"Enough!" Dobson was trying to get to his feet.

"Sit down, Inspector." Ethan's voice was flat and even. "Just sit there and do what you've been doing all along—nothing."

"Now—" Dobson started, but Ethan prowled closer.

"You could have investigated the fire. You could have examined the stairs. She's your friend. And you let her think she was crazy. So forgive me if I'm not in the mood to coddle."

Dobson didn't say a word but he eased back in his chair, a little chastised. A lot angry.

"It won't be long, Inspector." Maggie's voice was softer than Ethan's. "Eat a scone. Drink some tea."

"We are *out* of tea," he said with exaggerated diction and James went to make a fresh pot. "Get on with it, Wyatt."

Ethan turned back to the group. "Where were we? That's right. We have two real heirs and one fake heir—all of whom have excellent motives but no real opportunity to do all the crimes in question. Which is a problem, because who does that leave?"

As one, the entire room turned to look at James, who froze, teapot in hand. Looking very much the perfect English butler.

"James, are you a cold-blooded killer?" Ethan asked flatly.

"No, sir."

"Good enough for me!" Ethan clapped his hands, then turned back to Maggie.

"You see, there was one thing I couldn't shake." Maggie paced, unable to stand still. "Why did Eleanor change the lock to her office door?"

"You said yourself she knew someone was after her," Victoria pointed out.

"Recently, yes. But she changed that lock months ago. Right, James?"

"That is correct, ma'am."

"So why?" Maggie asked. "She was starting a new novel, but she's written at least seventy books in that office with the old lock. What was so different about this one?"

"No one's read it," Cece reminded the group. "I saw one page months ago and she was furious."

"Yeah. Well. About that." Maggie felt her face turn red. "I might have kind of . . . snuck the notebooks out of her office and taken a peek."

"She read the whole thing," Ethan told them flatly.

Dobson was furious. "I told you to stay out—"

"What was it about?" Sir Jasper asked.

"A woman who suspects someone is trying to kill her, so she fakes her own death and disappears." Maggie couldn't help but laugh. "Sounds familiar, right?"

"Well, who did it? You know . . . in the book?" Kitty put her knitting down.

"See, that's the problem." Maggie felt a fresh wave of energy pulsing through her. "The last notebook was missing, and then, sometime yesterday, the other notebooks were stolen out of my room."

"So who had access to the house and could steal those notebooks?" Ethan asked.

"And sabotage the stairs?" Maggie asked.

"And get close enough to lock Eleanor in the greenhouse?" Ethan said.

"And light it on fire?" Maggie finished.

"And who was free to steal a rifle from the gun room and then lie in wait for Eleanor to take her daily walk in the maze?" Ethan's voice was darker.

"And, most importantly, who in this house didn't know that Eleanor wouldn't be taking a walk that day?" Maggie was moving slowly, looking at them all in turn. "Because Eleanor was already gone?"

"Is the tea not to your liking, sir?" James whispered to Dobson.

"It stinks to high heaven." Dobson scowled down at the cup.

"Ooh! You forgot about the tea tray!" Cece chimed in helpfully. "Someone had to poison the tea tray."

But Ethan was shaking his head. "No one poisoned the tea tray, Cece."

Dobson huffed. "I believe Sir Jasper would disagree—"

"They didn't have to," Maggie cut him off. "Because someone had already poisoned the *tea*."

Ethan was inching closer to Cece. "What was it you told Eleanor through the door that first night? '*I found the tea you like*'?"

For a moment, Cece's face went blank. Then she remembered—"A box went missing! We thought we were out, but then I found it and . . ."

She gasped as the truth sank in.

"It was smart," Maggie said. "Eleanor was the only one who drank that blend. The killer could add the poison and be long gone by the time it was consumed." She looked down at the cup in Dobson's hands. "Until today."

Cece gasped and Sir Jasper scooted forward, his color coming back and his eyes going sharp as everyone in the room looked at Dobson.

"Go on, Inspector." Ethan crept closer. "Prove us wrong. I dare you."

But Dobson didn't look caught; he looked angry. "What reason would I possibly have to hurt Eleanor?"

"Murder," Maggie said simply.

"Fine." His face was turning red. "Why would I *murder* Eleanor?"

"No." Maggie could see her mistake. "I meant murder *was* the reason." She looked up at Ethan. "Was I unclear?"

"It was a little confusing," he told her.

"Oh no." She turned to the group. "What I meant to say was . . . well . . ."

It was like the whole room was holding its breath when Maggie pulled the final notebook from the box.

"I think you've been looking for this, Inspector. It's the ending of Eleanor's new book." She flipped through the pages. "Everyone knows Eleanor loves a twist, and I've got to say, it's a good one. You see . . . when I realized she was writing a story about a woman who fakes her death and disappears because someone is trying to kill her, I thought she was being meta . . . making a point. I thought it was a clue—and it was. But I was also wrong because this book isn't about Eleanor. It's not even about *now*."

Maggie felt herself drifting toward the windows that looked out over the wide expanse of snowy grounds. "It's about a young woman who walked five miles in the rain on a broken leg before collapsing on Eleanor's doorstep. It's about a girl who was so poor and a boy whose family was so powerful that no one would ever believe their golden son had beaten her unconscious and left her for dead. It's about a young woman who was so terrified she decided to just *be* dead—change her appearance and her name and disappear—because, sometimes, being dead is the only way to stay alive."

Maggie looked back at the group.

"It's about a girl who was so scared she never spoke her attacker's name—not even to Eleanor. But Eleanor was Eleanor . . . she always had her suspicions."

Ethan looked down at Dobson. "It's about the woman you thought you killed, Inspector. You know the case you came to Eleanor asking for help with forty years ago? The crime you thought you'd gotten away with? Well, Eleanor outsmarted you then when she got your victim out of the country. And she's outsmarted you now."

The color had drained from Dobson's face. It wasn't the look of a man who'd seen a ghost; it was the look of a man who'd just realized he was one.

He'd lived his whole life thinking himself a killer, believing that he'd gotten away with it. Maybe guilty. Maybe giddy. But absolutely certain that no one knew. But he should have known better. Because he knew Eleanor.

"She died! That girl died!" Was Dobson shouting at them or at himself? Maggie wasn't sure.

"You never found the body, though, did you?" Maggie watched him thinking, remembering. "Eleanor couldn't prove it was you, of course, but she always suspected. And she never forgot."

"This . . . This is insane. I . . ." He looked around, as if remembering where he was and what was happening. "How could I have known what Eleanor's book was about?"

"I don't know." Maggie turned to Cece. "You read part of it a few weeks ago. Did you tell anyone about it?"

Cece's eyes went wide. "Yes." Her hand shook as she pointed at the inspector. "I told him. He was visiting Eleanor one day and asked if I knew what she was working on, and I told him about what I'd read. I told him."

"And within days, someone started trying to kill her," Maggie filled in.

"This is ridiculous!" Dobson spat. "I wasn't even here when the two of you were shot at."

Ethan crossed his arms and gave his cockiest grin. "How's the ankle, Inspector?"

If possible, Dobson turned even whiter, but he didn't say a word.

"See, here's the thing," Maggie explained. "Last night, someone used the master key to break into my room and knock me unconscious. Then they locked Ethan and me in the greenhouse—"

"Ethan and *I*," Rupert snarled, sounding snide.

"Screw you, Rupert. And she's right; it's 'me.' Go on, baby."

Maggie blushed a little at the *baby*, but she kept her gaze on Dobson. "Someone locked us in and set the greenhouse on fire. Again."

"So unoriginal," Ethan muttered.

"Lucky for us, we escaped the same way Eleanor did—through the secret passageway that leads to the house. What we didn't know at the time was that the passage also leads to the little cottage on the grounds—the cottage where someone had slept and built a fire quite recently, three nights ago, in fact."

Ethan shifted but he never took his gaze off Dobson. "Someone who had to walk cross-country over rough terrain in high wind and blinding snow."

"In the dark," Maggie added.

"Right! Totally dark. Hard to see. Easy to, I don't know . . . sprain an ankle."

Dobson muttered and sputtered and finally settled on, "Of course I turned my bloody ankle walking in that blasted snow. I told you!"

"You did," Ethan conceded. "In fact, you said you did it minutes before you arrived, but your ankle was already swollen and bruised by the time we met with you in the library. No ankle is that color purple within minutes. No. You sprained it at least twelve hours before we saw it, Inspector."

"You sprained it while you were walking to the little cottage where you spent the night and, I'm guessing, left behind a newspaper and a whole lot of fingerprints."

"You sprained it before you snuck in and stole a rifle from this house. You sprained it before you took those shots, then walked cross-country back to your car, then down the road as if you'd just driven in from town that morning." Ethan folded his arms over his chest, bigger and stronger and oh-so-slightly smug.

"You sprained it before you knew Eleanor was missing and shot at the wrong people in the maze," Maggie finished.

For a moment, Dobson just sat there, chest heaving like he was trying to draw in enough air to blow the whole house down. "What about last night?" He pointed at the foursome who had been in the card game. "If they have an alibi for last night, then so do I!"

"Do you?" Ethan's words were a question but his eyes were a dare. "Or did you tie Maggie up in the greenhouse, then come in and throw on a robe and towel and act like you'd been in the shower?" Ethan laughed, then reached down for the teacup. "So what do you say, Inspector? Give it a sip?"

It happened in a flash. One second, Maggie was thinking that they'd made a good case and had a good theory but it would never hold up in court; the next, the teacup was flying through the air, scalding liquid arcing across the room. Ethan lunged, knocking Maggie out of the way, and she landed on the sofa—on top of Kitty and tangled in her knitting.

But just as quickly, a big hand grabbed her arm and hauled her to her feet. Dobson had an arm around her neck. The handle of Eleanor's second-favorite walking stick pressed into her throat as he gripped it with one hand.

She heard a *click* and felt cold metal against her temple. That's when she realized he held a small handgun in the other.

"Hey, now," Ethan said. "Don't do anything you're going to regret."

"You're forty years too late, Wyatt. Now I'm walking out of here." Maggie was his cane at that point, and he leaned against her as they inched toward the door. "I'm going to help myself to His Grace's vehicle. The phones will work eventually, then you can feel free to call for help, but I'll be gone."

"The bridge is out," Maggie reminded him, but she could almost feel him smile as he slowly shook his head.

"You mean we've been stuck here for nothing!" Dr. Charles sounded like that was the real tragedy of the situation, but Dobson was already dragging Maggie toward the doors.

"Maggie . . ." Ethan started.

But she was looking around the room, doing the math. It didn't matter how many shots Dobson had, he wouldn't miss. Not at that range. No one could miss at that range.

"I'm okay." And, amazingly, she was. The world was calm and quiet. It was like the faster things happened, the slower everything felt. Like she was watching the scene from a great height. Like she could see all the odds and play the angles. Like she could still win.

Like she was Eleanor.

"We should go through the gardens," Maggie said flatly. "It's faster."

"So helpful, Ms. Chase."

"No. I just want you out of here."

She felt his weight. He was still unsteady on his feet. If she could just get in the open. If she could run . . . But as soon as they stepped out into the deep snow, she felt less certain.

"The garage is—"

"I know where the garage is! I've been coming here for forty years!"

"Okay," she said calmly. "Let's go."

CHAPTER *Sixty-Four*

ETHAN

Ethan watched them go.

The French doors closed and cold air clung to the room, snow melting on the carpets. He watched Maggie wrap something around the door handles from the outside, gun at her temple and Dobson urging her on.

Then they were gone. For a moment, Ethan was frozen. Terrified. It was like there were two of him—one man who could do nothing but stand and stare and watch the best thing in his life slowly fade away. And then there was the machine who was nothing but training and intensity and a cold, maniacal willingness to do anything to get her back.

He didn't even remember walking toward the doors. He wasn't even aware of rearing back, starting to kick until a hand on his arm stopped him.

"Sir?" James sounded as if this was something they cover on the first day of butler school. "If I might make a suggestion . . ."

MAGGIE

Maggie didn't feel the cold. Maybe it was the power of her fancy new sweater, but more likely it was the adrenaline, coursing through her veins and keeping her warm and alert and alive.

She was definitely alive. For now. But the gun was still in Dobson's hand—the one that was draped around her shoulder like they were old friends. Like they'd had a night on the town and at any moment they were going to break into song as they staggered home, a little tipsy.

But it was daytime, and the sun was too bright as it bounced off a blanket of snow that shone like crystals. She had to squint against the glare as they traversed the uneven ground and knee-high drifts. She had to watch her step. Be careful.

"Hurry up."

She needed to be careful in so many ways.

"Where are we going?" Her voice didn't quaver and Maggie was proud of herself for that much.

"Just keep walking."

"The garage is that way." She pointed to the other side of the house, but Dobson leaned against her harder, hand shaking, cane slicing through the snow with a dull thud that echoed with every step.

She stole a glance behind her, but the doors stayed closed and the patio stayed empty, and Maggie felt nothing but the wind and a growing dread.

"Looks like he's not coming." Dobson sounded like he wanted to laugh, but all Maggie could think was—

Of course he's coming.

She'd been so wrong before. So very wrong for so very long that a part of Maggie wanted to give up and melt away, but she didn't believe Dobson. She didn't even believe Ethan. She believed *herself.* And Maggie wasn't wrong this time.

"Wipe that grin off your face," Dobson growled as he limped beside her.

"Make me," she dared and he stopped. He pulled back a hand like he could hit her—like he could hurt her. Like Maggie hadn't already lived through much, much worse.

Maybe that's why they didn't hear a thing until a voice rang out, saying, "Touch her and I'll kill you."

It wasn't a threat. Not even a promise. It was a destiny, something foretold that would absolutely come to pass, and the man froze as they looked into the blinding sun at the dark silhouette that stood fifty feet away.

Blocking their path.

A Remington rifle aimed right at them.

"Drop the gun," Ethan said.

"You first," Dobson shouted and then darted faster than a man with a bum ankle ever should, dragging Maggie with him and disappearing into the maze.

It had seemed different with the falling snow and looming questions. Back when she'd been looking for Eleanor and for answers. Back when she'd been alone. Except—she hadn't been alone, had she? Even before she'd known it, she'd had Ethan.

But now the tall hedges were casting shadows on the ground, and with every step Maggie wondered when Dobson would realize he'd probably be faster without her.

"Dobson!" Ethan shouted. "Send her out, and I'll let you go."

They were leaving tracks with every step. Ethan could follow. Ethan *would* follow. He had to.

So Maggie plowed forward, bumping against hedges and shaking branches, making as much sound as she could while staying silent. It was something that came naturally to her. Her whole marriage in a nutshell.

"Turn up here. Right. No. Left. Go! Go!"

They stopped. They froze. Because someone was standing in the way, saying, "Let her go."

CHAPTER Sixty-Five

ETHAN

"I said, let her go," Ethan said again.

Dobson was breathing hard and his face was pale. The ankle was killing him, a part of Ethan's brain said. Because a part of Ethan couldn't stop doing math and measuring angles. Calculating odds. *Good*, Ethan told himself. Because the rest of him—the bulk of him— was a frantic and terrified mess.

The only thing keeping him from launching himself at Dobson and strangling him with his bare hands was Maggie—both the gun at her temple and the look in her eye. She looked like a woman who had plotted this out, spotted the twist and knew what was coming. Like someone who had a trick or two up her sleeve.

She looked like Eleanor.

But she also looked like someone who trusted him. Who was waiting on him. Who needed him. Wanted him. Like they were a team. And for Ethan, a man who had spent his whole life trying to be enough, it should have been terrifying to realize that he was best when he was half of a whole. When the rest of him was her.

But Dobson had an arm around her shoulders and the small gun was still in his hands. He couldn't miss from that range. And even if he did—even if the gun misfired it would kill her.

So Ethan kept the rifle steady. It felt like an extension of him. Like he'd been training, waiting, preparing his whole life for just this moment.

"You're going to let her go and she's going to walk to me."

"Or what?" Dobson actually laughed, a cruel, cold sound that carried on the wind. But Ethan didn't say a word. He cocked the rifle, but that just made Dobson laugh harder. "I read all about you, Wyatt. Five years ago, you could have made that shot, but now?"

And then Ethan's hand wasn't just trembling. It was shaking. His whole body was. Because there was Maggie. She was so close, but Dobson was right. Of course he was right. Ethan couldn't make that shot with an old rifle that he'd never fired before. Even the Ethan of five years ago shouldn't have tried it. Not with Maggie in the way. Not with Maggie right there. Not with Maggie . . .

Slowly, Ethan lowered the rifle, and Dobson's grin turned into a sneer.

"Toss it!" he yelled, and Ethan started to drop the rifle in the snow, but Dobson jerked his head toward the hedges. "Over there. Nice and out of reach."

Ethan didn't want to do it. He couldn't do it. But then he looked at Maggie, who was nodding like *It's okay. It's fine. We've got this.* So he threw the rifle over the snowy hedge and heard it land with a soft *plop* on the other side.

It should have felt like failure, but he wasn't looking at Dobson at that moment. He was looking at her.

At the little grin on her face and the look in her eyes and the way her hand was moving, sliding, disappearing into the sweater's sleeve.

"You're right, Inspector. I'd probably miss." There was a quick flash of metal in the sunlight, and Ethan smiled. "But she won't."

There was a half second of confusion on Dobson's face as he looked at Maggie like *what could she do—she's no one.* But then the confusion turned to agony as Maggie slipped the knitting needle from her sleeve and plunged it into Dobson's thigh.

The inspector roared as he dropped the cane and tried to pull the needle free.

Maggie fell to her knees in the bloody snow.

"You bitch!" Dobson pointed the pistol at Maggie's head.

"Ethan!" Maggie picked up the cane and hurled it in his direction and Ethan didn't give it a second thought.

He aimed, and in the next moment, a small dart was flying from the end of Eleanor's cane and lodging in Dobson's throat.

The man choked as he stumbled backward, crashing into a hedge and then falling, frozen beneath a pile of snow.

"Maggie!" Ethan pulled her tight. "Are you okay?"

"I'm fine. I'm—"

"Let me look at you. Are you hurt?"

"I'm fine. I'm okay."

There were shouts on the wind, echoing through the maze.

"Don't ever scare me like that again." He was probably going to hurt her he was holding her so tightly, but he couldn't let go either. The pistol was on the ground, and he kicked it because he probably shouldn't kick Dobson, who was unconscious and bleeding, with that long, shiny piece of metal sticking out of his leg. Seeing it . . . Ethan wanted to laugh. Then he saw the blood again and wanted to scream. Then he looked down at Maggie, pushed that rogue piece of hair behind her ear one more time, and said, "So . . . knitting needles?"

"Knitting needles." She exhaled a frosty breath just as a helicopter appeared on the horizon. Then another. And another. Soon they filled the sky, circling like vultures, and Maggie had to shout over the noise. "Who did you call?"

She sounded worried, like he'd made some kind of crossroads bargain. Like he'd traded his soul for her safety and it wasn't worth it. But it would have been.

"No one." Ethan cupped her cheek and stared into her eyes while the blades spun shadows on the snow. "It's a Christmas miracle."

"Really?" she shouted and he nodded and then her voice dropped low. "Ethan?" His name was a whisper as the air turned white and her cheeks went pink.

"Yes, sweetheart?"

"I want to make out."

And so that's exactly what they did.

December 25

Ms. Chase: So, in answer to your question, Inspector Patel, yes, I have his blood on my hands.

Mr. Wyatt: She missed the femoral artery, though, didn't she? It's not like she killed him. Wait. Did she kill him?

Inspector Patel: No. The last I heard, Inspector Dobson is expected to make a full recovery. He'll be well enough to stand trial.

Ms. Chase: And Sir Jasper?

Inspector Patel: He'll be fine. Dr. Charles insisted on accompanying him to the hospital and has already reported in.

Mr. Wyatt: Was it poison? It was, wasn't it? It was—

Inspector Patel: Foxglove. And— I beg your pardon . . . Did you just fist-bump?

Mr. Wyatt: What about Cece and Baby Banes?

Inspector Patel: In custody. There's a warrant out for her arrest in the States and we're holding him for questioning.

Mr. Wyatt: So I guess that's it then?

Inspector Patel: Is it?

Ms. Chase: I'm sorry?

Inspector Patel: Funny thing . . . Four different branches of law enforcement received the same call this morning, informing us that the crime of the year was taking place at the home of Eleanor Ashley. But they didn't leave a name. I don't suppose either of you know who our mystery caller might have been?

Mr. Wyatt: Oh? Well, if I had to take a guess . . .

Ms. Chase: It was someone who likes a twist.

CHAPTER Sixty-Six

MAGGIE

Eleanor's office was exactly the same and yet everything was totally different as Maggie stood in the fading light that filtered through the frosty windows.

Christmas was almost over.

There were no more helicopters on the lawn or barking dogs on the grounds. No more Interpol and MI5. Even Inspector Patel, a woman with impeccable credentials, warm brown eyes, and the good sense not to fall instantly in love with Ethan Wyatt, had gone back to Scotland Yard, so Maggie returned to the scene of the sole remaining mystery.

"I don't think she's in here," a voice said from behind her and she turned to study the man who leaned against the doorframe because, well, when Ethan Wyatt leaned, *everybody* noticed.

He was giving her his sternest look—trying not to grin and failing. Of course, Ethan made failing look good because he could do that. Tease without saying a word, charm without making a sound. He would always have friends and he would always have fans. And Maggie . . .

"So there's got to be a secret passageway, right?" She scanned the walls and the shelves and the windows. "That's how Eleanor got out? Because she was definitely *in* this room! You saw her in this room."

"Maggie—"

"At first, I thought she must have thrown the bolt from the outside, but there's no sign of her leaving on the video, so she got out *through* this room." It was the nervous rambling of a woman who'd just realized that a man might kiss you in the swirling snow on Christmas morning, but, eventually, you'll wake up and it will be the twenty-sixth and someone will have to start shoveling.

"It's either that or the window. The snow wasn't disturbed on the sill, but if that top portion opens—"

"Maggie?" A big, warm hand kneaded the muscles at the back of her neck and she made a sound that was something between a moan and a sigh. A *migh*. A *soan*. "Sweetheart, what's wrong?"

"If we can figure out how she got out, maybe—"

"Margaret Elizabeth." He cut her off. "*What's wrong?*" he asked again, and Maggie's brain went into overdrive because Eleanor was missing and Christmas was almost over, and, soon, they'd be going home and Maggie didn't even know where his home was. She didn't know when she'd see him or *if* she'd see him.

They weren't in danger anymore. And they were no longer the only people they could trust, so maybe they wouldn't be anything? The snow would melt and the calendar would turn and he'd go back to being beloved and she'd go back to being alone. When all she'd wanted to be was . . .

"I don't want to be Eleanor anymore." She'd gone through the looking glass and she'd seen the other side of the fence—walked in Eleanor's shoes (or at least her pom-pom hat) and it wasn't all that perfect, even before the shooting started. "I used to think everything would be okay if I had money and a house and a family. I thought I just needed to be Eleanor. But I don't . . . I don't want to be her."

Those big hands were doing marvelous things to the back of her neck. She thought her head might pop off her body and float away. She thought she might just let it.

"Okay. Do you feel like telling me what you *do* want?" Ethan was being kind. And patient. And she was very, very mad that he wasn't giving her a reason to be angry.

"I want to be me." It was silly, but he didn't laugh. "I didn't think I ever would, but I know who I am now. And I like who I am. And I love who I am with . . ." She couldn't do it. Say it. Could she? "I love who I am with *you*, okay? And I think that might be because

I . . ." He said it first. It's okay. This is a safe space. ". . . you know . . . love you."

"Oh, you do, do you?" There was a smile in his voice, a too-pleased *I'm going to tease you about this later* tone that made her want to hit him. While also kissing him.

"I do," she admitted begrudgingly. "I love you, and it's so annoying!"

"Tell me about it."

"Right?" she exclaimed.

"I've been trying to be *not* in love with you for ages, so if you figure out how to stop, please let me know."

"Okay! I will!"

"Okay. Or . . ." He tucked her hair behind her ear for what felt like the millionth time. She hoped he never stopped. "Maybe we could try being in love together?"

"Okay," she whispered, trying not to cry because then her face would get all blotchy and her eyes would get puffy, so she studied his shirt instead. Another plaid flannel number. Turned out, she had a thing for lumberjacks after all.

And then there was kissing and whispering and somehow, she ended up sitting on Eleanor Ashley's desk with Ethan Wyatt standing between her knees. He tasted like good scotch and—

"Oh my!" They pulled apart at the sound of the voice. Ethan laughed into her neck while Maggie tried not to turn the color of cherries. "I'm sorry to interrupt," Victoria said, "but there were presents under the tree. Aunt Eleanor must have left them before . . ." Her voice cracked and her eyes went misty. There was something pinned to her sweater and she reached for it like a talisman made out of silver and pearls.

The duchess must have read Maggie's mind because she looked down at the tiny magnifying glass and said, "She never took it off. Ever. When I was a girl, I thought she must wear it to bed. I never thought I'd find it under the tree, wrapped up in a box with a stack of canceled IOUs and a revised will, but . . ."

Her eyes were red and she had to look at the light—like that might dry her eyes. Then she forced a smile and added, "I thought she was coming back, you know. I thought it was a game because that's what she does. She plays games. And she wins. I thought she was coming back. But . . ." Her grip on the brooch tightened and her knuckles turned white and she stood there, looking like a woman who'd just realized that, to Eleanor Ashley, clues *are* presents. And they're priceless.

Then she pasted on her duchess smile and resumed her duchess posture, handing them each a small package. "These appear to be for you." She started for the door, but lingered at the threshold, fingers on the busted frame as she gave a backward glance. "You're going to find her, aren't you?"

"You know your aunt better than we do." Ethan sounded resigned. "If she doesn't want to be found . . ."

But Victoria studied them carefully. Shrewdly. She looked like Eleanor when she grinned. "You're going to find her." It wasn't a question.

And then she walked away.

Maggie heard footsteps retreating down the long empty hall and then the rip of paper. Ethan was already prying open his present, that little boy look on his hot guy face again. "What do you think it is? Cash? Diamonds? Maybe . . ."

But Ethan's voice trailed off as he looked into the box—at the words staring back at him in black and white: *Off-Duty Secret Service Agent in Critical Condition Following Christmas Eve Collapse.*

Maggie had no idea how Eleanor had managed to get a physical copy of a Colorado newspaper in rural England, but that wasn't the important thing in that moment.

"Ethan?"

"She knew." He huffed out a startled breath. "My name wasn't in the papers. My dad and the Service . . ." He shook his head like he was trying to keep himself on track. "They don't publish the names of Secret Service agents because . . . She knew." That time he was smiling.

When he pulled the second piece of paper from the box, Maggie recognized Eleanor's handwriting as soon as she saw it.

"Here." He handed it to her.

"It's yours."

"Read it for me."

Maggie knew what he was doing—what it meant. There was a not-insignificant chance that those were the last words she'd ever read that were written by Eleanor Ashley, and for a second, she just held the paper in her hands, almost afraid—not of what they might say but of what they might mean.

"It's okay." His lips brushed her forehead, and she knew the truth then: this wasn't the epilogue of Eleanor's story. It was the prologue of Ethan and Maggie's. So she looked down at the paper and read—

"Dear Ethan. I have long been a fan of both your talent and your courage, though I must admit I was rather banking on the latter. I knew she'd be in danger. And I knew you'd keep her safe. Somehow, I felt certain you would not mind."

"She got that right," Ethan whispered.

"Take care of our girl." Maggie's voice broke. "Eleanor." Her eyes were hot and liquid as she realized that even if Eleanor's last written words weren't to her—they were *for* her. And that was somehow so much better.

"I'm not getting that letter back, am I?"

"No."

"You're going to frame it, aren't you?"

Maggie choked out a yes, and she felt Ethan wrap her in his arms.

"You know, this may be premature crying." He pointed her toward the second package. But unlike his, Maggie's name wasn't on it. The label just said *To the victor*. He nudged it in her direction. "Your turn."

It was just an ordinary present wrapped with ordinary paper and an ordinary ribbon, but it felt, to Maggie, like quicksand. A Venus fly-trap. An elaborate snare made out of fishing line and rusty springs. It felt like a trap. Because Maggie had wanted it so badly that it had to be a bad idea.

"Maggie? It's from Eleanor. She wants you to have it."

But Maggie wasn't ready for it. And she wasn't sure she ever would be.

."Hey." He tilted her chin up, forced her to meet his eyes. "I don't know how to break this to you, but you didn't win because you did what Eleanor would have done. You won because—"

"I had you," she said.

"No." He didn't tease or grin or smile. He was the most serious man in the world when he told her, "You won because you did something Eleanor *couldn't* do." Then he pulled back and held up the present, shaking it slightly. "Don't you want to peek? I want to peek."

"I want to find her."

"Okay." He gave a firm nod. "Then we'll find her."

So Maggie ripped off the paper and pulled off the lid, and together, they looked down into the box as the sun set on Christmas and the rest of their lives began. "Is that . . . an antique thimble, one silk glove, and a Harlequin romance novel from 1985?"

"Looks like it." He sounded too casual, too easy. It was when he was the most dangerous, when he looked like he wasn't even playing the game.

"I wonder what it means?"

He gave her his cockiest grin. "There's one way to find out."

LOCKED ROOM / OPEN CASE:
THE DISAPPEARANCE OF ELEANOR ASHLEY

In the early morning hours of December twenty-third of last year—two days before Christmas—one of the greatest mystery writers of all time disappeared out of a locked room without a trace.

Eleanor Ashley was the bestselling author of ninety-nine novels. She was eighty-one years old. She had recently injured her right leg and was reliant on a cane. Her home sat in the middle of twenty thousand acres that adjoined an even larger national park. And it was in the middle of a blizzard.

She hasn't been seen since.

Ms. Ashley had invited an eclectic collection of guests to her home for the holiday, and in the days that followed a number of arrests were made, including (but not limited to) her former assistant, her former attorney, and a local police inspector and longtime friend of Ms. Ashley's who was charged with multiple accounts of attempted murder, including the poisoning of beloved author Sir Jasper Rhodes, who survived the attempt.

But the disappearance of Ms. Ashley herself is still unsolved in spite of the international search that followed. Everyone from Interpol to online conspiracy theorists and true crime podcasters have spent the last year clamoring to answer one question: What happened to Eleanor Ashley?

Many believe she's dead, murdered and buried somewhere on twenty thousand acres. Another popular theory is that she fled her home that night and perished in the storm and (in spite of very extensive searches) her remains simply haven't been recovered.

Some think the story itself is the lie and Eleanor Ashley never disappeared and is, even now, hard at work on book number 101.

Many claim she never existed at all and was, in fact, the pen name of dozens of different authors employed by her longtime publisher Killhaven Books and then "killed off" in a way so dramatic it was certain to spike sales as Killhaven announced the one-hundredth (and presumably final) book by Eleanor Ashley, the aptly titled *They Never Found the Body*.

The novel features a foreword by bestselling author Maggie Chase, who headlines Killhaven's new Eleanor Ashley Presents imprint. In it, Chase writes, "Eleanor Ashley was born in a house with a dirt floor. Eighty-one years later, she disappeared from a mansion. Along the way, she changed a genre, built an empire, and inspired a generation, but despite that, her legacy will no doubt be one question: *Where is she now?* The answer is simple: she's here. In these pages and on our shelves. And that's exactly where she wants to be."

Only one thing is clear: it's unlikely that Eleanor Ashley will ever return to Mistletoe Manor. The historic home was recently sold to a charitable trust for the price of one pound and will soon be home to a shelter for individuals fleeing abusive situations.

When asked about the events of last Christmas, Ms. Ashley's niece, Victoria, the Duchess of Stratford, is the only person who was in attendance who regularly comments. "No one will find my aunt unless she wants to be found. It's a game, you see. And she always wins. One can only be grateful that, once upon a time, she chose to play with them."

EPILOGUE

One Year Later

They went someplace warm for Christmas, but the man holding her hand looked as cool as the breeze that blew off the dark blue water. The island was tiny and Greek, with narrow streets and steep hillsides, white stucco houses and views of the sea. If it hadn't been for the staticky carols coming out of an old radio in someone's window, Maggie might have even forgotten to be nervous.

It was the first time in forever that she hadn't spent the whole year worrying about December. Possibly because she hadn't had time. But more than likely, it had something to do with the man beside her.

His eyes were hidden behind dark glasses, and he was wearing a linen shirt with the sleeves rolled up, showing off his forearms and a brand-new tattoo.

"I still can't believe you did that."

"What?" He held up his arm and eyed the small circle with the words *From the personal library of Margaret Elizabeth Chase.* "I don't have a title page. It was the best I could do."

"You're ridiculous." She really needed to stop smiling. It only encouraged him.

"I know! But you're stuck with me . . ." He swung their joined hands, thinking a beat before finishing, "*Loralee.*"

Maggie almost tripped over her own feet. "What did you just say?"

"Loralee. Shayne." He spoke the words slowly, enunciating every syllable in turn and Maggie gulped.

"I'm afraid I don't know who that is."

"Really? Because the lip you always bite when you lie says otherwise." Maggie immediately stopped biting her lip, but it was too late. He knew. And, *oh*, was he smug. "I told you I'd find the fourth pen name."

"I don't know what you're talking about."

"Monster books, Maggie! Monster f—"

"We're not talking about this."

"Oh, we are *absolutely* talking about this." He pulled her closer and whispered in her ear, "Later. Later we are going to talk about this in very"—he kissed her—"specific"—he kissed her again—"detail."

"How did you even . . . How?"

"It's an anagram of Eleanor Ashley." He gave her a look that said *give me some credit*. But then, just as quickly, he stopped smiling, and Ethan Freaking Wyatt seemed almost embarrassed to admit, "Besides, I'd know your voice anywhere. You're my Eleanor."

"Oh." She straightened the collar of his shirt even though it didn't need it. "You keep saying things like that and I'm going to get a little crush on you."

"Promise?'"

They were midkiss when her phone beeped.

"Deborah?" Ethan guessed. "You didn't tell her where we are, did you?"

"Of course not!" Maggie was still digging in her bag. "She probably just wants to know if I'm going to blurb Sir Jasper's new book."

"Are you?"

"Uh. It's about a detective who is poisoned at a country house party, dies, and then comes back as a ghost to solve his own murder! It's called *The Specter Inspector*! Of course, I'm going to blurb it!"

Ethan laughed and said, "Good," just as she found her phone.

"Not Deborah." She held it up so he could see.

Duchess: Please let me know how it goes. If you find her, please tell her . . . I'm still here. And I'm ready to play.

Suddenly, Maggie's heart began to race because they were doing this. This was happening. This was—

"Hey." The hand holding hers tightened. "She's going to love you."

They were the same words he'd used a year before while zipping up her dress and looking into her eyes and reading on her soul what she needed to hear. He'd been right then.

"But what if we're wrong?" Maggie almost couldn't get the words out. "What if she's not here? What if—"

Ethan cut her off with a kiss.

"Then we keep looking. But we're not wrong," he said as his gaze drifted over her shoulder.

"But how can you possibly know that? The whole world has spent the last year looking for Eleanor Ashley! The best detectives on the planet and the craziest people on the internet. How can you stand there, utterly certain that *we* found her?"

But Ethan didn't say a thing. He just smiled as a bright, clear voice came flying on the wind. "Because she's right behind you."

It was a year to the day since Maggie turned to find Eleanor Ashley waiting on the steps of Mistletoe Manor, but she no longer looked like the Duchess of Death. This time, her home was small and white with stucco walls and wide-open windows. Gauzy curtains blew in the breeze as Eleanor led them inside, past the cane that was hanging on the wall because Eleanor didn't need her daggers anymore.

"Look who finally found us!"

Maggie and Ethan looked at each other and mouthed *Us?* just as James came in from the courtyard.

"I told you they'd be here soon." James gave Eleanor a swift kiss. "I suppose we should get started on dinner. Ellie?"

Ellie? Maggie and Ethan mouthed again.

But Eleanor never took her eyes off Maggie. "Can you get started without me, love? I'd like to show our guests the view."

The courtyard was small, with plants climbing trellises and scaling the side of the house, an arching umbrella of green vines and red blooms shielding it from the rest of the world.

Eleanor looked at peace in that dappled light. "They're called bougainvillea." She fingered a soft red petal. "And, yes, parts of them are slightly poisonous, but let's keep that between us."

Her gaze fell on Ethan's arm as it draped across Maggie's shoulders. Her lips tipped up and her blue eyes sparkled, but Eleanor Ashley would never be so gauche as to smile. No. It was a look that said *Well, what do we have here?* and *I told you so* and *You're welcome* all at once, and Maggie thought for the millionth time that she didn't just owe her career to that woman. She owed her for everything. But, most of all, she owed her for *him*.

"Well . . ." Eleanor raised an eyebrow.

Maggie had spent a whole year thinking about that moment, and she wanted to ask a million questions—say a thousand things. About the new imprint and the new books. About her life and her love and the way the world was more Eleanor-mad than ever.

Maggie wanted to ask her if she was happy. If it was worth it.

She wanted to say thank you.

But what came out was—

"How'd you do it? How'd you get out of the locked room?"

Ethan chuckled but Maggie couldn't even scold him, not with Eleanor standing there, breeze in her hair, mischievous smile on her face. She'd disappeared in a blizzard but was reborn in the sun and there was no doubt, no question, no chance that the world would ever know her equal.

So it was perhaps fitting that she just shrugged. And said, "I'm Eleanor Ashley."

And, somehow, that was answer enough. Ethan's arms tightened around Maggie, pulling her closer as the sun set on the far side of the sea. And when she leaned against him, she couldn't help but feel like maybe there are some mysteries that are better left unsolved, some questions better left unanswered.

Because sometimes it's enough just to have been there for the most wonderful crime of the year.

ACKNOWLEDGMENTS

I am extremely bad at writing acknowledgments. Probably because there are thousands of people who should go here, and we just don't have the time—or the paper—to include them all. But for starters . . .

To the three amazing editors who guided this book along its path: Nicole Fischer, Erika Tsang, and Tessa Woodward; copy editor extraordinaire Laurie McGee; and everyone at Avon and William Morrow, including (but not limited to!) Madelyn Blaney, Alessandra Roche, Kasey Feather, DJ DeSmyter, and Julie Paulauski.

I'd also like to thank the teams that bring my brilliant audio adaptations to life, as well as the foreign publishers and translators that make it possible to share the books around the world.

As always, I'm extremely grateful to Kristin Nelson and everyone at the Nelson Literary Agency.

For reading this book when it wasn't even a book, I thank Kassie Evashevski, Ali Lefkowitz, and the team at Anonymous Content.

Thank you, Shellie Rea, for eleven great years of bacon and shoe returns.

Thank you to my family.

I'm not sure if this one would exist without amazing friends who read early drafts and encouraged me to keep going. Rachel Hawkins, Carrie Ryan, Rose Brock, Sophie Jordan, and Ally Condie, I'm looking at you.

And, finally, to Sarah Rees Brennan, who walked with me down a cobblestone street in Monte Carlo one night, telling me about the time Agatha Christie disappeared without a trace. Sarah, my dear, you started this. It's all your fault.

ABOUT THE AUTHOR

ALLY CARTER writes books about people who fall in love (while trying to stay alive). After more than a decade of writing beloved YA titles like *I'd Tell You I Love You, But Then I'd Have to Kill You* and *Not If I Save You First*, she launched onto the adult scene with *The Blonde Identity*. A longtime lover of the holiday rom-com, Ally is also the writer of the Netflix original movie *A Castle for Christmas*.

She lives in Oklahoma.